THE FAMILY CONDITION

THE FAMILY CONDITION

CODY LAKIN

Katalpa Press

Copyright © 2022 by Cody Lakin

All rights reserved. No part of this book may be reproduced in any manner whatsoever without written permission except in the case of brief quotations embodied in critical articles and reviews.

Cover art by iStock.com/GeorgePeters
Cover design by Jules Alam

First Printing, 2022

ISBN: 979-8-218-04832-7
EISBN: 978-1-0880-3991-5

For my parents

"The church was dim at vespers.
My eyes were on the Rood.
But yet I felt thee near me,
In every drop of blood.
In helpless, trembling bondage
My soul's weight lies on thee,
O call me not at dead of night,
Lest I should come to thee!"

— *Servitude*, by Anne Reeve Aldrich

I

Night Owl

The first time her mother tried to kill her, Elodie was only a few days old. That's what she told me when she felt brave enough to open up to me about her family.

She told me, too, about the time she found her mother downstairs in the middle of the night, naked and pressed up against a window, staring with wide eyes out into the dark.

Before, I'd urged Elodie to tell me about her family. Imagine my surprise when this was where we started. I was falling in love with her, and when you love someone you want to know more about them, don't you?

That's what I told myself, anyway.

So, when Elodie felt brave enough, she tried to tell me why she didn't talk to her parents. She tried to tell me what was wrong—what was so deeply wrong—with her mother. She tried to tell me about the condition that made her mother into something not quite human—something like a reptile behind glass.

But even that was small, in comparison, to what came after. The legacy of her family, I mean. What I once thought I knew about the world and about myself... and what I eventually came to know instead.

And I'm telling you because I can't live with this by myself anymore.

It starts with Elodie. And if I choose to give this to you, if you're really reading this, you don't know anything about her.

Elodie Villeneuve. Yes, it's familiar to you because you've heard about her family. I'm sure you know about the farm, and about the rumors of wild, human-like creatures in the forests.

But we'll get to that.

Elodie was the first person I noticed at Night Owl that evening. I'd met plenty of people, exchanged so many paltry greetings, even collided with a few bodies on the pounding dance floor. But you know how it is some nights. You're surrounded but alone. Reality is a reel of film flashing before your eyes, perpetually in motion. Even though it looks clear up close, when you step back it's all blurry, far away, a whirring jumble of melding colors and shapes, and you can scarcely reach out to touch any of it.

It was one of those nights. Everything moving too fast. Everything numb and out of focus. Except for Elodie.

Kendra, my ex-girlfriend, was on my mind—in brief flashes

—when I first saw Elodie. Probably. I don't remember much about the night before Elodie entered into it. I'd been stumbling through a heartbroken stupor for so long.

When you've been waiting for the sunrise all night and it finally peeks its way up from the horizon, you forget all about your impatience and how long you've been waiting.

I say that as if Elodie is the sun. I shouldn't give the wrong impression.

As I drifted through Night Owl and the numb haze of my mind, trying to grasp something—anything—from the film reel flashing before my eyes in the form of dancing bodies, swirling lights of purple, red, and green, and the burn of alcohol in my throat, Elodie was a glimpse of the moon through a dusty window. It was a night when my heart could've burned a hole right through my chest. My mind was a mad, spinning carnival I couldn't shut out.

And then the moon peered through that dusty window, and I felt less alone.

"You're standing in my way."

The first words she said to me.

And they were true. I was standing in her way, taking up space at the bar when I'd already been handed my drink. Scotch, by the way—a particularly spicy brand. Tasted like burnt wood. Burnt mahogany—give me that much.

I turned from my drink and looked at her.

Elodie has a way of looking at you that feels like spotlights have been aimed at the corner you're trying to hide in. Her eyes are ashen, and you could cut yourself on the edge of that stare. She held eye-contact relentlessly.

I faced her with the rest of my body. "Excuse me?"

"You're standing in my way. Got a whole goddamn club to haunt. Shoo."

"*Shoo?*"

She raised an eyebrow, shifted her weight from one leg to the other.

What a bitch, I thought—the first thought I had about Elodie Villeneuve after the shock of meeting her eyes.

I was a few drinks in and felt numb inside. I'm not usually like that.

"Maybe I'm not done here," I said, turning back to lean against the bar.

"Fine then."

I expected her to leave, or to bother one of the other guys at the bar. Instead she shoved herself in beside me, causing me to bump against the man to my right. My glass of scotch nearly toppled over.

I regarded her with disbelief. "Ever heard of personal space?"

"What?" she said, resting her forearms atop the bar. "Kinda ruins your brooding?"

I opened my mouth to object, or to toss something back, but laughed instead.

She looked over at me, eyebrow raised again, and said nothing.

The guy to my right, whom Elodie had made me bump against, dug his shoulder into mine. "Fucking Jesus, man."

I apologized, but indicated with a gesture that there was no room.

"Take the fucking hint and bug off, faggot," he said. "Fucking hell." The man—several inches taller than I—looked down his nose at me. I wouldn't have had an immediate problem with him if it'd been merely annoyance, but he was apparently a bigot as well. And he had this look in his eyes. How to explain it? Like he was deeply annoyed that I was a man instead of a young girl. Emphasis on *young*, like my sister's age, so a couple years younger than me.

Elodie leaned over the bar so she could get a look at him around me. "Ted Bundy," she said, and I have to admit she was right—he looked a bit like Ted Bundy, if Bundy had started to go grey. "He's not your type. Deal with it or fuck off."

Ted Bundy scoffed, only shot his eyes in her direction fleetingly. "Get your woman friend to shut it, too."

"Oh, she's not my..." I looked to her and believed I saw the corner of her mouth twitch in the beginning of a smirk.

She asked of the man, "Do you wanna have sex with him?" Nodding toward me. "The gay bar in the next town isn't open tonight, so we thought we'd try our luck here. What do you think?"

I'd been to that bar—Badlands—with my sister; she considered it her haunt. And even though Night Owl was *my* haunt, that one was actually a lot nicer. I still laughed, partly from nerves.

The man was actively avoiding her gaze now, looking down into his drink and adjusting his posture, as if trying to hide himself. But he couldn't hide the crimson in his cheeks.

"I'm asking you a simple question, guy. What's your name, by the way?"

"I'm not a goddamn—"

"Just answer the question. Do you want to fuck my friend here?"

"Jesus Christ in Hell." The man stepped away from the bar, grumbling. He cast the two of us a deeply disappointed look and then stalked away across the dance floor, probably to find a booth or a lonely young girl to lure to his VW Beetle. Emphasis on *young*.

I barely noticed the looks from others at the bar. My attention was fully on the woman beside me.

"Well, I've never seen anything like that," I said.

She took my glass of scotch, raised it to her lips, finished it off, and clunked the empty glass back on the counter. She grinned at me. "Next one's on me."

"Thanks for that." With all the space now at the bar, I moved back a few inches so I could comfortably face her. "What's your name?"

"Yours first."

"Bennet."

"I'm Elodie." She signaled the bartender, a tall woman in a thin red dress. On her way over, she looked at Elodie as if she herself were a servant happy at her master's command.

Elodie cast a spell in that way. A fire burned in her that others could feel if they drew near, or if they met her eyes. The heat of that fire made you hungry for something you hadn't known was lacking.

I ordered the second round for both of us. When she told me she was a lightweight, I didn't believe her and she said it wasn't for lack of trying. When our third glasses arrived, I asked if she wanted to sit at a booth together.

And by then, she noticed something about me that a lot of people try to ignore: I'm not afraid to look at people. I've noticed, in the environments created by a nightclub, a certain number of people are careful with their eyes. Try it. Try looking at people and you'll notice it. Some of them are afraid to acknowledge their reasons for being there. The context is so blatant that it becomes shameful to admit, as if most people don't go out with specific, secret desires fueling their every move, their every word.

I used to be that way. That's how I know the look, having worn it so often myself. But when you've been numb as long as I had, something changes. It's the inhibitions, the filters, the feeling of necessary politeness. Those walls become transparent and suddenly so easy to break through.

I looked at Elodie freely, and not in the sense that I simply let myself check her out. I looked at her without trying to hide that she was someone I was interested in, someone I wanted to know better.

If I'd simply been checking her out, she would've known—and probably would've wanted nothing to do with me. Maybe it's part of being slightly on the asexual spectrum, maybe it's just who I am: I looked at her with an invitation in my eyes, without intending to objectify. And she noticed this. And was the first person I had met in so long—maybe ever—who looked at me the same way, as if in challenge. Who would look away first? What unspoken things lay writhing beneath the glances? How best to entice those unspoken things forward?

"Why do you want to know about my mother?" I said, pausing with my third drink of the night halfway to my lips. We had to raise our voices over the thumping music. "Kind of a strange question to ask. You barely even know me."

"And here I am trying to know you better." She sat reclined in the booth, at ease, one leg crossed over the other. A fake purple candle flickered in the center of the table between us, and the artificial light danced in her ashen eyes.

I said, "Should I ask if this question is Freudian in nature?"

"You mean, am I asking about your mother to gauge if you have mommy issues?" A playful grin spread over her lips. "So what if I am?"

"Is this what you mean by being a lightweight?"

"Stop dodging the question."

"I'm not. My mother was practically a saint."

"Was? You mean she's dead?"

"It's odd how we refer to people as dead in the present tense, as if it's some present condition, isn't it?"

She giggled. It was the first time I'd heard her laugh. As you can imagine, it was a mischievous sound. But it sounded like she was laughing at me, as opposed to at what I'd said. So much for trying to be clever. "Well, compared to being alive, dead *is* a present condition, is it not?"

"I'll give you that."

"Your mother. Since when?"

"Since I was twenty-one. Cancer."

"I'm sorry, Bennet."

I'm not sure what surprised me more—that she said sorry, or that she meant it.

"It was a long time ago."

"I understand."

I noticed how Elodie was a puzzle box. We'd been talking for maybe an hour, enough that I'd started feeling genuinely comfortable in her presence, and yet I knew so little about her. But sometimes she threw clues in, and I didn't know how to navigate those clues to unlock them.

I said, "You understand?"

"Yeah. I understand how time flexes and unflexes, curls and uncurls. On some nights, it doesn't matter where you are, what you're doing, or even if you're alone or with other people... things that happened years ago may as well have happened yesterday. Or how somebody's absence from your life goes from background noise to the only thing you can hear."

I took a drink. "You really have a way with words, Elodie."

"You said that at the bar."

"And I meant it."

"What about your ex that you mentioned? Katelyn's her name?"

"Kendra. That's a bit of a one-eighty from my mom."

"Not if this conversation is Freudian," she said, and I almost spat out my drink. She continued, though, more serious than before. "There are so many different ways to lose someone. It's still loss. Still grief." She took a drink.

I titled my head back. Inhaled deeply through my nose. Watched the multicolored lights from the dance floor swirl across the dark ceiling. Kendra was the last thing I wanted to think about, and the last thing I wanted to talk about with somebody new and interesting. But Elodie asked. And she wasn't the sort of person to ask unless she wanted a genuine answer.

A few months before this, I went to my soon-to-be-ex-girlfriend's house and there was another man in her bed.

It was my twenty-sixth birthday and I came to this very place—Night Owl, my usual spot—and Kendra was there. She'd told me she had plans with one of her friends, that it was one of those necessary girl nights. *See ya in the morning,* she said. *Will text you when I'm up so you can come over, babe. Happy birthday, btw.*

I should've seen it coming. We'd been together for almost three years and sometimes she seemed bored with me, as if prioritizing me caused her to miss out on some perpetually better experience in some perpetual other place.

I loved her, though. That's the problem. Like when you sit long enough and you get attached to where you're sitting, like you're stuck there and you don't mind. That kind of love.

That kind of love is terrible. It made me blind to things, like to the guy who texted her all the time, whom she accompanied sometimes to long brunches, but who she said was just a friend. The guy I'd later find in her bed.

I felt sour that Kendra was having a girl's night on my fucking birthday—and with the bullshit excuse that her friend needed her—and I was alone so I went to Night Owl. Night Owl was one of those bad habits I'd been trying to break, you see. I liked to go there for the atmosphere, for the music, for the dancing, for teasing my psyche with possibilities I'd never explore.

Sure, it's not a good thing to go to a club when you're in a relationship, but Night Owl was a haze of cigarette smoke and I was someone struggling—and failing—to quit. It wasn't about meeting people, and never really had been.

And I had no idea things were about to fall apart with Kendra. If I'd known, I would've insisted on meeting up with her so we could talk it through, work things out. Working on it —no matter what—was a given for me.

As for her? I saw her there, on the floor, dancing with another guy. Not just dancing, though. Grinding up against him, humping him, getting her face all in his, guiding his hands over the shape of her body. And it wasn't just some guy, either. It was the friend. The one she said was *just* a friend.

She has this wild dark hair that does something to me—all the times I've grabbed handfuls of it and pulled, or plunged my hands through it in the night—and to see it bouncing like that, another guy's hands running through it.

The images that flipped through my mind made heat burn through my body from my shoulders and my chest. I couldn't breathe. Images: this stranger's hands caressing her, squeezing her, fondling her; his mouth on her mouth, on other parts—my favorite parts—of her body; her moans for this stranger, not for me.

I stood there watching her, burning, seeing all of those things in my mind's eye.

But I was gone before she had the chance to notice me.

I showed up to her house the next day. Probably to end things, even though, like I said, I was foolish enough to believe maybe we'd talk and work things out. An explanation would've been nice, at least. I don't know. I hadn't slept a single minute that night.

Her roommate answered and gave me a look as I walked in. Kendra's door was closed. I nearly burst in, but considering what I'd seen last night, I knocked. When she opened her bedroom door, I saw someone else in her bed. The same bed we'd spent so many nights in. The bed we'd made love in. Had long, drawn out conversations in. Watched so many movies in, dinner plates on our laps.

The same guy from the dance floor was in that bed. And I still remember the look he gave me. He knew exactly who I was, and he waved. He *waved*. As if I were nobody, as if Kendra wasn't my girl, as if I hadn't been with her for almost three years. And although there was no superiority, no victory in the look he gave me, I still felt it. Whatever she meant to me, it didn't matter because he had fucked her in that bed, had slept beside her in that bed. I was left without her, left to suffer, while she had simply filled my absence with this man, this stranger. A man I'd met in passing, to whom I was the "ex" who happened to show up that morning to make things awkward.

It's a hot feeling, that kind of pain. Like fire on the skin. Months later and I still lost sleep over it, the image playing in my mind: the way she opened the door just a crack, obviously trying to block my view of the room; my eyes catching the movement behind her, seeing legs sprawled out on that bed. And then the guy sitting up, looking at me. And I couldn't breathe.

I consider myself guarded, philosophically stoic, but that pierced me. Even after I lost all interest in Kendra, even after she stopped occupying every thought of my waking mind—even after I stopped dreaming about her, months later—that hurt still boiled up from my chest, sometimes, and woke me in the night.

I didn't pause to consider the words. Looking straight at Elodie as she waited for my reply to her question—*What about your ex that you mentioned?*—I simply let the words out.

"Sometimes I think it'd be easier if she had died. That way, her not being in my life would make more sense than her not wanting me."

"Holy shit." Elodie knocked back the rest of her drink. She kept her eyes on the table for a moment.

If she were a puzzle box, I would've heard a click and one of the secrets would've been revealed. A small part of her shined through, deeper than any act she put on, too prevalent to hide behind any of her defenses or emotional walls.

This was something I would later come to appreciate about her, even if it always surprised me. Her sharp edges, as well as the willingness to be emotionally honest and vulnerable underneath.

"Sorry," I said. "I don't mean that. I just—"

"You do, though." She looked me in the eye, held my gaze in

that unwavering way. "You do mean it, and you shouldn't apologize for it."

"No..." Following her example, I finished off my drink and hoped she didn't decide to signal a waiter over for more. "I can't believe I just said that."

"Hey. We've all got worse shit than that somewhere underneath. Some people think it's ugly but I think it's beautiful."

I looked at her. It was all I could do. My heart beat heavily, my head spun on the inside, and I had never wanted anyone as badly as I wanted Elodie. Physically, I hadn't desired someone since Kendra.

So I told her about Kendra and me. Later I would go into more detail, but I told her about the other guy. The one in her room.

"My god, Bennet," she said. I hadn't expected she could drop into such somberness, such open sympathy. "I'm sorry."

I looked out for a moment at the dance floor, which seemed to exist in a different world from our shared booth. And I couldn't help the part of my mind that wondered—maybe even hoped—that Kendra might be one of the dancers, that she might glance this way and see me seated at a booth with this tantalizing woman named Elodie.

"What about you?" I said, tired of talking about myself. "Your family, I mean. Your mom."

She lifted her eyebrows playfully and clicked her tongue. "Oh, we are *not* going there."

"What?"

"You don't wanna hear about my family. And I don't wanna talk about them."

"An eye for an eye," I said, not entirely sure I was making sense. I'm not as much of a heavyweight as I like to think. "Nothing?"

"No."

Although it annoyed me then, later I would be glad she didn't tell me about her family. Not during our first meeting, at least. There are some things you are never ready to hear, just as there are some things you are never ready to talk about.

Maybe, if she'd told me about her mother while we sat in the booth, nothing would've happened between us. Maybe I would've been more than just terrified and would have simply avoided her from then on. Maybe. I don't know.

"If we're not going there," I said, "where then?"

"I have an idea." She stood from the booth. Her eyes caught light and, for just an instant, reflected back at me—but not the way eyes normally do. Her eyes glowed, if only for an instant, the way an animal's does in a certain light. Like jewels in low light.

I thought she meant to walk away—how she swung her hips as she walked, and shuffled as if ready to slip to the dance floor—but she turned and offered me her hand. To the dance floor is not where she led me.

I remember we talked in the backseat, on the way to her apartment. I don't remember what we talked about.

I remember it sitting in the back of my head, why she'd ask about my family—my mom, at least—and why she refused to talk about hers. But we talked about a lot of things, and she asked the kinds of questions nobody asks you the first time you meet them—if they ever ask at all.

I remember trying to bring up my slow pace when it comes to sexual attraction, how an emotional connection is what comes first for me. I didn't want her to think I was coming with her just because I wanted her.

I remember the way she moved slowly at first, having to hold herself back out of respect for my pace.

I remember she grabbed my wrist when I was on top of her, moved my hand to her neck, and told me to choke her. Told me *harder.*

I remember how wildly she moaned. Nothing after that except, maybe, my own moans, my own yells, and a few minutes later, lying on top of her, spent, catching my breath, and how she laughed softly in my ear and held me close. Held me close.

I remember the way she looked in my eyes in the soft, naked tangle of our lust.

And I remember waking up alone.

2

Don't Judge My Family

I sent Elodie a single text message telling her that I'd love to see her again, and didn't hear from her for the next two days. But, for those two days, she did not leave my mind.

The way she took control even while beneath me, telling me *more*, telling me *harder*, grabbing my hair on the side of my head and looking deeply into my eyes as her breaths grew more intense and she went over the edge. It had never been like that before, not with anyone.

Throughout the mundane rhythms of my work day, my hands remembered the soft swells of Elodie's breasts, the electric feeling of her body against mine. More than the physical, there was the way she had given herself to me, willful and yielding all at once.

I looked in my own eyes every time I saw my reflection and wondered what had happened that night.

The fire I told you about, the one that burns inside of Elodie. The hunger it inspires. It was beginning to feel like a bottomless pit. I didn't just want her, not just in that way. I wanted to be with her again. Wanted to play the games she played with her words, her looks. Wanted to contend with that. Like playing with fire.

Some of us, when presented with open flame, cannot keep our eyes away from it. Can't help but pass our hands over it to test the boldness of that heat.

I've always been like that. And Elodie was an open flame.

So when, in the middle of the night, she called me and asked me to join her at Farewell Lake, I didn't hesitate.

I was, however, concerned. Farewell Lake isn't like Lake Courageous. It's a half-hour drive from town, and then a fifteen-minute hike through the woods to the lake.

What Elodie was doing there in the middle of the night, I didn't know, but I didn't hesitate going to find out.

"There've been three bodies found here over the past two years," she said. The first thing she said to me as I came up to her in the dark.

Elodie had a way of imposing her own context on any situation.

She hadn't told me where to find her, so I had arrived at the lake under the dim glow of the moonlight without any idea where she was. The hike through the woods had shot my nerves into overdrive, so my whole body was tense and it felt like I could hear even the tiniest movements in the trees around me. Something about the silhouettes of the brooding trees was menacing. Surrounded by tall shadows that seemed to be reaching out with gnarled arms.

I came to the edge of the water, amazed by the quiet of this place in the dark. I'd come up here with friends on so many summer days, sometimes with girlfriends. Soft skin basking on warm rocks. Sunlight glittering in gems on the small lake's surface. Sound of splashing water, someone laughing from the other side.

Replace this with the night's silence and the water's darkness. It's like playing ominous music over a happy picnic scene. Something just doesn't feel right. Somehow it's both achingly sad and unexplainably unsettling.

I walked along the water's edge slowly, my eyes darting through the darkness, my ears peeled—all senses on high alert. After a few minutes I had the idea of turning on my phone's flashlight and holding it out, in case Elodie was in sight.

A moment later, I saw her flashlight high above the water, and I knew where she was.

She sat alone atop the rock, which jutted slightly out over the lake. I'm no good at estimating the height of something, but I'd jumped off this rock once before. It was probably twenty feet up, maybe not quite twenty-five. Friends of mine liked to say thirty, but I knew enough to know that people aren't good at estimating these things, plus the higher numbers sound more impressive.

Hair up in a wild bun, she sat cross-legged as if she'd been meditating here in the dark. She had lain out a towel to sit on, and scooted to the side to make room for me.

I sat beside her. She cast me a knowing smirk. Her eyes glowed subtly in the dark. I'd never seen a person's eyes do that before.

"There've been three bodies found here over the past two years," she said.

"I know. My friend Chris and I did a podcast on it just a few weeks ago."

"A podcast?"

"Yeah. It's called Pillowcase Stalkers. Ever heard of it? Our target audience is people who like to lay in bed and fall asleep to true crime podcasts."

She laughed. "That's brilliant. So you already know about the bodies."

"I know the local sheriff's office doesn't want to call it a serial killer just yet. But it seems possible."

Elodie leaned back on her arms as if to let the sun on her front, even though it was the middle of the night. "I come out here every so often and just sit like this, and sometimes I wonder if I'll hear a splash and it'll be someone dropping a body in the lake. I love that shit."

I laughed until realizing she wasn't joking. "You're serious?"

She responded by wrinkling her nose at me.

"Meeting a serial killer in real life—out here, alone in the woods—isn't the same as *loving that shit*."

She shrugged. But once the humor died away and she leaned forward again to peer down to the water, pensiveness clouded her features. She let out a slow breath. "You ever feel numb to things, Bennet? I don't mean literally... I mean, like... like you've missed out on some unnameable thing, and you were left outside while everyone else was welcomed in. And now you're standing at the window, wondering why you can't seem to get inside, and everyone treats you like you're already inside as if they can't see the windowpane that separates you."

"I know exactly what that feels like." I wanted to tell her about the other night, at Night Owl. About bouncing around the club like a pinball without feeling; about reality as a reel of film flashing by. And how she seemed to have woken me up.

But I'm glad I didn't say anything. She kept speaking.

"What about your father?" she asked.

"What about him?"

"You told me about your mom. What about your dad?"

I chuckled. "That's some way to pick up a conversation from a few days ago. My dad lives in Washington. I don't see him much."

"You aren't close?"

"He has alzheimer's."

"Oh. Bennet, I didn't know."

"It's relatively early stages. My sister checks in with him a lot, but... it'll be awhile before he needs to be, you know, put in a home or anything. But, uh... otherwise, I try to be close to him. I just..." I wondered why I was telling her this, why she was asking, but decided not to second-guess. "He and I never really know what to talk about. It's been like that ever since Mom died. Or... before then, really, when he basically just left me to deal with it all. Now, I never seem to ask the right questions, or when I do, he doesn't hear them the way I mean them. And it goes both ways. Plus, he doesn't know how to really open up about things... about his feelings, I mean."

"And you do?"

"Do what?"

"You know how to open up about your feelings?"

"Not with him. Not with a lot of people."

"So you two are alike in that way."

"I guess so, yeah."

"Makes sense," she said.

"And *your* dad?"

She blew air out through her mouth. "You do *not* want to hear about my dad."

"Why do I feel like we've had this conversation before."

"You don't want to, Bennet."

"I do, though."

She gave me a look. Even in the dark I could sense genuine resistance behind the playfulness in that look.

A puzzle box, like I said. But I felt I was making progress.

I dared to ask if she saw her family very often.

"It's been years," she said, and stood.

Just as I was thinking I had messed up and she was on her way out, back to her car—which, I'd noticed, was parked just down the hill from this rock, though I don't know how she got it here when the only route I knew was to park farther away and hike through the woods—Elodie surprised me when she took her shirt off and dropped it on the towel.

I looked coolly up at her in her small black bathing suit. Her softly brown skin had that glinting smoothness in the dim pearly moonlight. I wanted to reach out for her.

Her jeans came off next, which she stepped somewhat

clumsily out of. She moved away, facing me so she had her back to the rock's ledge, and reached a hand out for me.

"Coming?"

"You're serious?"

"Do I look serious?"

"You look like you forgot to remind me to bring a bathing suit."

"Don't need one. This one's coming off afterwards, anyway."

"Yeah?"

"Is that what you want?"

I laughed more from nervousness than from her words. "It's April. The water's probably freezing."

"Coward."

I stood, prepared to lift my shirt off even though my mind felt entirely unready for the jump. I couldn't imagine doing it at night, especially with the shock of cold water at the end.

In a teasing voice she said, "Come on, I'll even hold your hand if it helps."

"Wow. Goddamn it." I lifted my shirt off. My jeans next. Glaring at her all the while.

"That's it. Underwear next."

"I think I'll keep them on."

"Bennet. Take your underwear off."

Under any other circumstances, or had it been anybody else asking, I wouldn't have. But I did as told. Already I was shivering and regretting my decision to undress as it portended a commitment I didn't feel in the slightest.

Maybe I should've reconsidered what felt, already, like devotion to this woman. All my past relationships were slow-paced, carefully thought out. There was just something different about how I felt with Elodie. Stripping, even in the cold, was easy, when it shouldn't have been—not according to everything else I knew about myself and how I felt about being vulnerable with other people.

I forced myself to step toward her. She had her back to the rock's ledge, her back to the dark; two more steps and she would topple out over open air.

"I don't know about this," I said.

"It's okay, Bennet." She always called me by my full name, while most of my friends called me Ben. I liked the way she said it, though. "You don't have to jump. It's just... no one here will ever forget how much of a coward you are. And, you know, it's fine if you can, like, live with being reminded of your cowardice every day for the next..."

"Fuck you." I took two steps and leapt.

I heard her squeal in delight only seconds before she jumped out to join me.

I had enough time to wonder what the hell I was doing—and then to feel exhilaration spring through me—before my feet slapped through the icy water's surface and I was under, in a world of muted churning. Came up gasping, and Elodie followed seconds later. She wrinkled her nose at me as we treaded in the echoes of our splashes, surrounded by tiny air bubbles in the previously still water. It was a void beneath us where the shafts of moonlight couldn't reach, but that, too, exhilarated me.

The numbness comes to mind. The feeling Elodie seemed to

know well, too. Even in the icy water, I felt a warmth inside. When part of you has been frozen long enough, you tend to forget what it ever felt like before: it grows numb and then you grow accustomed to the numbness. We adapt so easily against our own self-interests. So many areas of my life had petrified in this way. But I was feeling something now that I only understood, by feeling it, I hadn't felt in far too long:

Like fire. Fire in the body. Under the skin.

When we climbed out of the water, trudging up onto dry shore, we looked at each other and didn't say anything. I wanted her so badly. She saw this—and the same feeling reflected back through her eyes.

"Look at me," she said, breathless, when she felt it rising in her—and subsequently in me. "Look at me."

I saw something in her eyes that I had never seen in anyone's before.

And it terrified me out of that numbness.

Maybe excitement is the wrong word.

It was so much more than that. Drawn from such deeper places—places that hadn't seen the light in far too long, if they ever had.

Like coming up for air at the exact point that you can't hold your breath any longer.

Like opening your eyes from the darkness of the mind and realizing you're looking at the stars.

This is how the notion entered my mind, as nothing more than a suggestion at first—hardly something I even noticed—that maybe Elodie was dangerous. Not a threat in the conventional sense, not because I'd been hurt before and feared being hurt again. Nothing like that.

I mean truly dangerous. For me. For the burning curiosity it inspired in me to pursue her. To understand her, and maybe be understood by her in return—what a feeling that would be. We'd only just met, really, yet I couldn't deny: I would follow where she led me.

It rose in both of us and if anyone had been within a mile of us in the woods, I'm sure they would've heard us.

"I've been in relationships with people who kept secrets," I said, the first to break a long silence in each other's arms. We were strewn across the backseat, nude, tangled in each other.

I hadn't been certain she was still awake, but she stirred on top of me, adjusted her head so that when she spoke, she spoke into the crook of my neck.

"We all have secrets," she said. "I don't think we could live without secrets."

I agreed. "But there are some things that need to be talked about. Things that fester if you don't."

"Just as there are some things," she said, "that never need to come out in the open."

Her hand glided gently across the hairs of my chest.

"Some things?" I said. She nodded. Although it took courage, I asked, "Is your family one of those things?"

She surprised me by not reacting in some visceral way. Nothing in her demeanor changed. She didn't reply by shutting me down or avoiding the question.

"You really wanna know about them?"

"I do."

She adjusted her head again so she could look up at me. Her chin jabbed lightly into my chest. I shifted myself so that, with the small effort of resting my ahead against the door, I could look back at her.

"Don't judge my family," she said, after a time. "That's all I ask."

"I wouldn't," I told her, and it was true. Opinions are a petty currency. *Judgmental* is, I hope, the last thing anyone would call me.

"The first time my mother tried to kill me," said Elodie, "I was only a few days old."

I looked in her eyes and knew she wasn't playing with me. There didn't even appear to be much emotion in her eyes. She was tired, but she said this with an even, unremarkable tone.

I said, "The *first* time she tried to kill you?"

Elodie nodded. "It wasn't really her fault. She just... she didn't know the difference between loving and... and hurting."

"What?" I couldn't believe what I was hearing. "Elodie... there's a difference between having a fucked up view of love, and trying to kill your baby daughter."

"It wasn't like that." Her tone remained flat, as though she needed to enter a daze in order to tell me these things. "She wasn't... There's something wrong with her."

"Yeah... I'd think so."

"But not the way you think. Listen. I ran away from home when I was fifteen, and it's not like she wasn't there all my childhood, and she was never put in a hospital or anything, but..."

Elodie shivered. And when she didn't go on, I let the silence continue. We were in our own untouchable world, windows fogged, quiet darkness beyond, soft moonlight and stars above. We had all the time we needed.

And after awhile—several minutes, though the silence made it feel longer—she found the words to go on.

"I don't know how to explain it without telling you more about them."

"About your parents?"

"My parents, my family... and my whole fucking childhood. I've, um..." Her breaths against my skin felt labored, as if the simple act of thinking about these things put her through unimaginable distress. The flat tone was vanishing under the weight of her emotions. I felt something in my stomach, a twinge, a sudden coldness. Regret, I think, for putting her through this.

And although I didn't know her very well yet, I recognized this as the first time I'd seen her so vulnerable—as if she were afraid. Before this, I'd been unable to imagine her like this, but here she was, fighting with her past.

I guess we all have our shadows to contend with. We all turn back eventually and are appalled by what we see behind us.

"You know, Bennet, I've never talked about them. Not to anyone."

"I understand."

"I still remember the first time I found my mother in the dark," she said, trembling. "I was maybe seven years old... seven or eight, and it was the middle of the night. I went downstairs to get a glass of water, plus I liked to sneak into my dad's study and read from some of his old books when I couldn't sleep. And when I went by the, um... the solarium? Like the little greenhouse room between the living room and the kitchen? Mom was there, naked, pressed up against the glass and just... just staring out into the dark."

Chills crawled down my back. "What the fuck..."

"I asked her what she was doing, because back then I still thought it made sense to talk to her, like maybe she understood me on some level even though I'm not sure if she ever did. My father would say otherwise, but... but I don't know.

"I went into the solarium with her, got against the glass alongside her, and I saw the way she looked. Her eyes were wide and just... blank. They're always like that. Like she's dead. But at the same time she looked completely intent on staring out there, like she was really looking for something out in the dark." Elodie trembled again. "Just staring. And with nothing behind her eyes."

The darkness beyond the car, outside the foggy windows, no longer seemed so far away, and this little world of ours no longer felt so untouchable. I thought of the bodies that had been found in the lake. Imagined hearing a distant splash and knowing a killer was out there. Conjured the sound of footsteps crunching gravel outside the car.

"What's wrong with her?" I heard myself ask. Not that I wanted to hear anymore, not now, but I needed to.

"It's part of the family. A condition on my mother's side, in the blood."

"She's sick?"

"You could say sick. But I've heard a lot of names for it. My father just says she's *different*, or *misunderstood* and other bullshit."

"So, what is it exactly? What's the condition?"

I'm sure she heard the connotation behind my question—*do you have it, too?*—but she chose, for the moment, to ignore it.

"Do we have to talk about that?"

"I'd like to know," I said. "But we don't have to talk about it right now. If that's what you want."

She rested her cheek on my chest. "Thank you, Bennet."

The questions reeling through my head only sped up in the silence. I sat in the darkness. Tried not to let my thousand curiosities burn me from the inside.

3

Shadows

"*So, what are we?*"

"*What do you mean, babe?*"

"*We keep doing this and, I don't know, I want to hear what you think.*"

"*I thought we talked about this. Labels and everything.*"

My partner on Pillowcase Stalkers—Chris, who tended to do most of the talking per episode, which was fine with me—seemed to have this argument with her girlfriend once a week. They were having lunch just outside the recording room, going back and forth—she with a serious-minded enthusiasm, Chris with a dry sense of detachment.

And I sat alone with a book in my hand—a Kurt Vonnegut novel I'd read four or five times before—and tried not to listen.

My first relationship had been like that. I'd been fifteen, she was seventeen. She hadn't wanted to put a label on it. Foolishly, I hadn't walked away then—having to find out later that she insisted on this for ulterior reasons.

I was fifteen, though. Something's wrong with you if you aren't ashamed of your fifteen-year-old self.

The night before, while lying on the floor of my apartment with Elodie naked on top of me—we always ended up that way together, strewn across each other, spent and out of breath—I had realized that Kendra no longer occupied my mind. My grandmother used to employ the old saying that the easiest way to get over somebody is to get under somebody else. I think there's something disgustingly shallow-minded about that, but we're all entitled to our opinions. But Elodie and I had been doing this thing for a couple months now. Kendra's presence in my mind was a balloon deflated, showing wrinkles along its flattening surface.

And when I thought of that cracked door of Kendra's bedroom, the hot emotions didn't ignite as strongly anymore. It hurt, still, and probably always would, somewhere deep down. But the fire was dim. A bonfire where once there'd been a volcano.

"You always call me by my name," I mused to Elodie.

She made a soft sound of affirmation. "I like your name."

"You can call me anything you want, you know. At this point."

"I do call you what I want."

You never know when to start calling someone by a pet

name—*babe*, or *hon*, or anything else—and I had played around with the idea in my mind. Kendra and I had started as early as possible. Well, Kendra had. I followed.

But the thought of calling Elodie something like *babe* just didn't feel right. So I called her by her name, too. There was something intimate about it, like how she called me by my name while looking into my eyes. Stoking a fire in my body for her.

"Hey, Ben," Chris called from the table by the recording room. "You and your girl should come over sometime. If you two are, you know, at that stage yet. We can do a double date."

Annie, her girlfriend, lit up. "Yeah, we should totally do that! Oh my god, I'd love to meet her."

I smiled. More of a grin, actually, trying to hide the delightful amusement I felt at the mental image of Elodie talking with these two. She and Chris would probably have a lot to talk about, at least when it came to serial killers.

"I'll see what her schedule's like."

I was occupied with other things. If Chris noticed it during the recording of the podcast, she didn't say anything. When, after we'd finished, she asked if I was good—her way of checking in, somewhat awkwardly—I told her yes, just tired. That's the answer I tend to give when something's wrong and I don't know how to talk about it. I'm tired. It wasn't untrue, it just wasn't the whole truth.

I was thinking about Elodie.

I was thinking about her family. How it was like a shadow

looming over her, darkening her every step, her every word, her every look.

Sometimes I could feel that shadow creeping up on me simply by nature of being near her. Sometimes the shadow took the form of a question I wanted to ask but knew I shouldn't. Sometimes it came in the form of a melancholy that settled over her eyes when she let her mind wander. I had watched her during moments when she didn't know I was watching. In the morning, with a cup of coffee in one hand, standing by the sliding-glass door. The shadow coming over her eyes as she was lost in thought. She tried to hide it when I hinted at sensing she was troubled by something. Other times she didn't say anything, simply leaned into me and closed her eyes and let me be a shield against whatever came.

I've known people with darkness in them. Darkness that follows them. I have my own. But I never met anyone with a darkness like Elodie's. It scared her. It never left her alone except for in the most fleeting of moments, moments she actively sought—like the moments of free fall after jumping into Farewell Lake at night, or the gasping moments of shared orgasm. Fleeting, I say, because none of those things—nothing at all that we can do—ever vanishes the dark that lives inside.

My desire for Elodie had deepened. If there'd been hesitation in my body before, slight though it was, none remained. And I can't deny this, either—my curiosity about her was consuming. Some nights it was hard to fall asleep. I wanted to know more about her, to simply know her better, to keep peeling back her layers. This had never happened with anyone else: this total ease of feeling like myself in her presence, mixed with the building intensity of my desire for her coupled with the desire to know her as deeply as I could. So that there would be more of her to care for. I'll say it—more of her to love.

And when you care for someone, when you really care for them and are willing to go to unthinkably selfless, unreasonable lengths to help them, or to comfort them, or to see them smile, you would do anything to help diminish the shadow that looms over them.

So I couldn't help it. Even if she resisted my efforts, I knew I needed to ask about her family. Needed to keep trying the turns and knobs and levers and buttons of the puzzle box.

How to best diminish a shadow? Expose it to the light. Bring it out in the open, even if you have to drag it kicking and screeching.

This was, of course, my mistake. From a certain point of view.

"You're joking, right?" she said, lifting herself off of me. Her breasts hung softly against my chest, and her hair fell along my collarbone as she raised herself to look me in the eye. "You're joking."

"Why would I joke about that?"

"That's what I'm wondering." The look she gave me asked the question: Do you really wanna go there?

And my look was answer enough, because she didn't wait for me to reply.

"Bennet, I haven't seen my parents in *years*, and that isn't a fucking accident. Why..." She pushed herself up, farther away from me. "Why would you even ask that?"

Even with the ecstasy of our lovemaking still holding me inert, this angle on her caused me to stir. When separate from her, my sex drive was minimal, but in her presence it was a constant flame.

"Look, Elodie." I lifted up on my elbows. "Would you believe I'm asking because I care?"

"No."

"Well it's true. I want to meet them. Or at least start talking about them with you."

"Oh my *god*. I can't believe we're having this conversation."

"That's exactly it. You can barely stand to talk about it except when you're either really tired or drunk or high as all hell. And that tells me something."

"Does it maybe tell you that I don't wanna fucking go there?"

"It tells me it's still an open wound. If it were healed, it would never even come up."

She lifted an eyebrow. "Fucking metaphors."

"You know what I mean, though."

"This isn't what you think it is."

"What do you mean?"

"You think I should come to peace with my parents, as if they're normal people who just happen to be flawed, and I'll regret it if I don't. It isn't like that."

"Isn't it?"

Her cheeks burned now, her voice wavered as if she were close to tears. But I saw only anger in her eyes.

"I don't wanna talk about it," she said, lifting herself even farther up until she was straddling me, looking down at me. In the low light cast by the lamp on my dresser, the shadows of the contours of her body made her look soft. I put my hands on her hips.

"Elodie, I don't want this hovering over us."

"Us? Hovering over *us*?"

"Yes!"

"Last I checked, they're *my* fucking family, Bennet. How exactly does it hover over you, too? Because you're curious?"

"Because I fucking care about you. Because we're together, aren't we? Or is that not what you want?"

In the same way that I could look at Elodie freely, wearing my desires on my sleeve, I held nothing back in my words.

And she was making me mad.

She saw this. Saw it in the widening of my eyes, in the tension holding my body as, beneath her, I leaned up toward her. A furnace was opening up in my chest, making me breathe more harshly.

I saw on her face—in the silence created by the last thing I'd said—a recognition, then. Something coming over her, as if my words had just then hit her, and my intentions were washing over her.

Because we're together, I'd said, meaning it, and she was realizing that my pushing her—my asking about her family—wasn't with the intention of making her uncomfortable. There was no corner I was driving her toward.

Her expression softened in such a way, it was as if I were seeing what she might've looked like years ago, younger and more vulnerable—and entirely caught off guard by the reality that someone might want to become acquainted with the darker parts of her life, her secrets, not to scrutinize what made her different, but because they loved her.

She noticed me beneath her then, seemingly for the first time since I'd said that I wanted to meet her parents. She responded with a mischievous grin, and then by pressing herself up against me.

She did this with a tugging movement of the hips, lowering herself and grinding. She leaned forward so her arms supported her on either side of me, and inched them forward with small movements until her breasts rubbed against my chest. All the while her eyes widely stared into mine, studying the effect she had on me.

I moved my hand toward her chest, my breath growing hot, but she seized my wrist and pinned it to the floor. Her lips twitched into a pleased grin as she readjusted her hips again, grinding closer until we both gasped.

I have never been the sort of person who is cynical about love. It's just that, for much of my life, I had little reason to be interested in it.

I loved Kendra for awhile, but there came a time when it wasn't love anymore. Not the way I see it. There were depths we rarely explored between us. Gaps of communication that became rifts between us. This went on for a long time before either of us realized those rifts were too wide to bridge.

I wasn't ready to admit to Elodie that I loved her. That I wanted her as badly, as deeply, as I needed her. That she was, by now, my person.

But she looked into my eyes in that studying way as she

drove herself against me and deeper again and again, not so much quickening as intensifying. She released my arms and put her hands on me, and I put mine on her, and I looked back into her eyes.

I cried out wildly, as if she had pulled the breath desperately from me. She cried out with me and broke eye-contact for the first time when she threw herself against me. And then, with more sounds of lingering agony—I call it agony because it's precisely that, an ecstasy that is agony—she pulled herself off of me and sunk, arms thrown across my body, hair splayed out.

We each had just enough energy to look each other in the eyes one more time before we collapsed and let sleep take us far more gently away.

"We're together," I heard her whisper sometime in the night.

The words reached me from just outside a dream. I opened my eyes.

Elodie was staring at me in the dark. She had moved off of me, now lay beside me, and her eyes were wide and sparkling.

I blinked at her. "Together," I echoed, and put my hand to the side of her face.

This one word was affirmation enough for her. She softened to my touch, reached a hand up and placed it over my hand.

She spoke again, low. "No one's ever tried to love me like this, Bennet."

"No one?"

She nodded. "Some people's idea of love is suffocation. Or control. But I've never let anyone in. Not like this."

"Then I'm a lucky man."

She restrained a smile. Rolled her eyes instead. "Slow the fuck down."

I laughed. After a moment, she did, too.

"Tell me about your mother," she said.

"Elodie, it's like... four in the morning."

"So it's the perfect time."

I gave her a look, but knew I would tell her. When she asked, it came easily for me, whatever it was.

"I thought she hated me at the end," I said. I'd managed to get through most of the story just fine, but the emotions were bubbling up from below. Flash of stifled fury.

It's odd how an emotion, when strangled for long enough, explodes when it's allowed to come up for air. My voice was strained. I hadn't cried about my mother in years.

"She didn't hate you," said Elodie. "I never met her and I know that."

"What, because of what I've said about her?"

"Well yeah. But it's obvious, isn't it?"

I shook my head. "If you had heard some of the things she said, when she was suffering—"

"I don't have to. And honestly, Bennet, haven't you ever said anything you regretted when you were mad? Or when you were hurt?"

I knew she was right. And it pissed me off.

Before I could protest in anger, however, I realized the irony in doing that.

"I know that. I guess I know that." And I'd known it for a long time. Sometimes you just need someone to say it. And then to say it again, maybe. And again.

Elodie put a hand on my chest. She smiled. "When I was twenty-two I had this sweet boyfriend. It was just for a couple weeks. He was a gentleman in some ways, but he had… he had certain ideas about the way I was supposed to act as his girlfriend."

"Oh god. We have to talk about your ex-boyfriends?"

"Shut up. One time, while he and I were walking somewhere… into town, I think, for lunch or something… I stubbed my toe on the sidewalk. Like, it hurt enough that I literally sat down and was just rocking back and forth, cursing through my teeth. And he…" She had to maneuver between laughter to continue the story. "He got down beside me and made this comment about how I should've noticed the crack in the curb… not even a judgmental comment, but just a… it was his tone. Not a big deal, really. And I was in so much pain, I told him he could fuck off and never talk to me again."

I gaped at her, trying to ask if this was really how she had broken up with this guy, whoever he was, but she didn't hear me over the sound of her own laughter. And, seconds later, I was laughing with her.

I also got her point.

When I brought my dying mother to a doctor's appointment —which would turn out to be her last—she told me she hated me. Told me something had been missing from me all my life, since birth. Said if I'd been born normal, I wouldn't do this to her, wouldn't put her through this.

And there's some truth there—at least about there being things about me she never understood. She'd never known how to talk with me about my sexuality, for example. But, in life, she had always tried, always listened, and had always been kind.

She came back to herself, at the end. Grew calm again. Looked at me the way she used to. Told me she loved me every chance she had. Demanded that I read to her so she could fall asleep to the sound of my voice.

But I never forgot the other things. The words that would sit like poison in my blood for years to come. Love and gentleness never leave the kinds of scars that hurt does. And, for so long after she said those things—the bad things—I was never sure if my mother had ever loved me.

Elodie looked at me and said something I knew already, but refused to admit—even to myself.

"You took it personally, the things she said."

"I did. She knew exactly what to say."

"That's not uncommon, you know. When it comes to people with terminal illness, when the cancer's in their brain. They don't act like themselves."

I tried to say yes, tried to say I knew that—and I did know it—but my voice wouldn't come out. I could only nod.

"I'm sure she would've hated the things she said to you, if she'd known. If she'd been herself."

Again, I could only nod.

I kept thinking, too, about my father. About how, even now, even with his gradually worsening mental condition, I couldn't think of him without a bitterness tightening in my chest. The resentment I still harbored that he had left me alone to deal with Mom's illness. That over the last several years, the chasm between him and me wasn't merely one of misunderstood words or misperceptions. I simply couldn't forgive him for how he left me alone with my dying mother, for how he left me alone in my grief.

Elodie was right about my mom, though. She hadn't been herself when she'd done everything she could to hurt me, to tear me apart.

And that was something new to contend with. A step forward, mentally and emotionally, for me—to begin reconsidering the memories of my mother.

4

To Actually Mean It

When I was eleven years old I went looking for a child killer.

My parents warned me about it by instilling a stricter curfew and reassuring me of the same things they'd told me since I was five: don't talk to strangers, don't get into a stranger's car, don't help strangers look for their lost puppies—stuff like that. Two children had disappeared over the past few months, their bodies found out by the train tracks, probably to try and make it look like it had been an accident. But I remember hearing the news that the kids had been murdered. Gruesomely. And their disappearances were ruled as abductions.

When my friends told me about a place not far from the railroad tracks—a little abandoned shack in the woods—I knew I needed to see it for myself. I brought a few knives, a small baton I'd bought off a friend, a flashlight, some snacks, and went out. By myself.

It's probably one of the stupidest things I've ever done.

But I found things out there, in that old shack. Clothes folded neatly on a decaying dresser. A few candles halfway burned to nothing. Six empty water bottles. A large blanket in a tangled mess on a torn, decrepit mattress.

I was certain I'd found the lair of the killer. I told no one. Especially not about the part when I thought I heard footsteps in the bushes outside and I ran—I ran until I was out of breath, sucking air, face red and sweaty.

When I look back to that time, I still wonder why I went. Why I did that. But it's like how it was with Elodie.

An open flame. An inability to look away. Something inside me drawn inevitably to a darkness I needed to see so I could try to understand it.

Nat, my sister, was telling me about how this guy she met at Night Owl a few nights ago had been more concerned with her consent than anyone else she'd been with in a long time.

"I don't know, I feel like I shouldn't let myself get too excited yet, since we've only seen each other a couple times," she said, pausing only to sip at her coffee. "But he actually told me that he stopped seeing anyone else since we've been talking. No one's ever been open with me like that. And I don't mean just in that way. That's just an example."

"Nat, that's great." I sipped at my orange juice, having sworn off coffee over the past few months—which, finally, wasn't as hard as it'd been at the start. Still, that dark woody smell wafting from Nat's cup danced like temptation in my nostrils.

"And, like... I know you don't wanna hear this, but he

checked in with me for consent like two or three times once we, you know, started."

"I'm guessing this was on the first date?"

She giggled, cheeks turning red. "Well yeah, Bennet, you know how important it is."

"Have you told Dad about him?"

"You know I have. He doesn't wanna hear it, but you know me, once I start. All he has to do is ask."

"Figured."

"And he, like, actually seems interested when it's a *guy* I'm dating."

"Well, there's Dad for you."

Nat had a way of bouncing between Badlands—the gay bar —and Night Owl. Sometimes she and I met up at Night Owl— sometimes for a drink, sometimes to try and help each other meet someone.

She asked, "Dad know about Elodie?"

I shrugged. "I called him a few weeks ago, told him about her. He seems worse, Nat. I doubt he'll remember anything about our conversation."

"Well, it's worse over the phone. You know that. It'd be good for him if you visited. Good for both of you."

"I doubt my visiting would make any difference to him, especially now."

She nodded, clearly searching for something to say in response. She didn't know how to talk with me about our father. She visited him a couple times a week, while sometimes months would go by before I called him or he called me. For me, it had always been part of us understanding each other. But

Nat wished we were closer. Family get-togethers weren't really a thing with us, except on the rarest of occasions.

"How's things going with her, by the way?" she asked, leaning forward with elbows on the table.

The smile that twitched across my lips must've cued her in, because her eyebrows arched up and she grinned.

"Benny! I'm so happy for you."

I hate when she calls me Benny. She knows that, but it seems to come out of her only when she's excited about something.

"We're pretty much living together. She stays at my house a few days in a row. Then we switch."

She reached across the table and mocked a punch to my shoulder. "Look at you! How long have you guys been together now?"

"Couple months.."

"You must really like her. All starry-eyed."

"I am not starry-eyed."

"Okay then. Rosie-cheeked."

"Please."

I resisted the urge to say something moronic—like how Elodie wasn't like anyone I'd ever been with before, how it was more than just liking her, how she drove me crazy. What I didn't tell my sister was about Elodie's family, or her resistance to my wanting to meet them. I didn't tell her these things because they were too raw, and after all, Elodie had been more open to talking about it lately.

Nat asked about the podcast and I told her it was the usual. Few nights a week for increasing returns. She wanted to know some of the details of our upcoming episodes and I was happy to provide. Like most of the women I know, she has a casual but sometimes addictive interest in true crime.

Elodie was lounged on the couch when I returned, wearing one of my t-shirts, looking like she'd only been up for an hour or less. She had a book from my shelf on her lap: *The Prophet*, by Kahlil Gibran. I sat down at the end of the couch so she could rest her feet in my lap, but she leaned up and pulled me on top of her, making sure my face was buried against her chest, beneath her collarbone. We laughed.

"Your ex came by the house today."

"What?"

"Hadn't met her before. Think she said her name was Kendra?"

I wasn't in the mood to laugh. "What'd she say?"

"You know, I'm not one to talk myself up too much, but you should be proud."

"Did she say anything?"

"I mean, like, not that anything's necessarily wrong with her, but she's got *nothing* on me. And here I was picturing someone capable of intimidating me."

I gave her a look and tried to suppress a grin. "Sounds like you two hit it off."

Elodie shrugged "I think I ruined her day. She asked me if I was your housemate, and then if I was your housemate's girlfriend. And then she seemed to get the point."

"Wow. And?"

"I told her I was your rebound and she... well..." The playfulness drained from Elodie's face. "She already looked like she'd been crying. Her makeup was... you know. But it was like the light genuinely went out of her eyes. Probably should've left the rebound joke out."

Readjusting myself so I was only half on top of her and could rest my head on her shoulder, I didn't know what to say. Felt as if she'd discovered a pile of very old, very dirty laundry of mine in some corner, and it occurred to me to apologize.

"She looked hurt?"

"Like I said, the light went out of her eyes. It's funny she's asking around for you."

"Yeah," I said. "Even after all that bullshit."

Elodie laughed. And that was that for her, although I could've easily mused on the subject of Kendra looking for me. Elodie asked, "How was coffee with Nat?"

"Good. She's seeing someone nice, finally."

"Bad history?"

"She was with someone named Erica a few months back. I think they were together for... almost a year? And then she found out how many months she'd been cheated on. I think the last good partner she had was in high school."

"Oof. I feel that. I want to meet her."

"Yeah," I said. "You'd like her. And I know she'd like you. She also said something about Kendra. Said she was over at Night Owl, asking about me."

"Sounds like buyer's remorse," said Elodie. "Or is that seller's remorse?"

"Cheater's remorse," I corrected. "And I couldn't care less."

"So I don't have to worry about you still having feelings for her?"

She said this with the lilt of humor, but I knew Elodie well enough. Beneath the spiky exterior she presented, there was... I don't want to call it insecurity, because that word comes with connotations that don't apply to her. At least, not as far as I knew. But I did know she hadn't been around many people who cared about her in a deeper, more genuine way. The longest relationship she'd been in hadn't lasted six months before crumbling apart.

A few days before, as we both sat in bed and she was settling from a laughing fit that came on spontaneously—which was only the second time I'd had the pleasure of witnessing her so exhausted she became loopy—Elodie asked me if I meant it when I insisted that we were together. As in, *together* together.

I write this in a joking way, but mean it that way, too. Some couples had the sorts of conversations that my podcast partner Chris had with her girlfriend—the *what are we* conversation that haunts so many young adults and, sometimes, the emotionally damaged promiscuous. I suppose Elodie and I had our own versions of that conversation.

It's not that she was insecure. It's that, after so long of being victim to thoughtless motivations and corrosive affection, it's hard to give yourself to something as encompassing as genuine affection, or love—or whatever the hell you want to call it.

And, in so many ways, I was learning how Elodie wanted to give herself to me. Even simply to trust that she could.

So when she asked me, in a lightly joking manner—a joke on thin ice—if she had to worry that I might still have feelings for Kendra, I knew what she meant.

And I didn't need to lie. "You were joking when you called yourself a rebound, right?"

She looked at me. "Was I?"

"You had to have been. Elodie." I scooted myself up so we were face-to-face. "I love you." It was the first time I said it to her out loud. The first time I'd said it to someone in years and actually meant it.

And she could tell. The smile that came to her face was the sweetest I'd ever seen, because behind it were tears she refused to allow.

"I love you too, Bennet."

She kissed me. My heart raced.

"You bring out the worst in me," I said. "You know that?"

She wrapped her arms around me and pulled me close, laughing softly. "You bring out the worst in me, too."

I told her not to be ridiculous.

After dinner that evening, while we were sitting around with glasses of merlot and discussing if we should put on a movie, her phone rang and her entire demeanor changed when she saw who was calling.

"What?" I looked down at her phone but it was just a number. "Who is it?"

She rose, eyes panicked. "I... have to take this."

"Everything okay?"

"I'll be right back." She went out to the back patio.

Before the door closed behind her, I only heard her say one thing:

"Hey, Dad."

5

Meeting the Family

On the drive to her family's estate, Elodie warned me about what to expect from her parents.

"I don't think he'll have my mother outside of the glass, so you don't have to worry about that." She had insisted on driving. This was her business, she said. Her family. So I sat in the passenger seat.

I turned to her, bewildered. "Outside the glass?"

"Her area of the house is glassed off. It's plexiglass. My dad had it designed sometime before I was born. When Mom got sick, I mean."

The more she talked about her parents, the harder it was to sit still. "What you're saying is your mom lives in a cage? Like... like an animal on display?"

"No." Elodie didn't share my humor over the situation, which was fair; it sprang from my discomfort and probably didn't come off as humor, anyway. She kept her eyes on the road, a solemn expression sitting on her face, keeping her features stiff, her eyes melancholy. "It's a living space. She's comfortable there... more comfortable, probably. And my father spends most of his time with her, anyway."

"Jesus. I've never heard of anything like that."

"Well of course not, Bennet. This is something unique to my family. I've never met anyone else, *ever*, with problems like mine."

When she put things this way, it helped me look at her differently.

How alone she must've been throughout her childhood. An only child. Parents that terrified her. A mother with a condition that turned her into some kind of animal, like a reptile.

And to have run away from that situation as a teenager. Not that she'd had much of a childhood, I'm sure, but she should've been focused on the fleeting problems of youth. Puberty, boyfriends, social image, whatever. She should've had friends she could relate to.

Imagine it. If you can, I mean.

"I think he'll let you meet her," said Elodie. "Actually, it's not up to him. It's up to me. And I'm leaving it up to you."

"To meet your mom? I'd like to. I'd like to be there with you, when you see her."

Elodie tried to smile. She reached over and put a hand on my thigh.

"She's protective of me." Elodie's voice was suddenly small, choked through. Her eyes glistened. "She's so protective of me. Always has been. So we'll take it slow. If she sees how comfortable around you I am, I'm sure it'll be fine."

"But something might happen?" I asked.

"I don't know."

"What do you mean?"

"I don't *know*, Bennet. Okay?"

I sighed. My heart raced and it felt harder to breathe. I'd been burning with curiosity about her family for so long, and now the chance was upon me and part of my mind told me to turn away from this situation—abandon Elodie—and never look back.

And maybe I should've listened to that voice. It isn't unreasonable to say that.

The darkness I told you about, the one that existed within Elodie, the one that followed her around like a shadow. That darkness wasn't an abstract inner darkness the way it is with me, or with so many of us. That darkness was palpable. Tangible. In the entity of her family. Her parents. The house they lived in.

Elodie's darkness was real. I may not have known it yet, not fully, but I was walking straight into it.

"While we're there..." said Elodie, "don't look in her eyes too long."

"Like with an animal?"

"Yes."

"So... just to clear things up," I said, hoping to lighten the mood, "you didn't orchestrate our entire relationship just so you could... you know... lure me to your parents' place and feed me to your mother, right?"

She huffed, and I knew I'd made a mistake. "Bennet. This isn't something I should have to tell you again and again. Don't judge my family."

I looked at her. "I'm not. I'm sorry. I think I'm just... nervous."

She met my eyes for a second, then nodded. By now she was used to my strange jokes, no matter how inappropriately timed they could be.

She said, "I used to spend a lot of time with her, separated by the plexiglass. I would look in her eyes when she was calm. And... and I would get lost there."

She fought back tears; I could tell by the tightness of her face, the tension in her jaw. I watched her, unable to look away, wanting to reach out and comfort her. This was new to me, this version of Elodie—the version she locked away.

She went on before I could ask her to. "And... you know how I said it's like I never really knew my mom? How I'm pretty sure it doesn't matter if you speak to her, because she doesn't understand? That's how it might be. You can speak to her, but it might not matter."

"So... sorry if this is a weird thing to ask, but I'm genuinely curious. Is she even aware of anything? You almost make it sound like she's catatonic."

"It's hard to explain. Maybe you'll just have to see for yourself. But she's definitely not catatonic. And she is aware. I know that much. I said she was protective of me."

"Right."

"I guess what I'm saying is, she can hear us. But... but it might not mean she can understand."

"Okay. And... and what about your dad?"

I had asked Elodie three times about her father. She tended to react differently when her father was brought up—I noticed the pattern after the second time I asked.

With questions about her mother, she satiated my curiosity incrementally with her small answers, offering cursory glimpses. And now that she was opening up about her mother, I saw how emotional it made her.

But something was different with her father—a different emotion sparked in her eyes when I brought him up. Something more like anger.

"You do *not* want to go there," she had said the first time.

"Seriously, Bennet, let's not talk about this now," she had said the second time.

And the third time, she'd been halfway through a joint I'd rolled for her. We'd been sitting on a rock overlooking an expanse of hills and trees. She leaned back on her elbows, took a large hit, shook her head. "The only thing you need to know about my father is that you should be afraid of him. Sometimes I think he should be locked up somewhere."

This time, as we drew close to the estate—twenty minutes away now—Elodie tightened her fingers around the steering wheel, took a deep breath through her nose.

"You're gonna want to love him," she said, surprising me. "He'll charm you. He can be so kind, and so courteous, and so fucking *perfect*. I'd be surprised if he didn't make this a pleasant visit for you."

"That's what I should expect?"

"Just understand that it's an illusion, Bennet. A magician's showmanship, or a salesman's persona. He has this way of looking at people... like he's trying to figure out what makes them tick. Or figure something out about them just by looking."

"How should I handle him?"

"Don't." She almost laughed. I felt insulted. "Just hold eye-contact with him as much as you can when he's talking to you. I think it'll be okay, otherwise."

When we pulled up to the paved driveway which sat nestled in the thick trees and carved a way through to a massive brooding house, I was struck by a dizzying perspective.

How many people assured their significant other that "everything would be okay" about meeting their parents?

How many of them meant it the way Elodie seemed to mean it?

The entranceway didn't boast the name of the family, which was the only disappointment. I'd been picturing something dramatic in that way, but it was a gate without any names. And the gate stood open, inviting us in.

I felt like we were falling toward a threat, asking to be consumed by a thing that awaited us baring sharp, poisonous teeth. And I wanted to ask her: should I be on my guard? How badly might this go? What happens if your mother doesn't trust me... how far do her protective instincts go? What did you mean by getting lost if you look in her eyes too much? What sort of mental minefield am I stepping into with your father?

Are we safe? That was the biggest one, flashing in my mind like a warning sign.

I didn't say anything. She might take it wrong, might think I was being judgmental of her family.

The Villeneuve estate rested in a cul-de-sac of the forest, enshrined by the looming trees and hills beyond. Most of the mansion was made from dark timber, the walls rearing up in a mountainous way, and a massive brick chimney billowed amongst the roof's dramatic vaults.

Beyond the mansion, the grounds were visible along the driveway. An expanse of garden interlaced with cobbled walkways. A number of statues carved from mythological, inhuman figures, and a handful of stone fountains. But even the beautiful grounds were encased by gates and a tall metal fence. Much of this fence appeared to be electric. But was it to keep something out—or to keep something in?

It struck me as bizarre that a house so dark could stand before a place so serene and colorful. But much of the house's darkness was conjured by the fear building in my own mind.

In truth, the place inspired awe.

As did the man who stood waiting before the mansion's front steps. His face was like an elegant brown stone. I could read nothing from those eyes. In his slim purple blazer over a glossy black and crimson vest, his pearly black shoes, dark walking stick, and hungry smile, Hugo Villeneuve was not a man I wanted to meet.

I remember the way he looked at me as I approached him with a hand extended in greeting. Look at people closely enough and you'll discover they're most honest with their bodies and their eyes. Hugo Villeneuve greeted his daughter with warmth and a big smile, and I saw what appeared to be sorrow on his face. The kind of sorrow that comes from too much joy. When you're so filled up, you know it can't last.

This is how I realized, upon the first impression, that he must truly love his daughter. In his way, at least.

He shook my hand firmly and looked into my eyes. Although he smiled politely, his face lost any signs of the joy he'd greeted his daughter with. The light seemed to drain from his irises and he cocked his head lightly to one side, a sign he was putting up with me.

Or was it my imagination?

"You must be Elodie's romantic partner," he said. He had a meticulous way of pronouncing his words. Calculated, I would say. Every word out of his mouth probably went through a series of filters before finding his voice.

I liked that about him immediately.

"I cannot say I looked forward to meeting you," he said, "but I can see you are not what I expected."

How to react to that?

"I've not heard much about you, but it's good to finally meet you," I said, keeping it simple. And we stared at each other, daring the other to look away first, before Elodie insisted we head inside.

"I think I need to see her first." Elodie said this to both of us

—her father and me. But she said it while looking at me, facing me on the elegant burgundy couch. I held onto one of her hands and nodded.

I told her I understood. "Come and get me when you're ready?"

"I will." She kissed me. Turned and met eyes with her father, who waited in his armchair which was somehow just as extravagant as the couch. "She's behind the glass?"

"She is," he said. "Likely in the solarium today. I told her she needed to come inside. You should have seen the way she lit up when I told her you were coming to visit."

I watched Elodie, waiting for an indication of what she'd told me before—that to her it didn't matter if you spoke to her mother because she probably didn't understand—but she appeared excited.

"Want me to go with you, sweetheart?"

"I'm okay, Dad."

She gave me a look of both worry and reassurance before rising from the couch. She disappeared beyond a set of pine doors which had a thick wooden bar for a lock. I supposed Elodie's mother's glass was beyond these doors. Her section of the house.

And although I've never been one to succumb to social anxiety, my nervousness spiked when I realized Elodie had left me alone with her father.

He and I regarded each other across the glass coffee table. Shafts of light fell into the house through the windows behind me, but the room felt encroached upon by shadows.

Hugo's attention, projected from the elegant brown stone of his face, settled unwaveringly upon me.

"This is a beautiful home," I said, uncharacteristically squeamish beneath his attention. "And the whole property—I only got a glimpse of it coming in, but I'd—"

"How long is it now, that you've been with my daughter?"

I paused, swallowing my smalltalk. "We've been together for a little over four months."

"Forgive me for prying, Bennet, but my daughter and I haven't spoken in nearly four years."

"I understand. It feels like time's flown by with Elodie, and like we've known each other forever."

Hugo smiled, nodding. There was a gentleness to his demeanor, a soft-spoken eloquence I had to admire. "I know the feeling," he said. "When I first met my Alodia, it was not so much a feeling of first meeting, but of meeting again. As if I had been looking for her for a long, long time."

Alodia, I thought, and realized Elodie had never told me her mother's name. *Alodia Villeneuve.*

Hugo spoke before I could ask him about her.

"Do you love my daughter?"

"I do," I said. "But there are a lot of different ways to define love, aren't there."

That smile again—a sort of twitch at the corner of his mouth, which his lips then conceded fully, with a sort of politeness. There was so much more emotion behind his face than he allowed to show through. For some reason I received the impression that he was greatly amused, might even burst out laughing if he let the mask slip.

"An educated answer," he said. "I'm sure you're aware of how the Greeks defined love."

"They had four different words for it, didn't they?"

"Oh, there were at least eight."

"Eight. Wow."

"If I were to ask of you the depth of your love for my daughter, I wonder which of the Greek words for love you might name?"

Difficult to tell if this was a question he expected an answer for, or some way of playing tricks with my mind. I decided to answer regardless—and, if I'm being honest, I wanted to impress him.

"I may sound educated, but if you asked me to name the Greek words for love, I wouldn't be able to. I just know that I love Elodie."

"You need her."

"Maybe I do. But I don't like to imagine that any of us ever really *needs* another person."

"Ah." The beginnings of a smile, though suppressed, on his mouth. "Spoken like a person cautious in love. This is a mistake, often made by those who plant the roots of their hurt and let it make them cynical."

"I've had bad relationships in the past, if that's what you mean. But I'm over that."

Hugo studied me. "So, you claim you do not need my daughter. Fair enough. You two are still new to each other. But you want her. You choose to be with her, not out of codependent necessity, but out of desire. Perhaps something even more than simple desire."

"I don't have your way with words, Mr. Villeneuve, but... yes. I suppose so."

"Do you satisfy my daughter?"

If things had seemed pleasant before, the illusion now faltered. This was more the sort of question I'd been expecting from Hugo, because of the way Elodie had warned me about him.

It occurred to me to state that it wasn't any of his business. To pretend like I didn't know what he meant and answer innocently, weaving my way around the question.

But why hide behind pretense? We were diving in, either way.

"Yes," I said, trying to speak confidently, trying to hold his gaze. "I hope so, at least."

"You've not made certain of this?"

My face glowed red. "Well, Elodie isn't the most forthcoming person. But as long as we communicate, I'm sure she'd let me know if there were a problem. And I'm sure she'd have left me by now if I wasn't satisfying her."

I felt pleased with my answer and managed not to shrink beneath Hugo's stare. His expression remained stony, unchanging, for maybe a whole minute. Elodie had said, on the first night we met, that time could curl and uncurl. This returned to me as I stared back at her father.

Hugo smiled. And laughed. A dry sound, a laugh like the scraping of dead leaves across asphalt.

And suddenly I preferred the silence.

"You seem like a good man, Bennet. I do not say this lightly.

And I see why she must be drawn to you. You do not pull your hand away when it gets too hot."

"No," I said, entranced.

"A rare quality in a man. Most of the men I have known are cowards. In fact, I'm sure Elodie would say something similar about the men in her life. But you. I do not receive this impression from you. Not yet, anyway. And you seek something from my daughter that you've not found elsewhere in the world. She ignites where others disappoint." He noticed how I gaped at him. "Am I wrong in this, Bennet?"

"I think these might be private matters, Mr. Villeneuve."

He laughed again—that scraping dead-leaf laugh—but his eyes widened and he leaned forward as if to better see me. "There are no locked doors in this house. I'm surprised you've not learned this by now."

Whether he meant this as code for something, or if he meant it as a form of philosophical play, I had no way of knowing. But I replied, hardly letting myself stop to consider what he might mean—what he might really mean, beneath the words he spoke.

"You're talking about your wife," I asked, but not as a question.

He showed his teeth, more a snarl than a grin. "Tell me, Bennet. What has my daughter told you about her mother?"

"I'm asking you, Mr. Villeneuve."

"Call me Hugo, if you would."

"Hugo. What's wrong with your wife?"

"Ah, Bennet, that is a matter of perception. You see, there is nothing wrong with my wife."

"That's not how it sounded when Elodie—"

"Elodie doesn't understand. She *refuses* to understand, is what I mean to say, although she knows differently in her heart. You'll see."

If Elodie hadn't come back into the room then, I may have excused myself and went outside to wait in the car. As scintillating as this conversation was, Hugo made me want to jump out of my skin. But the twin doors swung open and Elodie stepped through. There were tears in her eyes.

"We should go," said Elodie. She took my hand, pulled me up from the couch. Turned back to her father. "Thank you for calling, Dad. But Bennet and I need to be leaving."

I said, in a low voice to her, "What?"

She gave me a look.

Hugo rose from his seat and leaned into his black walking stick. "You've only just arrived. Bennet was just expressing to me his interest in meeting your mother."

Elodie glared at him, then at me.

I said, "We were talking about her. I... I mean, I'd like to meet her, if—"

"We came here for a reason," she said. "And now I've seen her and we can go."

"Elodie, I thought—"

"I got what I came here for. Now can we go? Please?"

"Elodie." Hugo spoke her name as if reciting the verse of a song. "How unbecoming. Your partner hasn't met your own mother and you're trying to rush him out the door as if this place is filled with poison gas."

"It *is* filled with poison gas." She let go of my hand, stood up to her father. "Mom had bruises on her arms."

"Oh, yes." Her father laughed. "From the other night. I assure you, she enjoyed it as much as I did."

"*Did she?*" Her voice held fire underneath, but I noticed the way one leg trembled with nervous energy and, with her arms crossed over her chest, her fingers tapped incessantly at her bicep. "Because she looks a lot weaker to me, compared to the last time I saw her. And I swear to God, Dad, if you've taken advantage of her—"

Hugo's eyes widened and his lips peeled back in a bestial sneer. The room shrunk and he became the towering center.

I had never seen such a violent shift in demeanor before. It flashed to the surface like fumes igniting, and although I stood across a glass coffee table from him, my reaction was physical: I stepped back, nearly forcing myself back onto the couch. My chest felt as though it filled with ice.

"Elodie, if you think I would intend to harm your mother in any way, ever, for *any* reason..." He inhaled sharply between gritted teeth, but seemed to hold it in, trying to let it simmer and calm. "How *dare* you, Elodie."

She had taken a step back like I had, crossed her arms tighter around herself. "It's obvious how much weaker she is. You have to be *careful* with her."

"And you think I don't know this, Elodie? You think I do not live with this reality every day? Or that I don't do everything I must to make sure she isn't harmed?"

"Bruises, Dad. On her *wrists*. Like you were holding her—"

"I am perfectly willing to discuss the details, Elodie, if that is what you wish. But take into account what your mother is capable of, and the care I must take for myself and also for her sake."

Trembling, she appeared to consider her father's words before she conceded a nod.

"I'm sorry. It's... it's hard... seeing her like this." She bowed her head.

And I couldn't believe what I was seeing. I had never seen Elodie back down like that, not from anyone—especially not from me. But that was it.

And suddenly I understood... there was so much more to this situation, and to her relationship with her family, than I ever could've prepared myself for.

The last of Hugo's fury became embers. He reached a hand out to touch her shoulder. "I know, my dear. I know."

And then he looked to me, and Elodie turned with him.

"Come, Bennet," he said. "Time for you to meet my Alodia."

6

Alodia

I was thirteen years old when I saw a dead person for the first time.

I'd been with a group of friends on the edge of town, wandering without direction, discovering shortcuts and backroads and hidden places—the secrets of our hometown from angles we'd never considered before—all in the name of what we called adventure.

You know how it is, I'm sure. It doesn't matter where you grew up, eventually you grew tired of it. We were young and didn't know what to do with ourselves. Sometimes we simply wandered. The discovery of a secret alleyway behind two otherwise familiar restaurants, or a field between the old McDonald's and the elementary school, become frontier paradises for a day if you've never seen them before. We sought ways to turn our stale, familiar town into something unexpected, something exciting, in every small way we could.

Which is how we discovered the dead man in the field of tall grass between the edge of town and the interstate.

The red tent became visible only from the parking lot of an abandoned building that must've once been a visitor's center. We sometimes met up at this decaying lot, although the excitement of the abandoned building had long died off since we had explored it so many times before. There were four of us including me, and I was the one who noticed the tent.

"You think it's Blackbeard's tent?" one of them asked. Blackbeard was one of the local homeless, distinct for obvious reasons. Rumors circulated that he was schizophrenic, or a heroin addict, or other things that were probably bullshit. And Blackbeard had been trespassed from so many places in town for setting up his tent behind businesses, in alleyways, near the railroad tracks. He seemed a harmless person except for the pictures of his sunburnt face posted behind cash registers through town, warning not to sell him alcohol.

And it looked like his tent. We thought it might be fun to see if he was around, see if we could scare him.

I don't know. We were kids. Guess that's the best answer I've got.

We found Blackbeard on the blanket outside of his tent. It might've been easy to think he slept but for the smell, the hollowness of his skin, the way his head had lolled to the side and his grey eyes stared vacantly, not seeing.

One of my friends threw himself away from the scene and threw up in the grass. Everyone else stood with their hands over their mouths, gone quiet in the presence of death. Maybe most of us had never seen a dead person before. I hadn't.

But I have never been able to look away. I have always needed to reach my hand out to test the heat. To make the flame dance with the passing of my hand.

This is why I was the only one to step forward. I crouched close to the body, then dropped lower onto my hands and looked into the dead man's eyes.

Except... this isn't really what I want to talk about.

What really comes to mind is my mother, in hospice, propped up in her bed.

How it felt when I went into that room, greeting her like I always did, prepared to sit down at the bedside, open the book under my arm, and read to her. I read to her a lot, since we didn't always have things to talk about in those last few weeks. She loved falling asleep to the sound of my voice.

But the time—the last time—when I looked in her eyes, and the realization struck me that she wasn't looking back—

It was the same with Blackbeard, sprawled outside his tent, eyes staring, unseeing, off into nothing.

It was the same with her. My mother. In a different way.

That's how it felt the first time I looked into the ashen eyes of Elodie's mother, Alodia Villeneuve.

I looked into her irises—ashen, I said, like Elodie's—and although those eyes were aimed in my direction, she didn't seem to look back. Not like a human does.

The room on the other side of the plexiglass wall still resembled a living space: generously cushioned couch by a fireplace that hadn't seen flame in far too long; a bed with a few tangled sheets; a dining table with two chairs; an abundance of healthy plants. The centerpiece was the solarium, almost large enough to be a greenhouse of its own, jutting out into sunlight on the far wall. The solarium had a bed as well, plus a few cushioned seats and a table. Plants draped their green fingers and splayed hands of leaves.

In dusty shafts of sunlight, among the hanging plants, stood Alodia.

I found out later how old she was. Hugo was in his late sixties, though he could've passed for a decade younger. Most of his wrinkles were laughter lines at the corners of his eyes and mouth. Alodia was in her early fifties, but she, too, didn't look her age. Not even close.

It wouldn't have mattered her age, either; she was simply one of the most beautiful women I'd ever seen. The shadow of her youth had not withered, was in fact an enduring legacy.

Alodia's wild hair must've once been much darker, but now boasted locks of striking grey and white slithering through. It reminded me of Elodie's hair, how it rose up without direction and then dropped, tumbling across her shoulders and down to her shoulder blades.

She stood facing away from us, looking out the solarium, out at the estate's expansive, colorful grounds. She wore a black leotard that hugged her slender form and ended at her thighs, leaving her muscled legs exposed.

Alodia's head twitched slightly when we entered the room, meaning she must've heard us. Her movements were swift and exact, not quite jerky, not quite robotic, but also not quite human, as she turned to face us.

And her eyes.

God. Her eyes.

I'm not sure when Elodie had taken my hand, but she squeezed it now, her fingers interlaced with mine. I squeezed back and would've looked to her for assurance, for courage—for anything—but in truth I couldn't tear my eyes away from her mother.

In a series of rapid movements, hunched and occasionally resorting to moving on all fours, Alodia slinked across the room until she stood only a few feet from us, separated by the plexiglass which seemed, suddenly, so thin and fragile.

Alodia raised her slender, toned arms above her head and pressed her hands against the glass until her palms turned white. The rest of her body followed, including her face. Her nose flattened and her lips crushed against the cold, clear surface, so that the view was, to us, somewhat comical. Or would've been comical, under other circumstances. Her breaths were rapid, fogging the glass.

I looked on, gaping, trying to remember how to stand, how to breathe, how to think.

Those eyes. Like the eyes of my mother after she had faded away. Like the eyes of old Blackbeard, baking in the uncaring afternoon sun. Blank. Staring but not seeing. Wide and alert and somehow empty.

Except they weren't quite like human eyes. Where human eyes were glassy and white, Alodia's appeared to have texture to them: a thick, yellow-tinted film across them. Her irises were a thin yellowish ring, leaving her pupils as wide black holes.

I said Elodie's father, Hugo, had a face like a stone. Perhaps it's more accurate to say that Alodia's *eyes* were like stones—polished dark stones, glimmering in her widely held sockets. Every few seconds her pupils darted off in another direction, but always, after a second, they flicked back to us—to me, it seemed. Or maybe she was looking at Elodie.

Maybe she was assessing me, the man who held the hand of her beloved daughter.

"Alodia, my love," said Hugo. His voice held none of the command he'd used with me; the tone was gentle, melodic, like singing moonlight. "This is Bennet, the man I told you about. The man Elodie is with. You see?"

Alodia's black-hole eyes shifted to Hugo and then back to me. The rest of her body, pressed up against the glass, had gone completely still

Like a reptile, I thought. You know what I mean. The way they move and then stop and are completely still.

Except for the eyes. Shifting here and there in reaction. Assessing. Analyzing. Watching. While her quick breaths fogged the glass.

Elodie squeezed my hand and I again became aware of my own body. Sweaty palms, the tension in my muscles, cold sheen of sweat forming across my skin.

Breathe, I reminded myself. Keep breathing.

"It's okay," Elodie whispered. "It's thick glass. And she's calm."

I tried to nod. Maybe I succeeded.

Hugo spoke. "This glass is designed with vents all along the bottom and top." Pride was eking into his gentle tone. "She can hear you, Bennet, if you wish to speak with her."

I managed to turn and look at him. His countenance presented the opposite of mine: calm, comfortable, genuinely at ease.

He flashed his teeth at me. "This is Elodie's mother. Don't you want to introduce yourself? Make a good first impression?"

What I wanted was to get the fuck out of here and never come back, never think about this place, never try to get Elodie to talk about it ever again.

No wonder she ran away when she was young. No wonder she'd responded to my prying with cold denial.

The thought occurred to me to apologize to her. Turn to her now, take her by the shoulders, look her in the eyes and say I'm sorry. I didn't mean to bring you back here. I didn't mean for you to have to face this again. I understand now. I do. Let's go. Let's start over.

Anything to get away from the plexiglass and the feral, dead-eyed woman on the other side of it, standing with her whole body pressed up against it like a reptile reaching for the light.

But when I remembered how to turn my head again and look at Elodie, she wasn't looking at me. Her eyes were on her mother.

And it wasn't fear in Elodie's eyes. Not like in mine.

She looked worried. Sad, even. Yes, sad. Especially that. But underneath the sadness, there was adoration.

And I knew what this meant to her.

"Hello, Alodia." I let go of Elodie's hand when I took a step toward the plexiglass. For a second I felt my legs go numb and I thought my knees would buckle beneath me, but I managed to keep my balance. My skin was slick with sweat now, my breaths felt labored coming up from my lungs, but I stepped until I stood a mere foot away from the glass. A mere foot away from those empty, staring eyes.

Did she have thoughts? Was there anything more than instinct behind those eyes, motivating those swift, inhuman movements?

"My name is Bennet," I said.

Alodia's diaphragm rose and fell, rose and fell; the glass fogged between her pressed lips. Her breathing appeared to quicken at the sound of my voice.

I spoke again. "Ever since I met Elodie, I've wanted to meet you. I hope you don't mind if I call you Alodia. It's a beautiful name." I looked over my shoulder. Elodie watched me, biting her bottom lip, trembling. Trembling with something like joy. Anticipation and joy.

I continued. Uncertain if it mattered to Alodia what I said, I tried to say what I hoped Elodie would want to hear. And I ignored Hugo.

"Alodia, your daughter is the most beautiful person I've ever met. She and I have... w-we've gotten to know each other better over the, um, the past couple months." I spoke slowly, annunciating every word—not because I wanted to make sure Alodia could hear me, but to make sure I made any sense. "And I love her, Alodia. I love your daughter."

Alodia's breathing stayed fast. If she were a normal person, she would've been hyperventilating. But somehow it was not so strange, nor so dire, for her. Things seemed to be going okay, however.

And then Elodie came up beside me and reached a hand out for the glass, meaning to touch it, to press her palm to it—

And I reacted instinctively, because even though I knew it was plexiglass, knew we were safe on this side of it, my brain had switched into panic from the moment we stepped into the room.

I swiped my hand out and blocked Elodie's hand before it could touch the glass, the way some drivers, just before a car accident, throw an arm out to the passenger as if to shield them—

And Alodia Villeneuve screamed.

Even through the glass the sound bellowed with enough vibrating force that I physically recoiled and threw my hands over my ears.

The feral woman's face had elongated as her jaw dropped and her lips peeled away from her teeth—and she screeched. A banshee's shrill screech, something you imagine hearing in the woods at night before shadows come rushing at you. Something you conjure in your imagination while reading ghost stories in the dark.

Alodia smacked the glass with one of her hands and the dull *thunk* echoed across the entire room.

I had fallen onto my hands, backing away on the floor, reaching for the twin doors. My heart raced. Breaths came in gasps.

Hugo had rushed to the glass and stood now between us, as if to block us from his wife's sight. He was muttering something to her, offering sweet nothings, soft assurances, in that sickening gentle tone. But Alodia wasn't looking at him. Even with the blankness of her eyes, I could tell she was looking past him —eyes held widely, lips peeled back in a snarl—at me.

Elodie stood back, arms crossed over herself, eyes aimed at the ground. After a moment, she turned and fled the room, not even casting a glance my way.

With panic flowing through me, I followed.

7

Moving Through the Dark

I'm not sure you'll understand, but I hope you do.

On that first night—the first night we both stayed at her father's house—I arose in the middle of the night and went looking for Alodia. Something in me wouldn't let me rest until I saw her again. A mere glimpse would do.

Hugo had set up a room for us upstairs, a room nice enough it could've been an old-fashioned hotel suite. Queen bed, two chairs and a table by one of the two windows, a private bathroom with two sinks and a tub large enough to fit four people.

I found Elodie by one of the windows, standing between the thick white curtains which framed her around the late afternoon light. She could've been a ghost looking down into a world she was no longer part of. Her arms were still wrapped around her body as though she were cold.

"We can leave in the morning," she said, not turning to face me. She stared blankly out the window. I sat on the edge of the bed and watched her, wishing she'd turn and look at me.

"I didn't mean to... to make that happen, Elodie. I don't know why—"

"It's fine." She appeared to hug herself tighter, as if she could make herself shrink. "We can leave in the morning and you don't ever have to come back here."

"What does that mean?"

She didn't answer. Didn't turn.

I felt as if something were slipping through my fingers, and the tighter I tried to hold on, the faster it dropped away.

"Elodie."

"What?" She lifted her head but didn't turn. Still, it felt as if she were glaring at me. "What is it?"

I asked, "What's going on?"

This time she turned.

Her eyes glistened, but her stare contained as much frustration as it did sadness.

"I haven't seen her in so long."

"Four years, wasn't it?"

She sat beside me on the edge of the bed. The light outside the window had grown dim, hinting toward the softer blue of evening.

Elodie rocked back and forth, one leg bouncing with nervous energy. I had never seen someone fight back tears with such insistence.

"You should've seen the way she reacted when she saw me,"

said Elodie. "The way her posture changed. Like... like she'd been *waiting* for me." She gave me a despairing look. "What if she was? What if, all this time... like when you leave a dog alone, and when you come back—no matter how long it's been—they die to see you. They can't stop crying and jumping all over you. I mean..." She lifted a hand up over part of her face, appeared to bite into one of her fingers.

"Well, if she's capable of missing you," I said, "then I'm sure she did. You're her daughter, and now that I've... now that I've met her, and know what it's like to be, you know, around her... I mean, of course she missed you."

She nodded, clinging to my words.

"But you can't feel guilty for leaving," I said. "Everyone leaves home. Everyone's got their own problems and their own lives. And if she can understand... I mean... she *can* understand what we say, right?"

"I guess I don't know. I really don't know." Tears finally slipped down her cheeks. "Sometimes I think I must be projecting, you know? I'd like to think she hears me when I tell her I missed her, or that I love her... but I could just be imagining it. Because sometimes it's like there's nothing there. Sometimes I'm sure there isn't."

Her mother's face flashed in my mind. Jaw dropping open, eyes striking wide, that shrill screech. The way a single slap of her hand on the glass seemed to make the whole room shake.

"Your dad seems to think she can understand us."

She didn't say anything.

"And, Elodie... if you don't want to leave in the morning,

I'm... I mean, I'm a little freaked out, but I'll be fine, it'll be fine, if you wanna stay longer. Another day or two, maybe."

She put a hand on my leg. "Thanks. But we should go. After breakfast."

I felt relief.

Elodie turned away from me in bed to stare into the dark.

I knew because of her breathing. Whereas I could lie awake in bed long enough to have watched half a movie before falling asleep, Elodie slipped into unconsciousness sometimes moments after closing her eyes.

Not tonight.

Tonight her breathing didn't change, her body never surrendered fully to its own weight. I could all but feel her eyes staring vaguely in the direction of the window. Maybe those eyes shimmered. Maybe she suppressed whimpers in her chest.

I waited an hour. Then rose from the bed and left the room. Walked through the dark hallway, found the stairs, descended.

Before stepping through the dark twin doors, I thought of my mother.

How often I thought of her in that wheelchair, snapping at me, her eyes no longer the eyes of my saintlike mother. Her words spraying like acid. Psyche peeling away to reveal a darkness I'd never known existed.

How often my soft memories of her were tainted by the poison of the things she'd said to me in agony. True, maybe she hadn't meant them. Maybe they'd been like the words that fly from the mouth after a stubbed toe, or a broken bone, or a cut deep enough to draw blood.

Or maybe they'd been the things she always wanted to say, the things she never let herself say.

I thought of Elodie as I pressed on the twin doors and they opened on darkness. I thought of what she'd said the first night we met when I told her my mother had died of cancer.

I understand.

And now I understood she'd been telling the truth.

The puzzle box opened on another, smaller puzzle box. But the reward for getting this far was here, beyond the twin doors, beyond the plexiglass, in the dark.

My eyes adjusted to the night on the other side of the twin doors.

The plexiglass had no glare to obscure my vision of the living space on the other side. At first glance the room appeared empty. There were no lights, no candles, only the darkness that seeped in from outside the windows, dim from soft moonlight.

My heartbeat and my anxious breathing felt loud in the pressing silence. Everything seems louder in the dark.

I stood for a long time in front of the plexiglass, scanning the room for signs of movement. Was she in here? I noticed there were two doors in the room, against the walls, which didn't appear to lead outside. She had other sections of the house glassed off. She might not be in here at all.

And it occurred to me that maybe she was allowed outside on the grounds at night. No doubt she was allowed during daylight—the fences around the property were a strong indicator. Maybe she was out there somewhere, among the colorful gardens beneath the stars and gentle silver moonlight.

I needed to see her one more time, before Elodie and I left for home in the morning.

Just one more time. Without anyone else around.

In pregnant silence I stood, studying the room, letting my eyes adjust, for as long as it took. When I determined I was alone here, I went to the plexiglass door, hoping it didn't require a key.

It didn't. There was a keyhole and a latch, but the latch was undone and the door opened easily.

It smelled like leaves and moisture on the other side of the plexiglass, probably because of the plants populating the walls and solarium.

I explored every inch of the living space, noting what looked like claw marks on certain walls and on one of the doors. In one of the corners, Alodia appeared to have stored leftover food. Bits of beef and chicken, some straight off the bone; half-eaten vegetables and fruit. Worse, however: the carcass of a rat covered in bite-marks. And insects without heads: a praying mantis, a large fluffy moth, a variety of beetles.

My hand flew to my neck and my throat tightened, constricted. I gagged, stepping away.

What the fuck? Did she eat insects, like a fucking lizard? Was she saving the rat for later?

What the hell was wrong with this woman?

Minutes passed as I calmed myself. The urge to vomit came and went.

I went to the bed of tangled sheets and torn pillows. Beside it, on a nightstand with markings that said it had been knocked over many times, sat a leather journal.

Hugo's name was inscribed into the leather.

I would've started to flip through it immediately if not for the feeling that I'd been in this room far too long. If Alodia was awake somewhere, what if she came back? What would she think when she saw me? That is, assuming she had thoughts.

Maybe she would remember me as the person who had kept Elodie from reaching a hand out. Maybe Alodia would remember the emotion that had caused her to screech at me.

So I took the journal instead. Tucked it into the waistband of my pants.

And would have simply left, gone back up to bed to be with Elodie, if I hadn't heard something outside.

A shuffling sound, maybe someone struggling out there on the cobbled walkway outside the windows. Followed by a very human grunt and the sound of panting.

Chills rippled over my skin. Breath caught in my lungs. With eyes wide, every muscle held tense, I moved toward the solarium, which offered the widest view of the grounds outside.

The noises grew louder. Grunting. Panting. I took a step inside the solarium, trying to peer through the windows.

What I saw made me gasp. Truly gasp. The sort of breath that forces itself through you involuntarily, makes you feel frozen inside.

Hugo and Alodia were out there, on the brick walkway. They were tangled in each other, both naked in the dark.

Hugo was on top, between Alodia's legs. He was humping her viciously, pressing with all of his weight and more. One of his hands held one of Alodia's wrists to the ground, while his other wrapped around her neck.

Her legs were lifted up around his back, keeping him in rhythm.

As I watched, their movements grew more intense—faster, harder—and Hugo moaned. It was a coarse, ravenous sound.

And then Alodia lashed out with her free hand, appearing to seize Hugo by his neck, and suddenly she was on top. It happened too quickly, more an attack than a movement of passion. Hugo lay beneath her, at her mercy, as she readjusted herself so she was crouching on top of him, one hand around his neck, the other digging into his shoulder, pinning him down. She slapped her body down against his again, again, again, quickening, intensifying.

I heard them come. Heard the choked sound of his penultimate cry. Heard another cry, one both bestial and undeniably feminine—high in pitch, a noise of release rather than fury or pain—from Alodia. She lifted herself up, arching herself back, head up and bent away so she could look at the sky, and her entire body spasmed and convulsed on top of Hugo.

He reached up for her, found her breasts, her shoulders, and he pulled her into an embrace. She went still, surrendering, perhaps out of energy—understanding in her primal way that she'd finished something and could rest.

I turned and ran, certain that, this time, I couldn't stop myself from being sick.

8

Rat Trap

"Elodie tells me you were in a longterm relationship with another woman before," said Hugo as he sat across the crimson table from us.

Although Elodie and I were already packed to leave, Hugo insisted on making us breakfast. He prepared a full board of food and set up in his dining room. The table could seat a dozen, but it was just the three of us.

I couldn't look at Hugo without the image of last night returning to my mind. And while that threw me off, so did his inquiry.

Elodie went red in the face. "Dad. Over breakfast?"

"Come now, Elodie." Hugo's eyes didn't waver from mine as he leaned comfortably back in his seat. "There are no locked doors here. And how else am I to know you, Bennet, if we cannot discuss truthful matters?" He flashed his teeth at me and the gesture was almost reptilian. I thought of the compliments he'd paid me yesterday—about how I don't move my hand away when it gets too hot. How I'm more interested in what lies beneath pretense.

I couldn't help but admire him. He'd lain a trap for me.

"I was with someone else for about three years."

"Ah, yes. You are someone who is unafraid of commitment."

"Well, when I say something, I mean it."

"And what of the things you don't say?"

I scooted to the edge of my chair, eyeing him carefully. "I try not to hold things back, if that's what you mean."

Hugo nodded. "This does not surprise me. You strike me as an honest man who cannot help himself."

"Well I appreciate the compliment, but I feel it's a basic kindness we should afford those we care about, don't you?"

He flashed that grin again, though I couldn't imagine why. It seemed he was increasingly pleased with my answers, as if he were peeling back my layers with meticulous intention, or playing a game of chess with me in which he remained several steps ahead at every turn.

"Another way of saying this, perhaps," said Hugo, "is that silence is its own form of dishonesty."

Had Elodie told him about Kendra? He knew I'd been in a relationship, but did he know what happened? I looked over at her but she was focused on her father—I saw no indication in her eyes. No. Hugo was simply figuring me out on his own.

As if to confirm this, he said, "And I receive the impression, Bennet, that this is how you have been hurt."

I don't blush easily, but I could feel my cheeks burning red. Too late to try and retreat from this conversation.

Hugo went on. "When you give yourself, you do so fully." This was a statement, not a question.

"Yes."

"And this other woman... she was dishonest."

"Yes."

"Considering your view of honesty as both what you say and what you don't say—this being a basic modus operandi, if you will, for those who are close to us..."

"And those we claim to love," I added.

"Yes, especially those. Considering these things, you are, despite a rougher exterior, quite the romantic, Bennet. A romantic with a heart that is mending."

"*Dad.*" Elodie's voice cut through the line of conversation. She stared at him with wide eyes that sent a dozen more messages than her words could. And I sensed, in how she avoided looking at me, that she was embarrassed. Or scared, maybe. Scared of what this must be like for me. Scared of how I must feel about her family, and about this trip.

I turned to Hugo. "She made me feel like none of our time together meant anything to her, which tells me all I need to know about who she really is and how much I should miss her. She broke my heart, if that's what you're talking about. But it's done. And it's been months since I've really thought about it."

Hugo visibly felt the weight of my words with the way his gaze softened and how he folded his hands in front of him, appearing to drop into thought.

"Can I offer you a small piece of wisdom, Bennet?"

I made a vague gesture in his direction, as if to say *Whatever*. He took this as a yes. "This woman did you a favor."

"I know."

"Truly, Bennet. Not simply because you are here now, with Elodie. What you say about honesty, it clearly means a great deal to you. And this other woman is not even capable of living on this level. Forget her, I say. Forget all those you cannot trust."

Hugo's manner of speaking with such formality made his more human moments feel shocking. And he didn't even realize how accurate his words were, not simply about the way things had ended between Kendra and me, but about the way she'd treated me in the months leading up to our ending.

The nights spent wondering why I felt so alone even when she slept beside me. The slow afternoons agonizing over why she didn't seem to want to spend time with me, even though she often said she did. All the ways I'd deluded myself into thinking I was the one who needed to do more for the relationship—as if I were at fault for her distance and her unhappiness.

"But do not get me wrong," Hugo said, his voice cutting through the theater of my mind. "Regret will live in your body and fester. Do not regret the time you spent with a person who did not deserve it. It will consume your present, and take away from those you are now with. Believe me, Bennet, regret can haunt you to your grave. Rejoice, instead, for what you are capable of. If you could love the wrong person with such magnitude to have been caused so much pain, imagine what it is like to love the right person. Or, perhaps you do not need to imagine it."

He gave a small smile, then rose from his seat and grabbed his plate. "Thank you for the conversation."

And then he was gone. Elodie and I finished our breakfast in stiff silence.

Neither of us said much to each other on the drive home.

I tried to imagine why she was acting like this, but everything I could conceive made me angry. And the anger was building up—which was ridiculous, since we hadn't even talked about it yet.

But the only thing I could think of was the moment when she'd been reaching out to her mother and I had swiped her hand away, as if I'd been trying to protect her. Maybe, I thought, it upset her that I'd done that. Maybe she perceived it as something I'd done out of distrust.

And if that's what she thought, she was right. Not that I distrusted her. No. I'd been on the edge of panic. Part of my mind had believed she was putting herself in danger by reaching a hand out for her mother.

I didn't tell her about what I'd seen.

I didn't tell her about Hugo's leather journal, which sat in my bag like a hand-grenade.

When we were a few minutes from town, I asked where she wanted to spend the night. She sighed, told me she felt like being alone for awhile.

For awhile, which could mean anything. Could be just for tonight. Could be a week.

Or worse.

I considered asking about tomorrow, about if I should head over or if she wanted to come to my place. But instead I let the frustration simmer under my skin.

And when she pulled up to my place, we both sat in silence for a long time.

I turned to her, trying to breathe calmly. "I have to ask you something."

She waited.

"You said you were eight years old when you found your mother in the solarium, in the middle of the night."

She nodded.

"Was she normal when you were born? Did you know her, as a person?"

Elodie turned away from me, her eyes shifting ahead toward nothing. "She was like this by the time I was born."

I wish I could say this answer satisfied me, but all it did was further disturb me.

The image played again behind my eyes, not fading the way memories do but seeming to grow sharper in my mind, blocking the real world out. Hugo between Alodia's legs. Skin slick in the moonlit dark.

Alodia flipping him over and humping him like an animal wildly reaching for erotic satisfaction.

Hugo, a man drawn to that. A man who'd impregnated that woman. And that woman giving birth to a normal girl named Elodie.

Well... *normal* is the wrong word for Elodie.

And, finally, Alodia—in her inhuman condition—holding a fragile baby. And trying to kill it.

Elodie broke up the images in my mind when she spoke. "I'm sorry about this morning."

I sighed. "It's fine. It was interesting, actually."

"My dad doesn't have boundaries."

"I figured that out on my own, thanks."

"And you know I don't need protection from my own mother, Bennet."

"I know that."

"Do you?"

We locked eyes.

"Forgive me for being a little on edge," I said. "The last time I was introduced to a girlfriend's parents, the issue was alcoholism, not whatever the fuck all that was."

"All that? All that, Bennet? That's my family you're talking about."

"I get that. But you're not even *trying* to see this from my perspective. None of that was exactly easy, or comfortable."

"You think it was easy for me? Or comfortable *for me*?"

"Elodie, your dad asked me if I was satisfying you. And when you left me alone for, like, ten minutes this morning, after that whole fucking conversation about my ex—"

"I went to the bathroom."

"Right, sure. But every time you leave the room, I'm left alone with him. And you know what he said to me? He said he didn't hear anything from us last night. As in, he didn't hear us having sex. And it *worried* him. That's what he said."

She turned away again.

Unrelenting, I slew on. "God. The way he grinned at me. And some of the things he talked about, like... stuff I didn't know. He told me you're really close with your Mom. That's not the impression I've gotten."

"She's my mom."

"Everything he told me about you, in between all the other weird shit he kept throwing in, everything he said about you, I'd never heard before."

"Bennet..."

"Why did it feel like I was stepping into some kind of trap? A minefield, or no, no, a fucking rat trap. There's your father, who comes off as some kind of sociopath. There's your reptile mother. And you just... you just left me alone in all that, to be surprised by so much of it and at a complete loss of what to do, or what to say, or.... or what to fucking..." My vision pulsed, began to darken red at the edges. I became aware of how heavily I breathed, how my heart pounded.

The absurdity of my own words—and of this entire situation—wasn't lost on me. But this didn't diminish the burning frustration.

Elodie stared at me with glistening eyes. "Bennet. I'm sorry." She said the words but I didn't see the apology in her eyes. "I'm sorry. I am. But you're not looking at this from my point of view, either." She looked away again. For some reason that was pissing me off. I'd managed to look her father in the eyes. Why couldn't she look me in mine? "I hadn't seen them in four years," she said. "Sometimes... sometimes I try to forget them. Act like

I don't even have a family. It's been like that for a long time. So it'd be nice if you could try to understand a little bit."

"If I could try?" I snarled. "Elodie, that's all I've been doing this entire time. Trying." I shook my head.

She was right. I knew she was right. I knew what I should've been saying, knew I'd lost control and was still losing control. But I could grasp none of it. Couldn't slow myself down enough to stop and hear her, see her, as clearly as I should have.

She didn't drive away immediately once I climbed out of her car. She waited until I'd reached the front door of my apartment. I cast her a single glance back, met her eyes across the walkway. And, still teary-eyed, she drove away.

I tossed Hugo's leather journal across my bedroom. It landed in the corner, behind the small plastic trashcan which always seemed to be overflowing.

I sat on the edge of my bed, head in my hands, and tried to focus on my breathing in order to settle the volcanic eruption under my skin.

Elodie and I didn't see each other for weeks.

9

Old Patterns

I don't know.

That was her response to the last text I'd sent her: **What now?**

I don't know.

By the end of the second week without seeing her, I became convinced she no longer wanted to see me. Maybe she hated me. Maybe she had never loved me and I'd been tricking myself into believing her all along. Some version of that, anyway. I've always believed I must be a fool. My rationality untethers too easily, my heart can be restless.

Except it had never been like that around Elodie. Only in her absence, left alone with my thoughts to spin through my head, did I begin to lose a grip on any sense of mental or emotional stability.

As if I were dependent on her. Maybe I was. I have always

been afraid that maybe that's what love is: when you give yourself to someone and you belong to them, and they belong to you, and whatever the hell comes with all of that anguish and uncertainty and seemingly masochistic bullshit.

So what did I do after I received that text, after I'd come to the end of my hope that she still wanted to be with me?

I did what any asshole would do. Slipped back into old patterns.

Started going back to Night Owl. Which is how I eventually ran into her again.

But not before I ran into Kendra.

I went to Night Owl not to find someone to go home with—Elodie was the only person I had ever gone home with from there. I didn't go because I felt the petty need to act out, the way some people throw fits and end up destroying their relationships or filling themselves with guilt for years to come. I went because Night Owl was my bad habit.

Which isn't to say I don't have other bad habits. Night Owl is just one of them. I wanted a drink so that's where I went.

And by one drink, I mean five or six as I sat alone at a booth with no one to share the glow of the fake purple candle in the middle of the table.

The dance floor wasn't its usual firework show of noise. The music still pounded, colored lights still spun across the club, but the crowd was thin, lacking weight—a deciduous forest in the midst of winter.

I tried to take my time with my sixth drink of the evening,

but within minutes the glass was nearly empty and I felt no better than I had before arriving here. If anything I felt worse. Empty and sere and desolate, as if my insides had been scraped raw and all I could do was sit, drink, and hope the healing process started soon.

This was as bad as I'd ever felt with Kendra, even after discovering her with another guy. This was speeding downhill and realizing I didn't have a steering wheel.

Or something.

And then, as if conjured by the now hollow memories of my ex-girlfriend—memories I could look at now with only the faintest stirring of emotion—she appeared, emerging from the dance floor and setting her eyes on me the way a hunter looks upon prey after a long wait in the high grass.

Except... not *quite* like that. Kendra wasn't akin to a predator—not in the way Elodie was. If Elodie was a tiger, Kendra was a house cat. In which case, I was a plaything disregarded some time ago, now rediscovered.

I pretended not to notice her until she arrived at my table. She must've been drinking, otherwise she might not have approached so boldly, nor stood with such a magnetic need for attention.

After heartbreak, after the love is gone, after the memories have either been drained of their power or have been poisoned, all that's left is lust. An empty, dry, ravenous lust. It's the last thing to go in the remains of what used to be. The memories between sheets. The unexpressed desires rising to the surface, able only to taunt in the emptiness.

Seeing Kendra in front of me, low-cut crop top, high shorts with torn edges, skin sweaty under the dancing lights, I felt no semblance of what I'd once felt for her. What I felt was purely physical.

How do I put it lightly?

I mean, not lightly.

I wanted to have her and then never see her again. Ever. When I become attached to someone, the memories sit in my head and, for much longer than they should, contain some hint of power. That was what I felt, looking over at Kendra. A semblance of old desires.

Six drinks in, and the way she looked at me, I knew it was possible. And I wasn't about to dismiss the possibility. I still hated her for what she did to me, but desire doesn't play by conventional rules. And desire loves vengeance.

Especially with alcohol.

"Haven't seen you in awhile, Ben." She sat across from me, inviting herself.

I nursed what remained of my drink. Decided I no longer liked being called Ben. Said nothing.

"I saw your sister recently," she said. "And your, um... your new girl."

I raised an eyebrow in her direction. "Yeah. They told me."

"And you haven't answered any of my texts."

I emptied the glass and hoped someone would notice so another could be brought to me. If not, that meant a decent opportunity to exit the conversation if it didn't appear to be going my way.

I looked at her. "Why the fuck would I answer your texts?"

"Well... I honestly didn't think you'd stop talking to me. The last thing I wanted was to lose you. You know that, don't you?"

My expression—quite beyond my control, after six drinks—must've cued her in.

"Ben, please. I'm sorry. I just wanna talk to you."

I couldn't let the last thing go. "The last thing you wanted was to lose me?"

"I never wanted to hurt you."

"Well you have a funny way of not wanting to hurt people."

"Look. I know I can apologize over and over to you. All I've done the past couple months is regret what I did. I mean... look at you. I fucked this up. I was just... I was unhappy, and you didn't..." She trailed off, surely unafraid of continuing.

Somehow I knew I should've expected all of this. Seeing her now—the word to come to mind was pathetic—I wondered how I ever could've expected anything less than what she'd done to me. From someone like her, I mean.

I made a gesture to one of the waiters, who gestured back, indicating they'd be over when they could.

"What are you doing here, Kendra?"

She reached across the table to take my hand. I refused.

"Babe," she pleaded. The tears in her eyes didn't look real. But the regret did. Either she was a great actor or she meant it. "Just talk to me. Don't shut me out."

"You been coming here a lot?"

She nodded.

"Seeing other guys?"

"Yeah... I mean... I mean no. Not exactly. I've been looking for you. And I've hung out with a few people but I haven't... haven't spent any real time with anyone."

"What about him?"

She flinched.

"Or is that none of my business?" I said.

Her eyes lowered. "No. I haven't seen him since that day."

I didn't believe her. Simple as that.

The waiter came over and I ordered another beer. My last, I told myself, but knew it'd be fine if I was lying. I'm great at lying to myself.

"What about you?" Kendra asked. "What about that girl I met when I stopped by your place?"

"I don't know."

The sixth beer was not my last. By the end of my seventh, my vision swayed so erratically that it split sometimes into two, creating ghost images spinning and dancing around the solider reality.

Kendra kept bringing up things from the past. Parts of our relationship that had been on her mind, apparently, and which she either wanted to talk about or even—strangely—hoped for an apology from me. But these things, put through the blender of my alcohol-hazed mind, barely registered. And I did no apologizing to her. I was done with that.

Kendra took my arm to keep me steady. She helped me into a car. We sat in the backseat and I tried to focus on the road ahead despite its dancing, swaying ghost.

And a bed. Sitting on the edge. Kendra helping me drink water from a glass.

And then Kendra straddling me, her hands on the sides of my face, fingertips cold as they caressed along my neck, around my ears. The familiar softness of her lips and warmth of her tongue.

Her hands pulling my shirt up over my head.
Her hands guiding my hands under her shirt to her chest. Her moans seeming to echo inside my brain.
Her hands again, sliding down my body, undoing my belt.
And then a pause.

"Is something wrong?" she asked. But she kept trying. Kept rubbing me, kissing me all over my face, caressing me. "I can slow down. We can take our time."

She tried to kiss me, tried to find my tongue with hers, but I pulled away. Looked at her with my brow furrowed.

"Kendra," I said. My voice held no more tenderness for her.

"It's okay, babe. Just relax. You've always had a hard time relaxing."

She'd always been like that—incapable of being positive about things. These memories were spiraling around in my mind, reminding me of everything I didn't like about her.

The way she used to throw emotional fits over small inconveniences and then cry to me about how cruel her life was. The way she would ignore the positive things I said to her—

even the loving things—because she perceived something negative in them.

I'd once told her that the best part of my day was coming home to her. And she'd responded by getting upset, saying she'd feel guilty now if she was out somewhere with friends when I came home.

I'd once told her that no one had ever made me happier than she did. She'd replied by huffing and telling me about how much pressure that put on her.

I gripped her by the shoulders and held her firmly away from me. Looked at her, doing my best to focus and keep my vision from dancing away.

Something wasn't right. The ghost image of her trying to swirl away, like the shadow version of her... it was the version of her that had broken my heart. The Kendra I had once wished were dead because it would be so much easier to rationalize than she having left me, not wanting me anymore.

But the other Kendra, the one on top of me, was acting different from that. Clashing with the one I knew to be real—just as real.

"Babe," she said, almost pleading. "It's okay. Just calm down and let me make it up to you."

And there the other Kendra was, taunting me.

"Kendra," I said again. "No. Jesus." I started to push her away. "No."

"Ben, if you'd just get out of your head for once and—"

"No." I stood up suddenly, nearly knocking her to the ground. "This isn't happening."

"Ben."

"You..." I pointed at her as I managed to stand on uneven legs. It felt as if I'd stepped onto a ship in stormy waters. "You, Kendra, your audacity. You think I actually want to do this with you? You don't fucking do it for me anymore. After what you did. And in this same fucking bed. I don't even... I don't even wanna be here. I don't love you anymore, like at all, I mean I don't even like you as a person, and honestly I can't even believe I'm... and I—" And then I realized I was going to be sick, so I threw myself into the bathroom and barely made it to the toilet in time.

I woke up on my bed, uncertain of how I'd gotten there.

My head pounded sharply, made it hard to keep my eyes open and dizzying to move. I couldn't remember much, but I remembered throwing up. Remembered telling Kendra she didn't do it for me anymore.

And, for some reason, the last conversation I'd had with Elodie spun through my head. The hurt in her eyes. The righteous frustration in her voice.

I suppose there's something to be said about the clarity that comes alongside a raging hangover. The voice in my head cycled through all the things I should've said to Elodie. All the things I wished I could say to her now.

There's something about distance, too. Space, I should say. Not that this was that, exactly—not in the healthy sense—but without being around her, without being near her, especially for this long, I missed her. Not just in my mind, but in my body.

And there's something to be said about distance, about the perspective it gives, how it allows you to miss someone.

I could only hope she felt the same about me.

And it occurred to me, after several minutes of sitting up in my bed, not moving, that it wasn't too late. We weren't done.

I hoped not, at least.

And, in retrospect, how shortsighted of me to think that Elodie was done with me. To think we could end that way, with a whimper.

Even through the headache, I managed the rational decision not to send a message to Elodie yet, not until I felt better. For now, I went to the corner of my room, found Hugo's leather journal, and began to read.

10

Context

We were recording a podcast about a serial killer who kept a double life for decades. A man who was capable of viciously murdering young women and then going home to his wife and two sons.

Chris was going on about how the wife claimed she never had any idea about her husband. I expressed mild skepticism, asking, "Yeah, but she had to have known something," which I said more as a way of setting Chris up for another point of discussion. And that's when it hit me.

I called Elodie as soon as we finished.

Over the past few days I read Hugo's journal with the seriousness of a desperate student during finals week. A few nights, unable to sleep, I opened the journal and reread passages, searching for something unnamable. Hugo wrote eloquently, recounting events as if they were a narrative of his own invention. But this was no fiction. It was the story of Alodia. Hugo and Alodia.

Many of the entries left me feeling disgusted. Sometimes I set the journal down and stepped outside to breathe fresh air and look at the sky, in need of something to pull my mind away from the images in my head.

But only during the podcast did it hit me, at last. Clicked into place. I understood what I'd been missing, and how I had misunderstood Elodie.

To my surprise she answered the call. Her tone was flat, not in the sense that she seemed unenthused to hear from me, but that she was, perhaps, so exhausted, so tired, she spoke this way naturally. She agreed to meet me, but not at the restaurant I suggested.

"Point Rock Lookout," she said. "Know where it is?"

I told her I did.

She told me when.

Elodie had a habit of wanting to meet me at unusual locations, often for strange reasons. Always at night.

Point Rock Lookout isn't as grand as its name suggests. Off one of the higher forest roads, it's a spot frequented by teenagers because it's picturesque: you can pull off the road, drive down a narrow path through the trees, and arrive at a spot that overlooks town. From that high up, when you go at night, the town of Wester is a pool of glistening lights amid a sea of darkness.

There were a few cars at the lookout, including Elodie's.

Most of the others in their cars were couples. I could see their shapes moving together. The place was too public for sex, but plenty of them were making out, making love in subtler ways.

Elodie wasn't in her car. But I'd been to Point Rock Lookout plenty of times—way too many to count, and for just as many different reasons—and knew some of the areas around it. I had a feeling I knew where she waited for me.

I was right.

Farther below the actual lookout, on a jutting rock all by itself in the trees, Elodie stood. A thin silhouette in the night, dressed in jeans and a slim leather jacket.

I felt as if I'd stepped momentarily into a memory. Silver moonlight on Farewell Lake. Jumping off into the water, nude. Encased behind the foggy windows of her car.

"There's something I didn't tell you," she said.

How I missed the sound of her voice. As smooth as a wolf's swooning howl at the moon, capable of the subtle rasp of a blues singer. A cool gulp of whiskey after a hard night.

Maybe Hugo was right about me. Maybe I have the heart of a romantic.

"Elodie," I said, approaching slowly.

She turned, eyes wide and watchful and seeming to glitter in the dark. She looked pensive.

"My mother's sick," she said.

"I know."

She shook her head. "Not like that. I mean she's *sick*. That's why my father called me, and why I needed to see her."

I said the first thing that came to mind. "Is it cancer?"

Elodie shook her head, turned her back to me again. I came closer. Stood beside her.

When she didn't answer, I decided not to wait. There was a lot I needed to say.

"I'm sorry, Elodie. I heard you and your dad mention something that implied that, but... I wasn't sure." I wanted to reach out for her, but for the moment restrained myself. "I'm sorry. About that. And about a lot of things."

"You don't have to say it."

"I do, though. I wasn't being fair to you." I turned so I faced her with my whole body. "I mean... they're your family. You asked me not to judge them and... well..." I tossed my hands up on each side with concession. When it comes to the important things, I've always been an idiot with words. "I won't lie. It freaks me out. There've been a few nights where your mother is in my dreams, but... they're your family, Elodie. And you're important to me. So this is important to me."

I saw her resist a smile. "I have dreams about her, too, you know. Dreams where she's just staring at me, and I keep talking to her, hoping she'll hear me."

"If you wanna go back there to spend more time with them..." I said, "I'll go with you."

"I didn't mean for you to feel like you were stepping into a trap," she said. "But you're right. You weren't being fair with me, either."

"I'm sorry."

"I don't know how to make you understand, Bennet. As frightening and unusual and as fucking weird as they are—both of them—I love them. Even when I think I hate them. Even when I stay away from them for years and... and try to pretend like they don't exist."

I nodded.

What I had realized earlier, during the podcast with Jeremy, is how Elodie was like the wife of the serial killer. The wife had said she never knew anything was wrong with her husband. Never could have suspected that, somewhere in their home, he kept a stash of photographs of butchered women. Never imagined he was capable of harming another human being like that.

He was quiet, she said. Kept to himself. But he was a good husband and a good father. And the love she felt for him, I imagined, would have to be reconciled with one simple fact: her husband was a monster.

I don't need to emphasize that this was a vastly different situation, but that story helped me see it differently. Helped me understand things from Elodie's point of view, which was the biggest obstacle we had faced in our relationship.

Maybe her family terrified me. The idea of her mother haunted every quiet moment I'd had to myself over the past few weeks, and the mental image of her father made me feel restless in my own skin.

But that had been Elodie's reality for the first fifteen years of her life. She'd been raised with a mother who wasn't entirely human, more comparable to a massive reptile. And her father, Hugo, was fiendish. You could say, a monster in love with a monster.

And if that was Elodie's reality, it must've taken so much

courage, so much willingness to change and step into the unknown, for her to grow apart from them, to realize they weren't normal, and to run away and try to make her own life.

And it must've taken even more courage to return—and to bring me with her.

How hard it must have been for her to live without knowing what constituted a normal life. Where would you start? How would you know what you wanted from other people, and from yourself?

I looked at Elodie differently now. Really saw her, it seemed, maybe for the first time since we'd met at Night Owl. No more preconceived notions. No more unconscious desires bursting underneath. I could look at her and see her.

"Elodie," I said. I reached out, took one of her hands. "If you were to meet my dad... and I'd like you to, I guess, at some point... if you were to meet him, I know what you'd think of him. You'd probably like him as much as I do, which isn't much at all. I mean... not to make this about me, but I can imagine what you'd say about him."

"What would I say?"

"You might think he's pathetic. Never talks about anything meaningful unless you force it out of him. Spends most of his time avoiding whatever else he could be doing with his time. Always looking for ways to distract himself from... well, from himself. And he's judgmental, and it can be abrasive unless you don't take anything he says personally."

"So, maybe I *would* like him."

I grinned. "That's how he used to be, anyway. Things are

changing with the alzheimer's, even though he comes through pretty clearly every now and then. My point is that you'd be seeing him from the outside, and all the things you'd notice and like or dislike, are normal for me. That's what I grew up with. What I'm used to. I mean... I at least know why he is the way he is, because I see his life from the inside. And I may not get along very well with my dad, but..."

I felt, suddenly, as if I was losing my main point. For a moment I panicked, trying to cover up my confusion with more words, before stopping and looking out at the dark trees ahead of us.

And something was different about Elodie. Later, this wouldn't strike me as strange. Elodie sometimes acted in unusual ways at night, as if passing briefly through waking dreams.

"What I'm trying to say is, I may have said some things a couple weeks ago, and I'm sorry. They're your family, you're doing your best, and I want to try. For you."

"Bennet, listen." She let go of my hand. "Thank you, for saying that. It means a lot to me."

I tried to burrow into her eyes with mine, tried to predict what she was about to say.

"I asked a lot of you," she said, "taking you to meet my family. The more I think about it, the more I wonder why the hell I did that. You've been unfair, but so have I. I brought you there and you weren't really prepared for any of it."

"To be fair," I said, "I don't think it's possible to be prepared for that."

"I know. But..." She sighed. "Listen."

I did.

And when Elodie left the rock and returned to her car, I didn't go with her. I stood, facing the darkness, feeling as if my insides had turned to stone.

11

Old Photograph

It was true—Elodie's mother appeared in my dreams.

Every night, somewhere in the chaotic turnings of my mind, I found myself surrounded by darkness in my dreams. Cold, swirling darkness. Somewhere far off, the echoes of an animal's shrill screeching. When I turned, Alodia was there. That feral, tantalizing, dead-eyed woman. In the dream she stood before me, naked, but there was no softness on her body. Her skin glinted, scaly, and the darkness conformed to the muscular shapes of her limbs.

Sometimes I tried to speak to her. Sometimes she approached me, always in her sudden, inhuman way, and sometimes she overpowered me. And then she was Elodie, making love with me, pinning me down, our bodies in a rhythm of impassioned bucking. And then it was Alodia again, forcing herself on top of me, holding me down, snarling in my face, eyes glaring but blank underneath.

Every night.

The last thing I expected and the first thing I feared was Elodie's denial of me. The way she pushed me away. I had missed something. My understanding—my wanting to understand—wasn't enough.

"Maybe it wasn't fair... it was too much all at once, to bring you there and expect everything to be okay," she'd said, *"but here's the thing. You're either all in with me, or you aren't. And no matter what you try to say, Bennet, or what you think you mean, I can tell."*

And maybe she was right.

So I turned to one of the main things that I could connect with her. It drew me to it by my curiosity alone, but fueled also by my longing for Elodie: the journal I had taken from her family's home.

Hugo's journal.

Of the many things I learned as I made my way through Hugo's journal, one began to occupy my mind: the matter of Alodia's side of the family. The Bailey family.

Hugo sometimes wrote about his side, the Villeneuve family, but seemed uninterested. When it came to chronicling his wife's family, however, he wrote like a psychological portraitist.

Reading the journal began to feel like an investigation. Reminded me of how it felt compiling notes for a podcast episode, gathering information on a crime and taking on the role of forensic investigator without any real stake. In this sense, Hugo's journal felt so much more real. I had never been this excited about the podcast, because none of it felt this real, not when we were doing it for the sake of entertainment.

Hugo's journal, however, was real for me. It brought me to life much as Elodie did.

I began doing my own research after reading Hugo's entries about the Bailey family. He wrote extensively about what he called their "family condition," which existed in the lineage of female members of the family. It existed in their blood.

On one page, he had enclosed a crackly old black-and-white photograph. It was of a woman dressed only in underwear. Around her neck, a collar and chain leash. The photo didn't appear old enough to be post-mortem photography, but at first I thought it had to be: the woman's facial expression was eerily blank.

Hugo had written beneath the photograph in his elegant, looping and curling scrawl: *I was unable to gather much concrete information from Ernest Bailey, but he provided this photograph with only a first name and date on the back. But this may be a photograph of Madelyn Bailey, circa 1939. Alodia's grandmother?*

Lifting the photograph from its plastic sheath, I recognized something in the woman's face. Took me a moment to realize, but it was the eyes. The woman's eyes were like Alodia's eyes. Cold. Dark. Staring but apparently unseeing. An emptiness there. A bestial countenance. And something animalistic in her hunched posture, as if she'd been pulling against the chain leash, trying to attack the photographer.

Elodie's alleged great grandmother.

Something told me Elodie had never seen this photograph. I couldn't be sure, but I knew I had to show it to her. Maybe this could be an avenue of reconnection. It was something, at least. So I tucked the photograph into my wallet and returned myself to the journal.

The photograph of Madelyn Bailey turned out not to be the most disturbing thing I discovered.

"Bennet," said Nat, leaning forward against the table. "What do you mean they keep them on a fucking farm?"

I had told her everything. As much as I could manage, at least. The reason? I couldn't sit with all of this by myself. I needed to talk to somebody about it, even just to say some of this out loud. And Nat and I told each other almost everything.

It was time I opened up about this shit. It sat on my chest like a block of ice.

"Like an actual farm," I said. And, luckily, I didn't need to elaborate or paint a mental picture for her. Hugo's journal contained photographs, especially across the sections dealing with the Bailey family and the Bailey Family Condition. I pulled out a black-and-white photograph from my wallet, handed it to Nat.

She studied it long enough for me to finish most of my coffee.

"Benny." She had lifted a hand unconsciously to cover her

mouth. She only called me Benny when she was either excited or scared. "Benny, what the hell am I looking at."

"The Bailey farm." I took the photograph back. Her eyes followed it all the way to my wallet.

If you didn't know the context, your first thought would likely be that the photograph was of a Nazi death camp. That's the first thing my mind went to, at least.

"They're on leashes," said Nat. She watched me, shaken, with stricken eyes. "Benny. They're on *leashes*. Like... like animals."

This was how the entire conversation had gone so far: I told her another part of my story, and she struggled to accept it, disturbed more viscerally with each revelation.

Once the initial impact of the shock had passed, Nat asked, "And those women... they have the same problem as Elodie's mom?"

"Apparently it runs in the family. On the women's side, at least."

"Oh my god, Ben. I mean... I had no idea you were going through all this."

I raised my eyebrows at her. "It's not really something that I'm..."

"I mean, things seemed to be going pretty well, and then... I can't even imagine what that must've been like. Finding that out, and meeting that family."

"It wasn't like that," I said, meaning the photograph. "It's... it's not..." Something hot flashed in my chest, gripped me from the inside. "This isn't exactly what's going on between Elodie and me. We're... we're working on it. This is just shit that I've been looking into, learning about. You know. Her mom's situation isn't really like this."

She nodded, though she kept her eyes low. When you know someone long enough, especially a sibling you're close to, you recognize subtle tells in their expressions or their body language. I could tell, from Nat's reaction, I was being an asshole. Overreacting, probably, the way I often did when it came to personal matters.

I've never known how to be open about my vulnerabilities, my developing problems, my mistakes. Kendra used to say I had a fatal flaw in the Shakespearean sense: I was alone in my problems by choice. If I let her in, she used to say, I wouldn't be alone.

And you know? She was probably right.

I should've apologized, but chose instead to shift the subject back.

"This isn't even really about Elodie," I said. "Maybe it is, on some level. But I also want to understand all of this better, for my own sake."

"Yeah. I would too. I mean... what the fuck is going on with that picture?"

I sighed. "There's more information in the journal about, um... about where the farm is. About members of the family and where they live."

Nat's eyes widened again. "Wait." Her voice seemed trapped in her throat. "You think... like... the farm's still a thing? Like this—the stuff in that photo—is still going on?"

After a few seconds I met her eyes and nodded.

Yes. The farm still existed.

And, thanks to Hugo, I knew where to find it.

12

The Baileys

On the evening before I had planned to seek out the Bailey Farm—a trip of roughly four hours—I ran into Elodie. We were at Night Owl. Hadn't seen each other since Point Rock Lookout.

I remember everything about our reunion. Like a splash of freezing water to the face, the quick gasp reaction to the cold. The details pop in the memory, sharply clear.

Constellations of lights dancing across the room, flashing sapphire, sharp purples, moody reds. Pools of bodies in movements both rhythmic and chaotic. The dark form of Elodie moving through it, her attention locked on me. Her ashen eyes luminescent, her features lit up in the sporadic flashes of colored beams shining through the dancing bodies.

Whatever I had been doing before faded from me like a

dream vanishing. I turned to her, religious in my willingness to give myself to her.

She came to me with a fiery smirk on her lips and a daring certainty in her eyes. Knowing, perhaps, that I would follow where she took me.

"Were you looking for me?" she asked.

"I look for you all the time," I said. "It doesn't matter where I am."

We had our hands on each other, let the pounding music move us.

I told her I had been looking at this all wrong. Told her to take me with her where she went. She was the most interesting thing in my life. To be without her was to look up at night and find the heavens starless.

I told her this, like the fucking romantic I apparently am.

We left Night Owl together.

How often did we find ourselves this way? Tangled in each other, panting, sweaty, our heartbeats gradually slowing, moans softening, bodies loosening. I was on top of her, let myself slide halfway off to rest my head on her chest. She ran her fingers through my hair, grinning mischievously.

Elodie was keenly aware of what she could do to me, and of what she could provoke me to do to her.

"Oh, I missed you," she said.

I looked up, met her eyes, grinned back at her. "I missed you."

She laughed. "I could tell."

Several breathing silences passed. Beside her, holding her, I told her the things I'd been dreading to tell her, but things I *needed* to tell her.

Ever since first laying eyes on the photograph of Madelyn Bailey, I had known I needed to share it with Elodie. Chance favored that she'd seen it before.

Except, I knew as soon as I told her: she had never seen the photograph.

Telling her was hard. It meant admitting I had taken the journal from her father's home. It meant opening up a part of her life she sometimes tried to pretend didn't exist. And although I expected an intense reaction, she surprised me with her tenderness.

And when I asked her if she wanted to see the photograph, I felt her tremble.

She sat up against the headboard, the sheets only reaching her stomach, her hair tumbling wildly across her naked shoulders. In the dim light of the bedroom, watching her like that, I wanted her again. But that could wait. This was important.

She held the photograph and stared at it for a long time. Maybe the room's silence made the seconds stretch out.

Some moments carry their own gravity.

You know what I mean. It's palpable, it is felt in the air against your skin, in how you're suddenly aware of every breath.

Gravity can warp time, and enough of it can turn minutes to hours.

Like Hugo and Alodia having sex on the garden walkway at night. That image lingered in my mind, seemed to replay in slow motion.

Like seeing someone else in Kendra's bed, after she'd discarded me and replaced me like yesterday's newspaper.

Like stepping into my mother's bedroom, the instant—as I called her name and she remained still—that I realized she was gone.

Like so many moments with Elodie.

They carry gravity, these moments.

And because this moment, with that old black-and-white photograph of her great grandmother pinched between her fingers, because this moment carried such palpable gravity for Elodie, it did for me, too.

In slow motion her expression changed. The melancholy in her eyes sharpened, her brow furrowed, and she drew in breath through her nose. I couldn't tell if this indicated frustration, or anger, or sadness, until tears sparkled in her eyes.

"Oh my god." Her voice came through broken. She shook her head. Turned the photograph over to where it read, in faint cursive: *Madelyn, 1939*. Someone had written that, unaware it would be read by a descendant decades later.

"Your father wrote a few things under the picture, in the journal," I said. "Her last name's—"

"Bailey," she said. "Madelyn Bailey. All I really know about her is..." She turned the photo back over to the picture. Looked at the feral woman from another time, from whom she carried noticeable resemblance—especially in the curves of her cheekbones and the shapes of her eyes. "She was my great grandmother. Sh-she died before I was born."

"Did you know Madelyn's daughter, though? Your grandma, I mean?"

Elodie nodded. "Grandma Everly."

"And she had it? What your great grandmother Madelyn had?"

"No. It skipped her. But she was..." Elodie cleared her throat, clearly struggling to speak. "Grandma Everly was a black sheep in the family. That's what my father told me, anyway. He said Everly was the one who convinced my mom to run away."

"From what?"

"From her own family, the Baileys. But I... I don't really know what that means. I used to wonder, and I used try and ask my mom that, you know. When I spent time with her, I still hoped maybe she could hear me... and that if I spoke to her enough, maybe enough of her would come through and she'd... she'd be able to tell me something." Elodie wiped tears from her eyes. I reached out, put a hand against her warm skin. "But by the time I was old enough to try and find out for myself, to learn more about the Baileys, I... I didn't want to know."

Elodie had never told me about this before, never shared much about her teenage years except how she ran away from home at age fifteen. So hearing her leading up to that, I gave all my attention to her.

"After I ran away," she said, "I told people I didn't have a family. That I was an orphan. And I tried for so... so fucking long to forget about them. To put it behind me and not go looking..."

She was trembling again. I pulled myself up so I could wrap an arm around her. She leaned into me. It was impossible for her to let tears come easily. She fought them, and her body shook with the effort.

"I have something else to show you," I said, when the time felt right.

She nodded. Pulled away to look at me. "What?"

I reached for my wallet again—for the photograph of the Bailey farm.

Elodie stared at this one, too, for a long time.

And when the shock faded, she let the photo slip from her trembling fingers so she could bring her hands to her face and sob into them.

But the way she looked at me, once the sobs passed, told me all I needed to know. I didn't even need to ask her if she would come with me to the farm. I knew what she would say.

And I was right.

13

A Stillness

Elodie told me what she knew about the Bailey family.

The condition had skipped her grandmother. She could tell me that much because she had known her grandmother, the black sheep of the family. This black sheep, Grandma Everly, had been on the farm with Alodia. And had apparently convinced Alodia to escape.

What Elodie didn't previously know, she learned from her father's journal. I brought it along on her insistence, and, in the passenger seat, she read it. She read most of it aloud to me, especially the parts I hadn't gotten to yet, ensuring we were in this together.

I had dreaded sharing the journal with her, because it meant admitting I had taken it from her father's house.

"I wouldn't have. I even considered putting it back," I had

told her. "But... this doesn't justify it entirely, but I kept thinking of something your father said while you were meeting with your mom. He said there aren't any private matters in his house. No locked doors"

Elodie nodded with a roll of the eyes. "Of course he fucking said that."

"Sounds like you've heard it before."

"He's a fucking hypocrite."

That had settled the matter of my taking the journal.

Here she was now, reading through it on our drive to the Bailey farm. The journal was our guide there, after all. It also happened to be the only information we could find on the place, so we were driving four hours with the chance that we'd find nothing.

"So, I've been curious about the women they keep on the farm," I said. "Is it every woman with Bailey blood? Or is it just women who have the condition?"

Elodie flipped back a few pages. "My dad wrote about that a few... a few lines ago—here. Right here. He wrote, *According to a few willing sources and any information I've been able to gather, the Bailey Condition—for lack of a better term—only develops at certain stages of life. There is only a single case of a baby girl being born with the condition. She deteriorated by the age of two, and never saw a third year. In every other case, it is one of two possibilities. Some women develop the condition alongside the onset of puberty. As their womanhood reveals itself to them, so fades their agency and mental sophistication. They digress across adolescence, but the reward isn't adulthood, it is the animal nature, the fruition of the curse of their bloodline. Sometimes the condition is delayed; some women made it into their later twenties or early thirties, with the condition revealing itself slowly, over the course of a few years. This is, by all accounts, considerably rare.*

"God, he writes like he thinks he's a fucking gothic horror novelist from the early 1900's," said Elodie, practically spitting her words as if to be rid of the taste of her father's writing.

Still, she continued reading aloud. "*Most common, however, is anywhere between the mid-thirties and late forties. In the same way that many mental illnesses manifest, so too does the Bailey condition strike when a woman ought to be settling into life's rhythms outside the fervent chaos of youth.*"

"You're right," I said. "He seems to enjoy writing about it."

"There's more. I don't wanna read it out loud. He says... blah-blah-blah... fuck you, Dad, rambling, rambling... okay. He says he had a source. A few, actually. In this case, a young man named Martin Bailey agreed to talk to him and tell him a little about the farm. Martin told him that sometimes they'll ask female family members to submit to tests throughout the years. Like, every few years they come to the farm where they'll be examined, like a doctor's checkup, which could take... oh, god. A few months at the most."

"Jesus."

"But if a Bailey woman is healthy, the farm has rules and codes, so they let them go." Elodie scowled at the journal as she read on. "Or... well, it looks like my dad crossed a few things out here... a few paragraphs, actually. Like he was interrogating Martin and couldn't get straight answers out of him. And he wrote that he didn't believe Martin was telling the truth about the *rules and codes.*"

"This is making me feel weird."

"Tell me about it. This is my mom's side of the fucking family we're reading about." She read on. "Wait. Listen to this...

"*Although Martin eventually refused further questioning and left infuriated, I was able to glean a few things about the nature of the farm that made him uncomfortable to talk about. I believe the Baileys may have inhumane practices and traditions that apply as much to healthy female family members as to those afflicted by the family condition. When I asked Martin if they keep healthy women on the farm against their will, for the purpose of breeding, testing, sterilization, or perhaps as a precaution lest they develop the condition and become a threat to the public and to themselves, Martin grew red in the face and accused me of unfounded conjecture. Quite telling, if you ask me.*"

"Jesus!" I spat the word. "What in god's name."

Elodie shut the journal slowly. Her hands trembled.

How hard this had to be for her. I couldn't even imagine. Even from my outside perspective I felt shaken, as if someone had taken a fistful of my insides and twisted them, pulled them, stretched them. My appetite, if I'd had one before, was ash in my stomach. But for her, I truly couldn't even imagine.

This was her family, after all. A side of it she hadn't even known much about before now.

"Could be conjecture," I said, trying to lighten the mood even a little. "Maybe your father was making guesses."

"Yeah. And maybe he wasn't. He's scarily good at telling when people are lying." She drew in breath. "I can't believe it."

"Can't believe what? That the farm actually exists?"

"That it *still* exists." She seemed to retract into herself as if she'd become suddenly cold. "An old photograph is one thing. But it's still happening."

"Like nothing's changed," I echoed, feeling the same cold.

Elodie shook her head. "I don't know if I'm gonna be able to keep myself from burning the place to the fucking ground."

"Ever committed arson before?" I said this as a joke.

Elodie simply stared forward and said, without humor: "Just once or twice."

"So," I said. "Your mom developed the condition when she was in her thirties or forties?"

Elodie was still reading from the journal, but hadn't been reading as much aloud for the past hour.

"My dad said she started having symptoms after they'd been together for seven or eight years. So... early thirties."

"And you weren't born until after she already had it? Like... after she'd crossed over?"

Elodie set the journal down in her lap. I only glanced over briefly, but caught enough of a glimpse to see how her eyes went far away. She said, "They decided to have me once they knew for sure she wasn't going to get better."

"Oh... god."

She nodded slowly. "By the time I was born, she was almost completely gone. But Dad told me she was still hanging on, still barely there, by the time I was born. So she was able to hold me and know who I was, and..." Her voice broke. She took a deep breath, closed her eyes. "Sometimes I think about that. That she got to really hold me, at least once."

Her choked silence filled the car. I didn't know what to say.

Although I drove with half my mind, the other half envisioned Hugo and Alodia's story, playing it across the theater of my mind.

"Please don't go, my love. Please don't go."

That is what Hugo wrote in the margins of his journal, dated around the time when Alodia was slipping further into her condition, succumbing. There was no fighting it. No known cure. Which meant she slipped away in full consciousness, aware that her awareness, her agency, her human nature, would grow clouded, grow foggier with each passing day. Like drowning with your eyes wide open.

And Hugo, deeply in love with her, having to watch. Unable to help her. Unable to reach a hand out for her to grasp.

I imagined him holding her, fighting tears because he needed to be strong for her. Awakening, perhaps, in the dim morning glow, turning to see her still asleep, running a hand

through her hair and whispering, "Please don't go, my love. Please don't go."

This is how I started to understand Hugo Villeneuve and his feral wife. This is how I began to see their story more clearly.

We stopped for lunch at a gas station town. Sat on a park bench with sandwiches we'd made at her house. The roads were quiet. If not for the meth-heads hanging out by the water fountains, this could've been mistaken as a nice place.

Still, with the sun overhead above the towering pine trees, we were content. But a shadow hung over us both.

"I've been meaning to bring up the night we met," I said, almost finished with my sandwich. It was good to feel that we weren't in a hurry. Our destination was just over an hour away.

Elodie raised an eyebrow. She sat on the other side of the bench. "If you're about to go into some romantic soliloquy, please just save it."

"No. You really think I'd try to soliloquize you? *You*?"

She smirked. "Fair enough."

"One of the first things you said to me was *shoo*."

She laughed, having to cover her mouth. "I'm so funny, aren't I?"

"Were you actually telling me to shoo, or was that your version of a pickup line?"

She laughed harder. "Oh my god, Bennet. You think I'd get many guys with a pickup line like that? By going up to a guy at a bar and telling him to shoo?"

"It worked, didn't it?"

"Well, yeah… yeah, good point."

"So you weren't testing me."

"I don't have the time or the energy to test people."

"That wasn't, in some way, a test to see if you'd meet someone who could keep up with you?"

Her eyes glinted mischievously. "Well, when you put it that way, I kinda like the sound of it. We'll go with yes. It definitely was."

"And what about the night at Point Rock Lookout?"

"Is this an interrogation about our relationship?"

"Yes. You were acting... different. And the way we left it... it just stayed in my mind. That's all."

She set her sandwich down for the moment. "Which part?"

"Well, firstly, the reason for having me meet you out there in the first place."

She laughed. "Right. I guess I should apologize for that. The whole thing, I mean."

"Nah," I said. "Wouldn't suit you."

"True. I guess I just have dramatic streaks sometimes. *Theatrical*, more than dramatic."

"Aren't those the same thing?"

"You met my father."

"Ah... gotcha."

"I'm my father's daughter. And sometimes I just feel better when I'm standing someplace high up."

"And jumping off those things?"

She wrinkled her nose at me.

I looked at her, confused, a bit concerned. "So, that feeling some people have, when they're standing somewhere high—like a cliff, or the railing of a skyscraper—and have the sudden urge to jump. Is that what it is?"

An eyebrow raised. "Should I ask if this question is Freudian in nature?"

"Oh, god, Elodie."

"No not *that* kind of Freudian."

"Then, sure."

"It's something like that. Something about being a step away from open air."

I saw that look in her eyes as she said this. The look she'd had at Farewell Lake. Like fire danced in her irises. Like she could set the world on fire and dance in the falling ashes.

This was neither the time nor the place—not that it ever mattered—but I wanted her. So badly. I wanted her, wanted to dance in those ashes with her.

Once we were in the car again, less than an hour from our destination—assuming Hugo's journal didn't steer us astray—I brought up another thing that had sat in my mind like a leaking barrel of acid. Something she had told me on our second night together, at Farewell Lake. About how her mother had tried to kill her.

"I thought I told you about that," she said. She was driving now. Hugo's journal sat in my lap.

I told her we hadn't talked about it yet.

"The first time it happened, I was a baby. A few days old. She was holding me, probably nursing me. This was close to the end of her, um... close to when she faded completely. She'd have flashes of being herself, and my dad tried to make sure she could hold me during those flashes, even if they were brief."

I could picture it too well as Elodie spoke.

Her mother was nursing her, cradling her in her arms, sitting upright in bed. Tears dripped down her cheeks, making them shine in the glow from the windows, but a bright smile rested on Alodia's features, shining through her eyes. This always happened when she held Elodie, in her fleeting moments of lucidity. Sometimes she wept.

To hold your child knowing you will fade away, and each time you return will be for a shorter amount of time, and one day you will never again emerge from the fog. To hold your child, to nurse her, cradle her, look down at her, hear her soft crying like music in your ears. To cherish every second with her. To cling, wishing love were enough to stop time so those moments could last forever.

That is what comprised Alodia Villeneuve's final days as a conscious human being. Awakening as if from a dense nightmare state. Her beloved husband coming to her, handing her the cooing baby Elodie, staying with her so she could hold her child and love her until the dense fog returned.

These images in my head stirred something I didn't expect to have ever felt for Elodie's parents.

I imagined Hugo sitting on the edge of the bed, looking at his wife—his beloved wife—cradling their daughter, and Hugo wanting to hold them both, wanting to wrap his arms around them and ward off any hurt that might come their way. Wanting to plunge himself into the reality of them and keep them just as they were. I imagined the way it must've felt when Alodia faded again and the feral woman returned. Her eyes would drop into blankness, no longer seeing anything, holding an inhuman stillness except for their random shifts in any direction. Hugo would have to take baby Elodie from her, leave the room, or whatever it was he did.

How that must've felt for him.

And how it must've felt for her. Like a muted scream on the inside.

These things, these emotions, were beyond my imagining.

Surely there were tears. And frustrated confusion. And burning rage.

"Please don't go, my love," Hugo had written to her, as if in desperate prayer. *"Please don't go."*

The first time she tried to kill Elodie, Alodia was lucid again, holding Elodie, nursing her. Tears marked Alodia's cheeks, and in between the soft things she spoke to her child, she sniffled, suppressed the sobs in her throat.

"My love," she whispered to little Elodie. *"My sweet, sweet girl."* She caressed her daughter's thin dark hair. Hoisted her up to kiss her forehead. *"Mommy loves you so much, dear. Mommy loves you so, so much, you beautiful little girl."*

Hugo, smiling sadly, stood from the edge of the bed, kissed his wife on the forehead, then on the lips. "I'll be just a moment." He went out to the gardens.

Alodia watched him. Watched as he stood under the sun, surveying the grounds. She noticed a difference in his posture, which had been worsening over the past several months. Hugo Villeneuve was a steadfast man, an anchor. To her, he seemed unmovable. But her worsening condition and how it ravaged her emotions had taken a toll on her husband. He tried not to show it when around her, but sometimes she caught a glimpse of him when he didn't know she was watching, and she knew. She knew.

She looked to her daughter, who looked back up at her with those striking ashen eyes.

With tears continuing to bubble to the surface, Alodia kept

whispering softly to her baby daughter. "You're the most beautiful girl in all this world," she said to her. "The world is full of darkness, but you can be a light. And I wish I could meet you one day, my love. See how strong you become. Hear what your laugh sounds like. I wish I could watch you dance on your wedding day... maybe out there in the garden, where your father and I like to dance." And Alodia felt a new emotion rise inside, something she hadn't felt before.

Suddenly she feared for her daughter, her sweet little Elodie.

The feeling came as a tightening in her skin, a swelling, cold tension in her limbs, making her feel as though her energy had drained her body in an instant. Her whole body shook.

And then nothing. Her mind swirled away into the dense fog.

She stared down with suddenly blank eyes at the baby in her arms. The baby started to cry.

Hugo, still standing out in the sun, heard Alodia wailing. The sound was shrill and pale, a predatory shriek, far from something that should've come from human lungs.

When Hugo flew back into the room, Alodia had one hand cupped over little Elodie's mouth and nose; her other hand was around the baby's neck. Alodia was wailing—sobbing, it seemed. And baby Elodie was choking for breath, coughing, and her small face was turning red.

"Oh, god." Glad I wasn't driving anymore, I lifted a hand up to my own throat. My mother used to say I was empathic. I've never put enough thought into it to know, but for a moment I felt phantom fingers around the skin of my neck, pressing against my throat. "God... Elodie." And I panicked for words. But what the hell could I say? That I was sorry? Sorry, Elodie, I'm so sorry your mother tried to strangle you after you were born. It didn't make sense to apologize, didn't make sense to offer any sense of comfort, or levity, or sympathetic apology. There are some things that repel words.

So I reached a hand out and put it on her thigh, and would've tried to meet her eyes if I hadn't been staring off into nothing, my mind filled with agonizing images.

Elodie sniffled. Only then I noticed the tears on her cheeks. But she stared ahead as if it were nothing.

Her voice came choked through. "Dad said it's because she didn't know what to do. She loved me so much, maybe it was her way of trying to... to protect me. Instincts and all that."

She didn't go on. Didn't tell me about the next time her mother tried to kill her. I trusted she would eventually tell me. But I didn't need to hear anymore today.

14

The Family Business

The town was called Olympus. It did not live up to its namesake. It felt like a one-street village that moved to its own clock, sheltered between brooding redwood trees. I had never heard of it before, never had occasion to pass through it. And I knew, once we stopped at a restaurant for some food and to ask around, I would never willingly come back here again.

When the opportunity arose to ask our waitress about the Bailey farm, Elodie took charge. I had planned on being discreet, but Elodie had her own plans.

"We're looking for the Baileys," she said, looking up at the curly-haired blond waitress who smiled sweetly with her eyes.

The smile remained there, in the waitress's eyes, but it tensed, grew strained, at mention of the Baileys.

"Oh, goodness, ma'am," said the waitress. She was young—probably still in high school. "Depends on which Bailey you're looking for. There's a whole lot of them 'round here. You mean the sheriff?"

Elodie performed a smile. "Is there a main estate, maybe? My cousin gave me directions to town, but didn't tell me how to get to their place."

"I'm sorry, ma'am. I don't really know. I know Eric Bailey, he and I, um... we hang out sometimes out at the water tower, when there's bonfires. But I don't know about the family farm."

"Yeah?" Elodie raised her eyebrows. I could sense her edges sharpening and I hoped she went lightly on the girl. "Kinda sounds like you know about it, since I didn't say anything about a farm."

The waitress swallowed. Her eyes shifted from one side to the other, latching onto the salt and pepper shakers, the utensils wrapped in napkins.

"I'm technically part of the family, visiting my uncle," Elodie added. "I've just never been out here before."

"Sorry," I said, giving the waitress a friendly look. "It's been a long drive."

"Yeah? Where you two coming from?"

"Wester."

"Oh, sure. Couple hours, huh?" The tension in her eyes lifted. "Well, I guess it should be okay, since you're part of the family."

She told us where to go. Within a few minutes, we were on our way.

If Elodie hadn't been driving, she wouldn't have been able to sit still. Her fingers were white around the steering wheel; her lips drawn into a tense, flat line.

I wondered what we were doing here, after all. Were we here to look? To survey the farm, make sure it was real, and then... leave? Would Elodie want to confront the Baileys? Meet the patriarch? Then what?

I asked her this. Asked what she wanted to do when we got to the farm.

"Let's just get there," she said. We were silent for the rest of the drive—a drive through the woods. And to the unremarkable locked gate that stood off the road, announcing our arrival.

"So," I said, pacing before the metal gate. "A small asphalt pathway leads into the forest, we can't see anything from here, the button on that intercom thing means we can ask them if they'll let us in, and we have no reason to give them for being here. Great prospects. But, hey, at least there's cameras." I gestured to the gate's stone pillars. "So we know they're watching us. At least there's that."

"Shut up." Elodie elbowed me before moving to the intercom.

"You think that's such a good idea?"

"What else should we do, Bennet? Climb the gate? Get shot before we even see anything?"

"Would it make it better if we *do* see something *before* we get shot?"

She gave me a look, more playful than harsh, before standing on her tiptoes for the intercom's camera and pressing the button.

"Anyone there?" she said. "I know you can see us." She released the button. We waited for a minute in silence.

I thought about the four-hour drive. Normally, a drive that long implied something worthwhile at the end. A nice view, at least.

Worst of all, I couldn't even be angry with her. Like walking into a wall and stubbing your toe, you want someone to blame but can only be mad at yourself. This trip was my idea, after all.

No answer from the intercom. No sounds from the forest except a gentle breeze rustling through the treetops.

Elodie paced in front of the gate a few times, hands firmly on her hips, lips twisted to the side. She paused when something occurred to her, then returned to the intercom.

"We aren't going anywhere until you talk to us," she said, her tone matter-of-fact. "And I'm pretty sure I have a right to at least talk to someone. My name is Elodie Villeneuve. Recognize that name? Maybe you know my mother, Alodia. Alodia Villeneuve. Formerly *Alodia-fucking-Bailey*. Ring any bells?"

Apparently it did. A man's voice returned over the intercom.

"Wait there."

That was all.

Ten minutes later, a green Jeep pulled up on the other side of the gate, emerging from the asphalt road that snaked into the trees.

Two men exited. One of them stood by the car, staring cooly from a pair of sporty glasses that made him look like an asshole. The other guy wore a crocodile-hunter-style hat, a plain white shirt, and ratty jeans. His cowboy boots clapped the asphalt with each step. He came up to the gate, one hand on the right side of his hip, over a holstered revolver.

My first impression of the Bailey family. An impression that would prove all too accurate for my future encounters. I hate it when first impressions prove correct.

"Now," said the man in the hat. He chewed on a piece of gum, slapping it around in his mouth with each chomp. "Normally I'd have this here .38 in my hand, and I'd tell you two to get the fuck away from here and don't even think about calling the cops. My brother Percy's a deputy, and our Uncle John's the sheriff. So you'd just be calling the fucking cops on yourself. But you." He pointed a finger at Elodie. "You say you're a Bailey?"

The man's tough cowboy act, or whatever the hell it was, struck me as ridiculous to the point of amusement. And Elodie didn't flinch in the slightest. She returned the man's stare with coals burning in her eyes.

"No," she said. "My mom was a Bailey."

"Well, close enough I guess. There's a lot of Baileys around town. Not a whole lot of them like to come out to socialize. And I've never seen you around here before, one way or the other."

"You wouldn't. I'm not from around here."

"And how am I to believe you really are a Bailey?"

"How about you let us in and we can talk about it in a more comfortable spot?"

"Don't think so, woman."

"My name's Elodie. You've probably heard of my mother. Her name's Alodia."

"Sure, I know who Alodia is. Most of us do. A namedrop

ain't gonna get you anywhere, especially not past this gate. And especially 'cause I ain't never heard of an Elodie Bailey."

This caught both of us by surprise. Elodie didn't let it show, but I caught it in the subtle readjustment of her posture.

"Here's a name for you," she said, spitting the words. "Howard Bailey. Why don't you ask him?"

The man raised one eyebrow, appeared to smirk. He cast a glance over at his partner—his guard, I assumed—and then turned back to us. "Sure, I know Howie. What's he to you?"

"My uncle. And I'm sure he'd love to hear that you turned away his niece at the front gate of the fucking Bailey Farm."

They took us past the gate in the backseat of their Jeep. Instructed us that there'd be consequences if we took out our phones for any reason, or snapped any pictures.

The asphalt road wound through the trees for a mile before leading to another gate. This gate was more grand, obviously well-maintained, surrounded by an abundance of flowers. Arcing above it, in gold, was the name *BAILEY*.

This was an estate, but not like Hugo Villeneuve's. There was a large house, but it was dwarfed in comparison to the expansiveness of the rest of the place.

There's a lot I don't remember about the Bailey Farm. At the time, my senses were on high alert and I was trying to absorb everything at once, every little detail in case one of those details might prove crucial later if we found ourselves in danger, or if we needed to make a quick escape. Theatrical thinking, no doubt, but it's the way my mind works. Always looking for a way out. Eye on the exit. Always preparing for some unnamable thing. Makes it hard to relax. Hard to feel entirely comfortable.

But I remember the corral.

If not for the humans within the enclosure, the corral could be mistaken as being for horses. You know—the sort of corral where people ride horses in circles, or train on them. Like that. And it was connected to a building that could only be described as a massive stable but with the industrial appearance of a slaughterhouse.

But the creatures within the corral, enclosed by the chain-link fences, weren't horses. They weren't farm animals at all. You already know what I'm talking about. You've seen the old photographs. You don't need me to tell you.

I didn't even realize the car had stopped moving. My eyes were glued on the corral, on the women who wandered within it. Some of them wandered, I mean. Others were completely still. Standing in place. Sitting in strange positions, or lying in the dirt.

Others were along the chain-link fences, dispelling any illusion that they were there willingly.

Some of them had climbed partway up the fence, clinging to it with their whole bodies. The fences were bent inwards at the tops, lined with barbed wire. I'd never seen anything like it. The women were aware of this because none of them were near the top, they had merely climbed as if they could press themselves through the tied links in the fence.

They had collars strapped around their necks. Most of them

were naked, their flesh glinting in the sunlight. Glinting because the Bailey Condition has certain physiological effects that I'd read about in Hugo's journal. Effects like the capability for their skin to harden, to temporarily undergo a controlled transformation similar to ichthyosis.

For some, it came in the form of scales. Like reptile scales. But for most of the women, the effects were lighter, subtler, noticeable mostly in how their skin glinted in the sun and would be hard to the touch. I thought of Alodia. Everything about her, even just the way she carried herself, lacked any human softness.

Perhaps it's my sexuality, simple as that, that women's bodies, for the most part, seem to bely a softness. Not in the juvenile sense, not even in a sexual sense. Maybe it's just me, but that's how it is.

But it wasn't that way with Alodia. Not a single part of her body implied softness or warmth or tenderness.

It was this way with all the Bailey women behind the fences, as they climbed, as they crawled, as they wandered—in tattered clothes, in collars, in harnesses.

Men were positioned around the perimeter of the enclosure. Two or three of them carried tranquilizer rifles. The rest carried cattle prods.

Just like in the old photograph.

Elodie took my hand and squeezed. I squeezed back.

There was nothing we could think to say, so we said nothing.

We were told to wait. The guard stayed with us while the

man in the crocodile-hunter hat went, I presumed, to find Howard Bailey.

When he was out of earshot, Elodie and I wandered hand-in-hand toward the massive enclosure. The guard simply watched us.

"You never told me about your uncle," I said.

She stared straight ahead, eyes flitting from one feral woman to the next, to the next, to the next. "I've never met him," she said. "But I've heard my dad say his name before. And I read about him in the journal."

I had never seen her with such pain in her eyes. Such thrashing torment.

This, I thought, was the shadow she carried around with her. The shadow that followed her like her own, beneath every step.

This was her bloodline. What she had come from. The legacy of her mother's maiden name.

And all I could do was hold her hand and hope my presence was enough. Hope I could be there for her after all this, in some way. But, from where we stood, the idea of there being an *after*, a life outside the shadow of this place and its reality, was beyond our conceiving.

One of the women pressed her entire body against the chain link fence. Arms raised, fingers clutching through the fence as if she meant to climb. Her skin was brown, hair a pile of wild curls. Clothing hung from her body in shreds.

We weren't allowed within three feet of the chain link, but we stood and watched her, and she looked back with utter blankness in her eyes.

When I say blankness, I don't mean she lacked expression. There was an urgency in the void of those eyes. Something manic. Something thoughtless, purely instinctual.

"All I've ever known about the Baileys," said Elodie, her voice strained, "is that my father hates them. He never talked about them much. But when he mentioned them, I could tell. Just from his tone, I could tell." She crossed her arms over her chest, hands clenched into fists. "Now I know why."

I felt it too, but didn't know how to say it. Didn't know if I had any right to say it. I hoped she felt it from me, though, in how I gripped her hand like it was all I had to hold onto, and how I couldn't tear my eyes away from the women in the corral.

"I wonder what her name is," I said, nodding toward the woman pressed up against the fence.

Sometimes you witness something and you know, at the very moment of your witnessing, that it will haunt you for the rest of your life. It will be something that will come back to you in quiet moments or in dreams, and you will have to wrestle with it when it comes. You may wish it could leave your head, or wish you had never witnessed it, but those will be errant wishes.

Some things need to haunt you. They should never be forgotten. They deserve to evoke deep enough pain—pain that echoes on and on.

When I recall standing at the chain-link fence, the brown, half-naked woman before us, I seem to recall a conversation with Elodie. Emotional confessions. An intimacy of vulnerability expressed, pain shared.

But I don't think she or I said anything as we stood there. The conversation I almost remember must've been, in reality, a series of unvoiced impressions as we stood there, linked by our hands, sharing the experience—the witnessing—and being close enough that we didn't need to say anything.

Our trance was interrupted when the crocodile-hat man came to take us to Howard Bailey, Elodie's uncle, whom she had never met.

15

Frozen in the Spotlight

"Ah... don't tell me," said the massive Howard Bailey from the other side of a large mahogany desk. "I'd know you anywhere, sweet girl. You look so much like her."

Howard Bailey was important on the Bailey Farm. A supervisor, it seemed. He was a thick man, dense and broad. His deliberate, lumbering movements were the first thing I noticed: he moved as though he had to stop and think about his every action: *take step forward, smile, look friendly, shake hand.*

I don't know how else to describe it. The smile that stretched across the bottom of his large, bulbous face didn't show in his eyes, which had a stiltedness holding no joy, only calculation. Howard Bailey, I thought. A man trying to imitate human male behavior.

"My dear." His voice was higher, more nasally, than I'd expected from a man of his size. He lumbered around the desk, stepping on heavy heels. I imagined he could knock me over with a single punch. He approached Elodie, completely ignoring me, and moved to put his arms around her. "You know something, Elodie, I've spent so many years imagining who my sister's child was. I didn't know if you'd be a little boy, or a little girl, or, *huh*, I didn't even know if you even existed. But here you are." said Howard. "I just can't believe it's really you."

Elodie, not one to sacrifice her comfort for anyone, stepped away from him before he could hug her.

Disappointment flashed across his face, but he masked it with a smile so wide I wanted to believe it was genuine.

"Damn it, Howie," he said to himself. "Moving a little fast. I understand that. I get it, sweetheart. You know who I am, don't you?"

"You're Howard. My uncle Howard."

"And you're Elodie. My long lost niece. My sister Alodia's daughter. Please. Oh. Both of you, sit." We did. Howard waved his two men off, and they left us alone.

Howard had made it halfway back to his seat on the other side of his desk before suddenly stopping, his eyes going wide. He slapped a hand to his temple. There was something forced about the gesture. Like he was back there pulling strings on this awkward human puppet. "Well, Jesus Christ now, Howie," he said to himself. "This just isn't right. Forgive me, Elodie, and, um... I'm sorry there, boy, I didn't get your name." He met my eyes for the first time since we'd walked in.

I raised an eyebrow at him. "Bennet."

"He's my boyfriend," said Elodie.

Howard came back over, fidgeting, extending a hand. It was like shaking a grizzly bear's paw.

"You must be quite the gentleman, accompanying her to meet the family, especially family she can't exactly warn you about since we've never met." He made something of a chuffing sound, which could only be an attempt at laughing. "Now, I'd feel silly if we stayed in here, like I was interviewing the two of you for some sort of position, am I right? Not that we don't have plenty of work that needs doing around here! How about we take a little walk? Get some fresh air. Get you better acquainted with the place before the tests."

Elodie and I locked eyes for a moment, just a moment, long enough for Howard to notice. He continued to smile, however, meaning he might be oblivious.

But in that brief moment of meeting eyes, Elodie and I broadcast the same question: *Tests?*

"Fresh air sounds good," said Elodie.

With his polite smile, fidgety hands, and lumbering gait, Howard led us back outside. Back out into view of the corral full of feral women.

"Your mother and I grew up here together," Howard said to Elodie. He had just shown us the mess hall for the workers, and we were on our way to another small building. "Well, not here exactly. Our house was a few miles west, but we came here all the time. Dad worked out here, guard duty mostly. Honorable work on the farm. And because he worked, Alodia didn't have to stay in the quarters with the rest of the girls. In The Hotel, I mean." He pointed to a building. "She was able to come home. Most nights, anyway."

It was appalling to me the way Howard spoke of hideous things with such a casual tone. But it helped me realize: this was his world. This—all this—was normal to him.

Far worse than any monstrous medical condition, this was the Bailey Family Condition. I began to realize this, began to look at the farm in a different way. My stomach churned, felt hard as if I'd swallowed a brick. Head spun on the inside, making me feel nauseous.

As Howard toured us around the farm, I began to wonder: what if, somewhere in one of these houses or buildings, more girls were being kept and tested on? What if that part of it wasn't a thing of the past?

Worse, though I hardly let my mind go there—what did that mean for Elodie?

What had I done by bringing her here?

A panicked restlessness bubbled under my skin. The impulse was to run. To take Elodie and run and hope none of the guards around here decided to make use of their rifles.

"I can't tell you, Elodie," said Howard, "how happy it makes me that you're here. Maybe I already said this, but I had no idea you even existed until today. I had my suspicions. Alodia always wanted to be a mother. I just... I was never sure it ever happened for her."

Elodie's arms were crossed over her body. We stood outside the main farmhouse.

"To tell the truth," she said, "I wasn't sure if this place was real."

"That so?" Howard furrowed his brow at her, genuinely surprised. "Good old Hugo never talked about this place?"

Elodie hesitated before shaking her head. "No. Not... not that I recall."

"Ah, well... I suppose that ain't much of a surprise. None of us ever got along with old Hugo Villeneuve back in the day. Myself included. Can't say I ever trusted the man. Gave me the creeps, if I'm telling the truth."

My cheeks turned red. Elodie's burned. I saw something flare in her eyes, saw her try to tame it and keep it down.

Despite everything I knew about her father, Elodie was loyal to her family. I always respected that. *Don't judge my family*, she had asked of me. Demanded, rather.

She managed to sound calm when she asked Howard, "Why didn't you trust my father?"

Howard shrugged awkwardly. The man couldn't act natural no matter how hard he tried. The past half hour of his tour around the farm had proven his wide-eyed, touchy awkwardness. I couldn't stand still around him.

"Eh, well," he said, "there's something wrong with the guy, for one. Now, don't call me judgmental, I know the story he tells about how he met Alodia, and, if you don't mind my saying, it sounds like a load of horse's manure, doesn't it?"

"I'm sorry," I said, needing to interject. Elodie gave me a look; I ignored it. "I don't think I know the story." I said this to Elodie. "Of how your parents met."

We were given sandwiches from the mess hall and Howard had us sit at a bench overlooking the corral. Neither Elodie nor

I had any appetite, so we took a few bites of our sandwiches and then set them down and hoped nobody noticed.

And Howard told us his version of Hugo's story.

"So, um… so Elodie knows this story, already. Don't you, sweetheart? You've probably heard it plenty of times. Alodia managed to escape from here. That's a story in itself, and I, uh… to be honest, I'm not at liberty to give too many details about that. By my own account, I mean. It's not a story I like to tell. But anyway…

"We sent out a couple of search parties. A few in basically all directions, mostly for protocol's sake, you know. I took three others, including my cousin Les, and we started to track her. Les and I both have a knack for it—plus, I learned a lot from him when we went out tracking deer every weekend, back in the day—so we got on her trail and we followed it for a few days. Worst fucking backpacking trip of my life, let me tell you. Not that it was strictly backpacking… well, anyway, there I go, rambling off the wrong details. Anyway.

"When the trail went cold, we started doing more detective work, right? Asking around. Figuring stuff out. Believe it or not, after a couple weeks, we managed to get back on the trail. She'd started hitchhiking. I don't wanna imagine how she managed it… especially since she started off with only the pair of clothes on her back and… and that's about it. Gotta admire my sister like that. Little spitfire. Goddamn.

"I could go on and on about the details of it, but we eventually ended up around your neck of the woods. Wester. And a few hours northeast, when we found the little town called Hilltop. Started asking around there. Which is how we heard about the Villeneuve Estate, and figured, why not? The trail had gone cold again, and in my spare time I was literally going door-to-door, asking questions, being a damn nuisance. Not my finest moments. Not my element, if you take my meaning.

"And then we met Hugo. He was... what, late twenties back then? No, no... I forget."

"Thirty-six," said Elodie.

"Ah... thirty-six. Not quite prime, not quite past." Howard winked. "Alodia was twenty-two. Way too young to be out on her own, if you ask me. Especially in her state. She was always a special case on the farm, and not because she was allowed to go home every night rather than stay with the rest of the girls. I mean, Alodia was always... chaotic. Had a dancing star inside her soul. And a shadow on the edges of her eyes." Howard's own eyes went somewhere else when he spoke about Alodia.

You start to notice things about people when you don't give them the benefit of the doubt.

With Howard Bailey, I was repelled in the same way I felt repelled by the serial killers I talked about on the podcast. The man made me want to claw at my own skin simply because I'd been looked at by him.

And when he spoke about Alodia—about the dancing star in her soul—I realized something I knew I'd have to share with Elodie, if she hadn't already noticed it herself.

"If you'd known her back then," he said, "you'd understand. Even at that age, she commanded a power over people. I'm telling you. Never seen anything like it. Not in a healthy Bailey woman, and especially not in a sick one. And sure, some of her behavior was because of the condition, you know... it sits like fire in a woman's blood. Gnaws at them. Feeds on them, or parts of them. I know that much about it. But Alodia owned it. Walked with it, I suppose. Sometimes it seemed like the way she moved through the world was one continuous dance. Or, like a fire walk. Yeah, that's it. Like she was walking on fire."

Undeniable. It was so clear in the heightened tone of Howard Bailey's voice, and in the twinkle of his eyes as he spoke about his sister. Something inside him came alive when he spoke about her—something that nothing else seemed to spark.

If it had been up to me, men like him would've been the ones inside that corral, forced to press against and try to climb the chain-link fences, motivated by cattle prods.

"And you know what Hugo told us when we questioned him about my sister?" said Howard. "He told us he found her in his garden late at night, dancing under the moon. And he said they fell in love. There we were, looking for my missing sister who's only twenty-two and doesn't know a thing about the world, and here's this older fellow talking to us about love, when all he really had was a friggin hard-on for my sister." Howard shook his head. A darkness had crept into his eyes, turning his awkwardness into something else. He was like a malfunctioning machine trying to act human. He huffed. "Made me sick."

I cast a glance at Elodie. Her eyes had misted over. Her mouth was a taut, thin line.

When Howard turned from his thoughts and looked at us, a wide grin had curled across his mouth.

"All my yammering, bringing up the past, made me forget my manners. I sure am sorry about that. Been meaning to ask the two of you, especially you, Elodie. Why the visit? Tony told me you sounded pretty eager to get past the gate when you arrived." He chuckled. "Doing a little genealogy research? Looking up family history? That it?"

I gaped at him. Was he actually teasing us?

Elodie spoke before I could. "I found an old photograph of this place and... and wanted to learn more about it. Because, like I said, my dad never really talked about this side of the family. And it's not like my mom ever got the chance to talk about it."

"Oh, I'm sure she didn't," said Howard. He licked his lips. Beads of sweat popped across his forehead, all the way back to his receded hairline. But it wasn't hot enough, I thought. A warm, nice day, but not that bad.

"But really we just came for a visit," said Elodie. "For today."

"Just for the day, huh? Thought we might have a conversation about that."

My entire body reacted to this by stiffening as though bracing for a hit. And the quick glance Elodie cast me, how she reached out for me under the table and took my hand, told me she knew.

The tests. He wanted to talk about the tests. The ones they conducted on the healthy women to see if they were really healthy—to monitor for signs of the condition.

My mind refused to imagine the invasiveness of those tests.

"Tell me first, though," said Howard. "You, uh... you talk with your father, still? Seems like it'd be quite the family situation."

Elodie held relentless eye-contact with him. "Actually, we came from his house. And we'll be going back there today." A pause. "He's expecting us."

Howard looked away and nodded slowly. "Ah... shame. Would've been nice if you could stay a bit longer, but I know how it is. Guess we'll have to have them conversations the next time."

Both Elodie and I could breathe again, for the moment. Both our hands were slick with sweat, holding onto each other under the table.

Before I could change the subject and rise from the bench, hoping to leave, Howard kept speaking. "Your father ever tell you about what happened after he refused to give Alodia back to us?" Howard was looking off toward the corral, ignoring us. A stillness had come over him, so pronounced compared to his fidgety awkwardness it was like he'd injected himself with a stimulant. "I never should've underestimated the man. Keeps a sword inside that walking stick of his, for one. What kind of man carries something like that? Someone not worth trusting, if you ask me. Gave us a lot of trouble over the next couple of days. So much trouble, there really wasn't anything we could do about it."

"Howard," I said, cutting him off, and cutting off whatever Elodie had been trying to say. "It's been a pleasure meeting you, and getting some background on this place after all the questions Elodie had. But, um... we can set a date or something for a better time, for the next time we visit. But we should probably get going before it starts getting dark."

"Funny thing about your mother," said Howard, ignoring me as he continued to stare off toward the corral. "She had symptoms none of us had ever seen before. On some nights, she'd kinda... kinda get bad. Like a goddamn fairytale, come to think of it. The princess turns into a monster at night, but is magically restored during the day." The man smirked, contorting his massive face. "I swear, there still hasn't been another case like hers. Didn't happen every night—in fact it only happened sometimes, though I think it was getting worse the older she got—but some nights she'd get bad. Get that blankness in her eyes. Slip into the condition like into a pretty dress. And *apparently* go dancing in the moonlight."

"Howard," I said. Elodie and I stood up at the same time.

Howard clenched a fist and slammed it down on the bench's wood, making the whole thing rattle. "Les, Tyler, and Ron snuck onto Hugo's estate one night. This was about a year after she escaped. We kept trying to appeal to Hugo, but he wasn't having it. Wouldn't even listen to what I had to say. What kind of man does that? Doesn't even listen to what another's got to say? So we were forced to... well, what I mean to say is, he forced our hand, if you will. Took some harsher measures. Certainly tried to, is what I'm saying.

"So Les and Tyler and Ron, I sent them in the middle of the night to get to Alodia. You know, sneak her off, make a mission out of it, get her out clean and then deal with the fallout. Whatever the hell it took. Really I just wanted my sister back. Wanted her safe, away from that creep Villeneuve."

"That's my father," said Elodie. "Fucking ironic of *you* to call *anyone* a creep."

Howard went on as if he hadn't heard her. "Ron's the only one of the three that came back from Hugo's estate. You know what happened, don't you? He ever tell you about it? Hugo *murdered* them. *Slaughtered* might be a better word... yeah, that's the word alright. When he discovered them trying to haul Alodia away, he... well, I can't even go into the goddamn details of it without feeling sick. So... so I won't talk about it. But Ron did say that Hugo didn't kill the other two immediately. Ron said he saw Hugo tying them up. Said it looked like he was gonna question them. In fact, that's exactly what he thought was gonna happen, that Hugo was gonna question them, maybe torture them a little and let them go. So Ron waited outside the estate for them to come out. Waited until morning, is what he said, especially when he realized there wouldn't be any cops coming.

"And you know what he said he saw? Said he saw Hugo dragging them out beyond the garden, into the trees. Heard them screaming.

"Ron came back here to the farm—was the only one to come back, remember—and he just... he wasn't the same after that. Went a little crazy in the head after witnessing something as horrendous as that.

"But that weren't the end of it. Not quite. Few mornings later, one of the guards comes running into my office and says I gotta see something at the front gate. So I go. You know what

Hugo went and did? He left one of those men—I think it was Les—he left his body at the front gate, just to show us what he did to him. Poor Les, I tell you. His fingernails had been yanked off, some of his teeth were gone, one of his eyes gouged out..." Howard went pale and lifted a hand up to cover his mouth. "Excuse me. I don't like to go into it."

Elodie and I had backed away several steps, joined tightly by our hands.

"So you think about that on your way home, Elodie Villeneuve. You think about that." He turned to us finally. And I swear he looked like a different person. Something about the eyes. The stillness that had settled over him. "You say hello to your father now. And we'll be reaching out. Still got some tests for you, sweetheart. You come back to us now, you hear?"

Elodie and I, as if of the same mind, threw off any notion of manner or appearance. We turned and walked away. We nearly ran, I mean, at least until we reached the first set of gates where the guard named Tony waited for us with his Jeep so he could take us back to our car. He was laughing at us.

Howard Bailey watched us, all the while, from the bench. Just watched us. We rode away from the farm in sweaty-palmed silence.

16

Strangest Dreams

"Did you notice," I said, "the way he never even seemed to care what Alodia wanted? It was all about what he wanted. All about getting her back to that fucking godforsaken place."

Elodie, in the passenger's seat, shared my anger. We'd been on the road for almost an hour, and in that time she had said very little.

I could see, in how she looked out the window with misted eyes—her body completely still—something had broken inside her.

"And the things he said about your dad. To hear someone like him say things like that about someone else… and your dad, of all people!"

"I know, Bennet."

"I mean, your dad's one of the strangest people I've ever met, but he doesn't keep your mom in chains, without any clothes on, behind a fence. He doesn't use fucking cattle prods on her and he... I mean... he loves her."

Elodie stared ahead. "I know."

The drive went on this way for some time. My appalled expressions of disbelief. My attempts at grappling with what we had experienced back there. And Elodie sharing my rage in stunned silence.

Howard Bailey's face kept appearing in my mind, his voice echoing behind my thoughts.

"What kinds of tests do they even do? They'd just keep you there for however long they want, doing what the hell they want?"

She crossed her arms over her chest. "Whatever they do, it's more than just to see if the women are healthy."

"I know, but... I mean, is it some kind of surgery? Your dad's journal almost made it sound like they have ways of tracking the healthy women. Keeping tabs on them. Like, what if they just perform experiments? I sure wouldn't expect them to have any idea what the fuck they're doing—"

"I *know*, Bennet. I just... I don't really wanna think about it right now."

I cast her a cursory glance, noticed her closed-off body language. Best to move on from that. I didn't really want to think about the tests either, whatever they were. But Hugo's journal had mentioned things. Sterilization, for example. "I can't believe he let us go," I said. It wasn't something I'd necessarily meant to say aloud, but as I said it aloud I realized the absurdity of it.

"It's because of what I said about my father. Howard's scared of him."

"You think so?"

Elodie nodded. She didn't say anything else.

"Can I ask something of you?" she said this as night came on. Home was only two more hours away.

"Anything."

"Would you come with me to my parents' tomorrow?" Her eyes reflected the night outside the windshield. Her face was dimly lit by the glowing buttons on the dashboard.

Tomorrow I was supposed to record a podcast with Chris, and then have lunch with Nat. Nat wanted to talk about plans to visit our dad. And Kendra had called me this morning, which I didn't really care about but it seemed like something that needed resolving.

I looked at Elodie, then back at the road. Was I ready to return to that house? To be confronted again by her nebulous father? And by the inexplicable entity of her mother? "Yes," I told her, and meant it. "Tomorrow morning?"

"Tomorrow morning."

"I need to ask you something first."

She looked at me. Her open silence invited me forward.

"A couple months ago, you barely wanted to answer my questions about your parents."

"I know."

"Now you want to go back there."

"Bennet, I don't expect you to—"

"All I wanna know is what changed."

On all sides of us, the ocean of darkness blurred by—silhouettes of towering trees eclipsing most of what we could see of the night sky. The road was a thin line illuminated by the car's headlights.

Elodie sat, quiet, for a long time. She sighed. "After we left their house, they were all I could think about. I saw her face when I closed my eyes, the way she'd looked at me when I stepped through the doors and stood in front of the glass. And my dad... when I got a moment alone with him, he... he had all these stories he wanted to tell me. He just wanted to catch me up on everything I'd missed." She looked over at me, and I couldn't tell if it was merely the reflection of the headlights in her eyes, or if she was fighting tears. "I'm tired of running away from them. I guess that's what changed. I want to try."

I reached over and put my hand gently on her. She took it and held it with tenderness, with gratitude.

We arrived at Elodie's place after midnight. With almost nothing to unpack, we fell into her bed, stripped most of our clothes, and held each other under the covers, in the dark. Held each other in breathing silence, our fingers whispering across each other's skin.

I felt her tremble. She pulled me closer, burrowed her face against my chest, and let herself cry.

It broke my heart when Elodie cried. It didn't happen often, and she fought her tears whenever they came. But despite all the faces she wore, all the masks she liked to switch between, Elodie was always a sensitive and vulnerable girl. So I recognized the importance of her vulnerability with me, her willingness to engage with her own walls, to let them down for me when she could.

Even if, sometimes, she didn't do it willingly.

She let the tears come this time. Put up no resistance. Wept against my chest, clutching at my body, pressing as if she could disappear in my arms.

I held her. Whispered things into her ear. Whispered that I loved her. That I was sorry. That it was okay, even though it wasn't. Nothing was. Not when a place like that farm existed, and those women were inside that dusty corral, encased by barbed wire and often at the ends of needles and cattle prods.

Elodie and I had started our relationship in a night club, then in a bed, having wild sex, flinging away our pretenses for the burning desires underneath in the same way we had flung our clothes aside. And here we were now, so far from where we'd been, holding each other in the dark, almost naked. The intimacy was the same yet so much deeper. I had never experienced eroticism of this kind, and yes, I do mean eroticism. The eroticism of being entirely naked in front of another person, completely in their arms both literally and metaphorically—emotionally, I mean—in the sense that they have your heart, they can hurt you deeper than anyone or anything else in the world.

It is an intimacy that goes deeper than any physical act—it is, you could say, what physical intimacy strives to imitate. And it is sacred.

So when I told her I loved her, I meant I loved her forever, having no idea what would come.

"I don't know how I'm supposed to sleep," she said as I held her, maybe an hour after we'd told each other goodnight.

I was spooned up against her, and she cradled my arm against her chest the way she so often did.

She hadn't needed to ask if I was still awake. We could feel the other's consciousness in the dark.

"I can't stop seeing them," she said, her voice almost broken. "Whenever I close my eyes."

"Me too," I replied. And squeezed her tight, pulled her closer to my chest.

I thought about the first time I had laid eyes on Hugo Villeneuve's brooding estate. The massive house. The beautiful grounds. And the gate and electric fencing.

When I'd first seen the fences, I hadn't been sure if they'd been there to keep others out, or to keep Alodia in. But now I knew. Now I knew the difference between Hugo Villeneuve and Howard Bailey.

Howard Bailey's fences were there to keep the Bailey women inside, like animals in a cage.

Hugo Villeneuve's fences were there to keep intruders out—to keep Alodia safe.

Eventually, holding each other, Elodie and I both slept.

I opened my eyes in the middle of the night, having felt Elodie stir.

She was awake, her head on the pillow beside mine. And

with her face only inches from mine, she was staring at me—staring at me with wide eyes in the dark.

My heart leapt, my breath caught in my throat, nearly forming around a gasp. It had appeared, for a moment, as though her open eyes were black, empty sockets, but a breath later and I could see the glimmer of her ashen irises.

I smiled a little nervously, ready to laugh at myself for having been startled.

Her face remained as it was. Expressionless. Blank. Not like Elodie at all.

I brushed strands of hair behind her ear. "Elodie," I said in a whisper.

No response. Nothing. Only the blank stare, the sound of her steady breathing in the night's quiet.

I said it louder this time, panic finding my voice and lilting it upward in tone. "*Elodie.*"

She took in a sudden breath. "Bennet," she said, and the rest of her body came alive. She lifted a hand to the side of my face. Her fingers were cold. "Oh, Bennet. I was..."

The emotion seeped into her eyes, returning light to them.

She touched her hand along her bottom lip. "I was having the... the strangest dream."

"You scared me."

She kissed me desperately. For a moment I couldn't give in, but a few seconds of her open mouth against mine and I was hers. We slid our bodies close together again, touching all the way down, hands finding each other beneath the sheets.

There are no polite descriptions for it, and no need to dance around it. She fucked me like it was the first time, but first times don't come with the understanding of longer relationships. We knew each other's rhythms, understood each other's responses. It could've been minutes, could've been hours. We finished together loudly, our bodies slick with sweat, staring into each other's eyes.

But as we lay together, heart rates relaxing, breaths slowing, my mind flashed the image again, reminding me before I drifted into unconsciousness—

Our heads sharing the same pillow. Her lack of response to my saying her name. The blankness of her eyes in the dark.

17

To Lose Her

"I heard it from that sick fuck," I said to Hugo as we sat on a bench in the gardens. "But I want to hear it from you."

Hugo was staring off into the distance, a thoughtfulness in his eyes. Something like a smile came across his lips. "I dream often of the night Alodia and I met. This is why it is easy for me to recount."

Elodie and I arrived at her parents' house in the early afternoon. Hugo, expecting us, waited on the front porch of the house, top of his black walking stick held firmly with both hands. He smiled with more warmth than before. Or maybe it was me. The first time I met him, I remember the way he towered above everything else, and how the gleam in his eyes seemed hungry. But I saw only invitation on his face this time.

Hugo Villeneuve was a man—an eccentric man, yes, but not a monster.

Still, I remembered what Howard Bailey had said about him. About the men who had broken into his house to try and steal Alodia back to that fucked up farm.

Was Hugo Villeneuve truly capable of killing? Or, as Howard had described it—slaughtering?

I didn't want to think so, but even with Hugo's newly warm greeting, I looked at him with caution. What was the man truly capable of?

Hugo hugged me rather than shaking my hand. "Still keeping my daughter satisfied, Mr. Bennet?"

In a flourish of inspiration, I patted him on the shoulder, grinning, and said, "Still keeping that beautiful woman of yours under control, Mr. Villeneuve?"

Hugo reacted with a pleased cackle as he raised his eyebrows at Elodie and pointed at me. "You've chosen a good man, Elodie. A good man."

"What can I say, Dad? We bring out the worst in each other."

When Elodie told me she needed to see her mother alone for awhile, I recognized the somberness in her eyes. Of course, I said. This would've troubled me before, being left alone with her father. But I felt ready.

So when Hugo asked if I would walk with him—that's how he phrased it, *Would you walk with me, Bennet?*—I said yes. There were things I wanted to talk with him about. Questions I needed to ask him.

First and most important, since it had gnawed at me since

leaving the Bailey farm, I needed to hear his version of how he and Alodia met.

And I discovered Howard Bailey had been right about one thing, at least, although this was something Hugo freely admitted: the story sounded like a fairytale.

"In the years since that night," said Hugo, speaking as always with meticulous pronunciation, "I have not often been afflicted with insomnia. But before Alodia, I wandered often at night, unable to rest. I cannot say why, in truth, but I like to think part of me was waiting for her. If you take my meaning.

"I do not recall what I was doing that night—perhaps reading in the solarium, or simply checking the locks. I still do this, but only on occasion. And I happened to catch a glimpse of her through the window. She was out in the gardens, nude, twirling and pirouetting, seeming to float amongst my godetias and lilies and fuchsias. I stepped outside and it was most ethereal under the moon. In my dreams the moon is full, but in truth it wasn't quite. Even so, it is so easy to remember the way her skin glinted under the silver glow. The way she drifted through it like a fairy dancing in glowing mists."

Hugo's eyes misted over as he looked out across the garden. The memories must have taken the place of the reality before his eyes. His sunlit garden must've darkened in his mind as if illuminated by the dimmer light of the moon. The stillness across the grounds must've been replaced by the mesmerizing image imprinted in his mind of Alodia dancing naked along the cobbled walkways.

"I went to her," he said. "My intent was to ask her why she was here, and perhaps inquire if she needed help. I had no intention of making her leave." Hugo grinned. "I am an educated man, Bennet. And I believe in the agency I have over myself in this life. It is something I value. But I cannot—and was never able to—resist Alodia. I was drawn to her as if in a trance, completely under her spell from the moment my eyes fell upon her. Did it help that she was naked?" His grin widened. "I'm certain you know the answer. I am not afraid to admit this."

I sat, listening, unable to withhold the shock from my face. I couldn't believe Elodie was missing this.

"Perhaps you know something about what I mean," he said, leaning forward as if to look more deeply into me. I've heard the term "piercing stare" in the past, but had never truly felt its meaning until that moment. "Perhaps," he went on, "when it comes to my daughter, you know what I mean: how it feels to be inexplicably, inexorably drawn to her. As if it is your instinctual nature to go to her, to want her."

"Mr. Villeneuve," I choked over my own voice. Stuttered, making sounds rather than words.

"There is no need to deny it, Bennet. I've seen the way you look at her. To know that she receives this kind of love from you is wonderful to me. Makes me feel a fullness here, in my heart. For so long I've known she was alone in this world. But she has you now. And I am glad."

The turn from strangeness was so abrupt I stared vacantly at him for a moment. "Mr. Villeneuve..."

"Have I not told you to call me Hugo?"

"Right. Hugo. I'm... I'm happy to hear that. It's just... forgive me." I straightened, slowed down, composed myself. "I've never met anyone like your daughter. Elodie's everything to me—the most important person in my life. And this situation with you... and, to be honest, this conversation... it's unusual, to me."

Hugo laughed, and the sound reminded me—as it had the first time—of dead leaves scraping across concrete. "Your willingness to admit this to me is a good sign, then. Honesty is infectious. Our pretenses are walls that do not belong in this house. This is how I try to live my life."

"Without pretenses?"

He shrugged. "I learned from my parents how to withhold. I learned from the rest of my life, and from love, to release. To open up. And when I am honest with you, you feel you can be honest with me. I apologize if this is uncomfortable."

"No, please. It's fascinating."

In response, Hugo grinned. "You do not pull your hand away when it grows hot," he said, echoing something he'd said about me before.

It occurred to me that I had no control in his presence. And as much as he talked about being open and not having secrets, the shadows were deep around the edges of his eyes. There was so much about Hugo Villeneuve that I would never know, and even more that I would never want to know.

"You feel it is strange," he said, "to discuss Elodie in a suggestive context."

I laughed, unable to help myself. "Yes. I do."

"This is because I am her father."

"Yes—and no. I've always been like that, but also, yes, because you're her father. You don't think it's strange?"

"I feel it is stranger that these topics are so often avoided in conversation. You ever think about this, Bennet? So much of our nature is tied inextricably with our sexuality. It sits, hungry, behind every word we speak, every posture we assume, every thought we entertain. Philosophers and theologians and the religious like to pretend to rise above these things as if there is a victory in the denial of what fundamentally drives us. Wouldn't you agree?"

"I'm not sure I've ever thought about it," I lied. And immediately corrected myself. "It doesn't drive all of us, Hugo. I haven't told you anything about, um... about my own sexuality."

Hugo raised an eyebrow as if I were suggesting the silliest thing. "Please, Bennet. When I speak of sexuality, I hope you don't do me the disservice of assuming I mean *conventional* sexuality. What I mean to suggest is, there are forces beneath our skin that dictate so much more of our lives than most of us are willing to admit. For some it is sexual desire, for others it is emotional desire, for others still it falls somewhere between these. And beyond this, the spectrum is endless."

I listened, trying not to grin. This man was full of surprises.

"And what I mean to ask," he said, "is that there is no victory in imagining oneself as being above one's own nature. Above one's own desire, if you will. Do you agree?"

I thought of Elodie walking toward me through a dancing crowd.

Elodie without clothes, arching back, her breaths turning to heightening moans.

The way she looked at me sometimes, an invitation in her eyes. The way I looked back at her, unmasking myself, inviting her to unmask herself at the same time.

We learned how to make love with our glances. It didn't matter where we were. I looked at people in a certain way, choosing to do away with the pretenses. I had looked at Elodie that way on the night we met, and she hadn't shied away like so many others.

"Yes," I said to Hugo, correcting myself. "I agree. The only real way to connect with someone is to acknowledge what's underneath. The ugly things, you know, that don't often see the light of day."

Something ignited behind Hugo's sharp eyes. He leaned his head back and exhaled slowly, grinning.

"You speak my language, Bennet. You perceive a great deal more than you seem to. I appreciate a man willing to keep quiet, especially a man also with the knowledge of when to speak and what to say." He wiped a hand across his lips. "What I said about Alodia. About being drawn to her, as though by some fundamental force. Pulled, like by gravity."

"Yes," I said.

"You know what I mean. When it comes to Elodie."

"I do," I said. "In my way."

Hugo nodded. "Thank you, Bennet. You're a good man. I am glad you love my daughter. She has deserved true, deep love, her whole life."

"She's incredible," I said.

"And you appreciate the phantoms beneath our actions and our words. You understand the nature of what must be pulled from under the surface and dragged out into the light."

If that was Hugo's way of describing desire and the dropping of pretense, I had to appreciate his poetic flare.

I expected him to go on—he seemed to be fascinated by this, fueled by an interest in his daughter's love life that was making me, with each sentence, more and more uncomfortable—but his pause dragged on through the seconds. The garden's silence—marred only by the snapping of small insects and the fluttering of hummingbird's wings—was easy to fall back on, but something about Hugo made it difficult to relax. Let me put it this way: *a lot* of things about Hugo made it difficult to relax. Maybe it was his posture, which seemed both at ease and somehow like that of a lion crouching in tall grass, stalking prey. And when I looked at his face... that's what surprised me.

He had grown suddenly pensive, cold, as if a cloud had passed over his sun.

"I do not know how to ask you this," he said, after staring for a long time at nothing. "You love my daughter, Bennet. Even without the words you have given me, I know this. It is apparent in your eyes. It is the way you look at her. How you search for her, even when you know precisely where she is."

"Hugo, as much as I appreciate—"

"No, Bennet—listen. You must know you are going to lose her."

It didn't matter, then, how hard it was to hold Hugo's gaze. I made myself look in his eyes and not turn away. "I lost her once already," I said. "Briefly, but I felt it like it was the last time. I won't let that happen again."

"And I trust you say this from your heart," he said. "But you must understand, if you don't already—if you haven't yet seen the signs—that it will happen no matter what you do. No matter how tightly you hold on. It is out of your control. In fact, maybe it is happening already. Slowly. A shadow infecting her from the inside, embracing her in slow motion."

I knew what he was talking about. How could I not? It had occurred to me the first time she had ever opened up about her mother's condition. A question I'd thought to ask but had elected instead to push from my mind.

Do you have this condition, too?

I thought of the night before, after we returned from the Bailey farm. When I had awakened in the night and she was beside me, across the pillow, staring at me with wide eyes, utter blankness in her stare.

"You will lose her one day, Bennet." The warmth he'd had for me seeped away. He looked at me now as a suspicious stranger who had wandered into his life. And the house again felt like something dark—a yawning mouth lined by sharp teeth. "And we will see then, Bennet, what kind of man you really are. If your heart matches the words that seem to come from it."

18

Family Dinner

The last time we had visited Elodie's parents, Elodie and I had been allowed our own space and Hugo kept a polite distance. Except for the strange conversations I'd had with him, the visit had been like sitting in a pot of water over a piping furnace, but the temperature was still lukewarm, only hinting at the boiling heat to come.

The water was near scalding now. I had walked through the doors of her father's house thinking I knew what I was walking into. I can be arrogant that way, in the assumptions I make. Elodie knew this, and my fault was in misunderstanding her attempts at helping me adjust to the water.

I noticed something was wrong when she entered the room. She'd been downstairs talking with her father. She moved stiffly, keeping her back rigid, as she crossed the room to sit at the edge of the bed. And she was looking deeply into her thoughts, mouth slightly ajar, eyes not seeing anything; the expression on her face suggested she didn't quite know what to say.

I stood between the white curtains at the window, facing her, phone in one hand. The moment I saw the pallor of her skin, I forgot what I'd been doing seconds ago.

"You okay?"

She lifted her head in my direction; her eyes followed, lagging behind. And she just looked at me without saying anything.

I moved toward her. "Elodie?"

Her mouth opened, closed, opened again. Her eyes were in my direction but didn't seem to be focusing on me. As if I were far away from her, waving my arms to try and get her attention, and she could barely see me.

And then she saw me. Her eyes snapped into focus. She took a deep breath.

When she reached her arms out to me, tears already forming, I went without hesitation to hold her. She placed her head against my stomach, just under my chest.

"We're gonna have dinner with them," she said. "Both of them."

"Both of them?"

"Bennet. You know I love you."

She stayed sitting, her arms around me and mine around her. I looked down at her. "I love you, too."

"You know you don't have to do any of this for me."

"Elodie. I wouldn't do this if I didn't want to. They're your family."

"I know. Sometimes..." She pulled slightly away from me, as if to make room to gather her thoughts. "Sometimes I feel like I can almost picture myself as someone else. Someone who had a completely different life, with a completely different family, someone who doesn't know any of this, or what any of it's like. Sometimes I can see that girl, and I wonder who she is. And I wonder what it'd be like to just..." The tears welled up. "What it'd be like to hold you, Bennet, and not have this weight in my life. All of this... fucking baggage.

"And when I try to think of myself like that, I feel like I can see it all more clearly. Like I look at them, my parents, and I see how *unthinkable* it all must be to you, and how fucked up all of this is."

"Elodie, that's not what—"

"So I need you to know that I understand how much it must be for you to take on, how hard and... and scary, if it's scary... and I know you don't have to do this with me. None of this... none of this has to be part of our relationship. I... I think I'd be okay, you know, trying to keep this, all of this, as a separate part of my life."

Though I stuttered trying to interrupt her, before she could go on I moved my hands to her shoulders and held her firmly. Made sure she looked up into my eyes.

"Don't ever say that again. For one, I know you don't mean it."

"Bennet—"

"No, okay? I know you think you mean it, but... what kind of life would that be? This is your family. And it's part of your life. And when I say I love you, I mean I want to be part of your life. All of it. Everything about it that I can."

She really started to cry then, but it was with a smile shining through. She reached a hand up to the side of my face and pulled me close, held me close like that, in tears.

"Even after all of that. Those people... the farm."

"Yes."

"All of that, and h-how much stranger it's all going to get."

"If you mean dinner," I said, smiling. "I think I can handle dinner with your parents."

She laughed, wiping at her eyes and nose. "Where the hell did you come from?"

"I could ask you the same thing."

"By the way," she said, "you have no idea what you're in for with dinner."

We both laughed. Except she wasn't joking.

*

After he reached over to his wife's side of the table and slapped a bloody chunk of raw meat on her cedar cutting-board of a plate, Hugo asked: "And old Howard Bailey—the sick man—before he let you go... he told you he'd be reaching out?"

I didn't hear the question. Alodia's presence at the dinner table was like a magnet to my attention. I sat, physically unable to relax, across the crimson tabletop cover from her. Elodie was at my side, but the table felt small and I felt alone. Alone except for the feral Alodia Villeneuve.

She wore a tight black bodysuit, one that hugged to her steadfast muscular form. And she sat just like any of us, in a chair, but with a harness strapped to her torso. Her harness was attached to a wire—a leash, essentially. She couldn't move around the table if she chose. Couldn't climb across to lunge at me, although my mind insisted she could. My mind told me I sat across the table from a dangerous predator, an unpredictable wild animal.

Worst of all, she stared right at me. And although the expression on her face was blank, I could see something glow in her eyes.

Something.

Like a closeup video of a lioness. They don't have facial expressions except for those we project onto them. They could be relaxed and lounging about in tall grass, or they could be ready to pounce—the look on their face would be exactly the same.

Except, maybe, for something in the eyes. A subtle difference. The dilation of the sharp pupils. I don't know how else to explain it. But that's what Alodia's eyes were like, trained on me from across the dinner table. Not to say they portended hunger for me. But she was unmistakably watching me. To her, I was the outsider. She didn't trust me with her daughter.

Hence the harness and leash, which Hugo apologized to her about every few minutes.

As I watched Alodia watching me, it occurred to me that all mothers must feel this way for their children. Deep down, they may never completely trust the life partners of their offspring.

And if Elodie's mother were a normal person, she probably

would've welcomed me in, been open to me, but also been analyzing me to make sure I was trustworthy, someone worthy of her daughter's devotion.

I would've preferred that.

Because, in comparison, Elodie's real mother didn't simply distrust me, or analyze me. Instead, she looked as though she would have no hesitation in reaching across the table to try and rip me limb-from-limb if I appeared to pose any form of threat to Elodie.

In contrast, none of the problems of my old life—not even my past heartbreak over losing Kendra—seemed to carry any more weight. Anxiety, the sense of losing both a friend and a lover, and the toxic weight of betrayal—those concerns were such paltry things when compared to sitting across the crimson tabletop from Alodia, Elodie's feral mother, with that gleam in her reptilian-like eyes that suggested murderous thought.

The small slab of meat on her cutting board was fleshy pink, leaking red onto cedar. She had already consumed another chunk of meat, a few minutes ago. That image, too, was seared into my mind. This woman, across from me, digging her fingers like claws into the meat, dropping her face down and chomping into it, pulling at it, tearing it into pieces. The way she chewed loudly and quickly, ravenous, predatory, eyes wide.

Hugo had laughed to see my stricken expression.

"When you do something," he said, as if reciting a poem, "do it entirely. When you fuck, fuck as if it is the last time. When you love, give your heart without fear. When you eat, eat as if it is your final meal. Alodia demonstrates this with such fervor, wouldn't you say?"

He was right about that. She appeared not to have any thought in her head except to eat as she consumed her meal. And when it was finished, she returned to an erect sitting position, though now her lips shone with blood and grease, and her eyes returned to me. I noticed, too, how she panted.

Later, Elodie would tell me this was unusual. Physically, her mother was healthy, capable of prowess and showings of strength and endurance far beyond what was expected of even great athletes. But she was sick, getting sicker. And the simple act of eating—with her energetic animosity—made her pant now.

As she was given a second helping, Hugo brought up the subject of Howard Bailey.

"You say that he simply let you leave?" asked Hugo.

"Yes," said Elodie. Whenever she spoke about the Bailey farm, especially Howard, she drew her shoulders stiffly in and kept her eyes low. "He just… let us go. Even though it seemed like…"

"Like he would've stopped us," I said. "With what he was saying about having tests for you."

"That's right," said Elodie. "He kept bringing up the tests."

"Ah, yes." Hugo nodded. "I remember." He reached a hand over to Alodia, placed it on her leg. "Alodia told me, decades ago, about the tests. How the family monitors the healthy females, no matter where they are, no matter how far away. And they are called back every few months for these tests, if I remember correctly."

"To test if they're healthy?"

"In part, Bennet. But they are treated as though they are sick. Like they are sick animals. And it is up to the discretion of the family, and men like Howard Bailey, whether the healthy Bailey women are allowed back into society." He paused—and not merely with his words. His entire body went still. "If I were to make an educated guess, I'd suppose that Howard Bailey did not mention the abuse, or the surgeries, or the sterilizations." He turned to Elodie, who had gone pale.

I merely gaped at him, reacting physically as if he'd thrown something at me. "That really happens?"

"Indeed, Bennet. The tests we speak of, they are not simply for the sake of health. You see, any sick Bailey woman is sterilized. And some of the healthy Bailey women, if they are considered high risk, are only allowed back out into the world if they consent to these procedure."

"What the *fuck*." I set both hands down on the table harder than expected.

"Count yourself fortunate that you were not shown the surgery rooms. The floors stained by so much blood, there is a *scent* of it that cannot be eradicated, and the stains themselves have been too thoroughly soaked to ever be washed out. Some of the younger girls there, I hear they called it *the pink room*."

Neither Hugo nor Elodie seemed to notice, but Alodia visibly tensed, her eyes still trained on me.

I turned to Elodie. "Did you know about this?"

Her eyes were watery. She shook her head, said nothing more.

"Do not underestimate the psychopathy of these people," said Hugo. Then, with a flourish of his hands—as he picked up his silver utensils—he changed the subject. As if it were hot asphalt he wanted to step away from. "And old Howard Bailey—the sick man—before he let you go... he told you he'd be reaching out?"

Elodie nodded, still dazed from what her father had just said.

The memories of the farm kept replaying, over and over, in my head. Those women we'd seen along the fence, in the corral.

Howard Bailey and his veneer of politeness, the way he'd attempted to greet us with such casual warmth.

The way he'd looked out at the corral, at the women encaged within, as if it meant nothing to him.

The encounter was clear enough in my mind that it could've been earlier today.

Howard, a hulking man—so stilted and awkward yet with an eerie stillness coming over him—as he told us about the men that Hugo had supposedly killed. *Slaughtered* was the word he used.

And there had been the increasingly paranoid sensation of helplessness—the fear that Howard Bailey and his fucked up family would try and take Elodie, and that I might never see her again if that happened. I wouldn't have been able to do a fucking thing to save her.

"And," said Hugo, "he said this to you as you were leaving?"

Elodie nodded again.

Hugo responded with a simple "Hmm," and he clinked his utensils down onto his plate. Folded his fingers in front of his face and, for the briefest of moments, closed his eyes. A foggy silence descended over the table.

I spoke when I felt I realized why he reacted this way.

"Hugo. He's a dangerous man, isn't he?"

Hugo was staring down at the table, as if studying the burning candle a hand's reach from his plate. "When we are children, we fear the monsters that lurk in the shadows of our imagination. In the bedroom's dark corner. Lurking in the closet among the coat hangers. Beneath the bed, where the moonlight doesn't reach. But we grow out of these things. We learn there are no monsters. Until the day we learn that yes, there are monsters in the world, after all. And they are among us, shaking our hand, sharing our tables, passing us on the sidewalk." Hugo's eyes shot up at me. "You understand what I am saying."

"He seemed friendly at first. But even at the start, it was an off-putting kind of friendliness. Awkward and... accommodating."

"Something about his eyes," said Elodie, shivering. "And he grew stranger, the longer we were there."

"Howard Bailey is like a beast wearing the body of a man," said Hugo. "He can scarcely maintain the façade for long stretches at a time, as you clearly witnessed."

"Sure, I get that," I interjected, remembering Howard's eerie stillness. "But, I mean... there was something clearly *wrong* with him. Not just in the philosophical sense—I mean, sure, he's a fucking psychopath or whatever—but I mean, it seemed like something was seriously wrong with him." I turned to Elodie. "Didn't it?"

She agreed with her eyes. She had stiffened to this conversation, the same way she had withdrawn more and more the longer we'd stayed at the Bailey farm.

Hugo gave his wife a long, loving glance. She had finished with her second helping of raw meat and was now sitting still. Her eyes remained on me, but she didn't appear as prepared to lunge across the table at me. She was relaxed. At ease. Or simply digesting her food.

Then Hugo turned to me again. "You bring up an intriguing point, Bennet. This is an issue I have written extensively about, although my findings have not proved as fortuitous as those on the female side of the Bailey family.

"You see, Bennet, as I'm sure you've read in my journal by now..."

I turned pale, exchanged a cursory glance with Elodie. She gritted her teeth at me.

Hugo's expression didn't change. "Yes, I am well aware you took my journal, Bennet. We will come to that.

"As I was saying—as you read in my journal, the Bailey condition expresses itself exclusively on the female side. You witnessed this on the farm, as you told me. However, I believe the condition *does* indeed exist inside of the men, as well. Some doctors I've spoken to about this, they believed it to be dormant in the men, and they gave interesting but uninterested opinions about how the condition may latch onto certain chromosomes that females express and males do not. You know what I mean, yes. These are simple hypotheses."

"But," I said, "you think the men have it, too."

"I noticed the same things about Howard Bailey on the

occasions that I was *fortunate* enough to have met him." Hugo flourished his hands as he spoke; he had a way of communicating his sarcasm with tilts of his eyebrows or a subtle movement of the hand. "I myself have only hypotheses about this, but I believe you can see it in the Bailey men. We already know what the condition does to the women." He reached over to Alodia again, placed a hand on her leg. "But it seems to act strangely upon the male brain, in a different way. Turns them monstrous, makes them unhinged. Perhaps you get my meaning."

Neither Elodie nor I had to say anything. We both knew exactly what Hugo spoke of. We had seen it in the eyes of Elodie's uncle, had heard it in his manic voice.

"And as for Howard Bailey," he said, "I'm afraid he is a man of his word. If he told you that he would be reaching out, it means you might expect a visit from him. Soon, even."

I didn't say it aloud, but I had been expecting this. Probably Elodie had been, too. It was why she'd wanted to come here, why she probably felt safer here. Just because we'd left the farm didn't mean we were beyond that family's toxic reach. We were in their heads now. Howard Bailey would be thinking about us. He'd be thinking about Elodie, about the tests he wanted to give her, about wanting to sterilize her—about the audacity she had, being of Bailey blood and going about in the world, free from his control.

I thought of the way he had spoken about his sister. As if he were infatuated with her. Maybe more than that.

And Elodie was her daughter.

I reached over to Elodie. Put a hand on her leg. She placed her hand over mine. I felt her tremble.

Across the table, Alodia continued to stare, wild eyes locked on me.

19

Clouds Clearing Away

On the night before they came for us, Elodie and I made love. It was the first time we had done so in her parents' home.

Something Hugo had said to me on our first visit recurred to me as I moved on top of Elodie, my hands sliding her clothes away, our bodies wrinkling the sapphire duvet. Hugo said he hadn't heard Elodie and me having sex, and it had *worried* him. Made him wonder if something was wrong between us, if we'd been fighting or having issues.

And it occurred to me that, for Hugo, this was a perfectly normal thing to inquire about. That's simply how he was. Never the father to make his daughter feel shameful about sex. Never the father to pretend such a part of her life didn't exist. He was, sometimes literally, the opposite of that.

Thoughts of him and Alodia flashed through my mind, but faded as I covered Elodie's body with my hands and my kisses.

Her moans filled my ears, and the rest of the world melted away.

We found ourselves tangled together, breathless, nude. Sometimes the rest of my life felt like intervals between these moments with her.

She plunged her hands through my hair, messing it up over and over, sometimes lifting my head so she could look into my eyes and give me a mischievous grin—flashing both playfulness and passion.

"You really meant it. What you said earlier."

I gazed into her eyes. Doing this was easy. "When have I ever been dishonest with you."

"Never, that I know of." She bit her bottom lip when she saw me lift an eyebrow. "Really, Bennet. I never pictured anything like this."

"Never pictured you'd be sitting with me and your family for dinner?"

She nodded, a softness in her every movement. This was a side of Elodie emerging that I never would've conceived upon first impression. Vulnerable. Open. Softening from those sharp edges I'd first encountered.

"Can I be honest?" she asked, though it wasn't really a question, and she didn't wait for an answer. "I keep expecting you to give up. To turn and walk out the door and leave."

"Thanks for all the credit to my trustworthiness."

"It's not like that," she said. "It's just part of my mind, spinning in its endless circles."

"Will you tell that part of your mind to shut the fuck up?"

"Oh, believe me." She chuckled.

I pulled myself up closer to her so I could rest my head on my arm. "I will say, though... it was hard to relax at dinner."

"Because of what my dad was saying?"

"No. I mean... not really. That stuff's been on my mind anyway. I meant the way your mom was looking at me."

"Oh. Right."

"I know it might be ridiculous, but I felt like she wanted to leap across the table and throttle me."

Elodie put her hand to my cheek. "She just doesn't know you yet."

"It's a little more than that though, isn't it? She doesn't trust me. At all. She looks at me like I'm a threat."

"Bennet, I've been alone for most of my life. You know that."

I did. A couple months ago we had opened up to each other about our past relationships. Except it was more like I opened up about past relationships, and she opened up about her lack of them.

"*I've never been in a very serious one,*" she had told me. "*Not one that lasted more than a couple months, anyway.*"

And I knew what this meant.

I traced her neckline to her shoulder with my fingers. "Hadn't thought about it like that. I'm the first guy she's ever seen you with."

Elodie nodded somberly.

"You probably never even brought friends over, when you were a kid."

"No." She almost laughed. "I didn't really have a lot of friends."

"So she doesn't know what to make of me."

She shook her head.

The absurdity of this situation wasn't lost on me: to think we were discussing what Elodie's reptile-like mother thought of me.

An idea came to me then, arising in my thoughts like the sudden swell of an ocean wave. Maybe it was a bad idea, but no —it didn't feel like a bad idea.

I asked, "Are you planning on seeing her again tonight? Before we go to sleep?"

"I think so. At least to say goodnight. Or to read to her for a little bit, like last time. She likes it when I read to her."

"Okay." I sat up. "How about we both go? Right now."

She sat up with me. And the look she gave me melted my heart.

Elodie and I set a blanket down as well as a few pillows, and we sat beside each other, shoulder-to-shoulder, in front of the glass.

On the other side, crouching and pressing her hands and face up close, was Alodia. She appeared more alert than at the dinner table. Her eyes flitted back and forth between Elodie and me, but seemed always to linger on me for longer. Her hair was a tossed and strewn mess.

I got a different sense from her here than at the dinner table. She seemed more comfortable now, as she better understood this environment—understood she couldn't break through the glass. And although I'd learned that trying to read her expression was a wasted effort, I didn't glean from her face the same animosity as before. She appeared more curious. An intelligent, attentive animal trying to make sense of what was happening. Trying to figure out the dynamic—whether to be on guard, or to relax.

I was deliberate with my every movement, lest I should elicit from her—as I had at our last visit—a violent reaction.

Elodie had brought a collection of poetry to read aloud, and was just finishing a poem from William Butler Yeats.

"I am haunted by numberless islands, and many a Danaan shore,
Where Time would surely forget us, and Sorrow come near us no more;
Soon far from the rose and the lily and the fret of the flames would we be,
Were we only white birds, my beloved, buoyed out on the foam of the sea!"

As she stretched out her pronunciation of the poem's final lines, her mother's eyes fixated on her. And I swear I saw adoration in those reptilian eyes—eyes that appeared almost to catch golden light, dimly luminescent in the dark. Her mouth twitched oddly at the corners and her lips peeled back slightly, as if she were trying to imitate a smile.

A chill flooded my body, raising goosebumps on my arms, up to my shoulders, and then all down my back.

If there had been doubts in my mind before about Alodia's consciousness, about any remnants of the woman she had once been, those doubts dissipated like thin clouds clearing away.

Elodie reached a hand out and placed it against the glass, opposite Alodia's open-palmed hand. "She likes romantic poetry," she said, sadness weighing on her voice. "Dad always reads romantic poetry to her."

"Does she have a favorite?"

"Baudelaire. Or Poe, if you can call him romantic."

Somehow both of those choices made sense.

"She looks paler," I said, "from our last visit."

Elodie nodded with her lips pursed tightly together. I couldn't tell if it was a trick of the room's low light, but I thought I saw her eyes glisten.

"It always happens to us, at some point." By *us* she meant the women of her bloodline. "Some of us grow into old age just fine... like that photo of my great-grandmother. She must've been in her seventies."

The pale photograph flashed in my mind. The woman's dead eyes, the chain leash around her neck.

Elodie went on. Now I was certain there were tears in her eyes. I could hear it in the strain and lilt of her voice. "I've spent most of my life avoiding my family in every way I could, and that meant trying to just... to shut out anything I was told or anything I learned about the condition. But I know this much. I know most of the women in my family who develop it... they don't live past sixty. If they even make it close." She turned away from her mother to look at me. "It kills us. Eventually it kills us."

Alodia was in her early fifties—maybe fifty-five, at the most, even though she didn't look it. And the pallor of her skin, the sunken appearance of her eyes, the way eating dinner had left her out of breath—all of these told me what I needed to know.

I put my hand on Elodie's arm, scooted closer to her.

And then I turned to Alodia, who watched us from the other side of the glass. Alodia, who was weakening, who would someday be gone. Whom, despite everything, Elodie would miss with her whole heart.

Alodia's breathing quickened. And her eyes flitted back and forth, back and forth, between Elodie and me.

"Alodia," I said, addressing her clearly. I couldn't be sure if she listened or if she understood, but I'd been paying attention to the way both Elodie and Hugo addressed Alodia. They spoke to her in the same way someone might speak to a comatose loved one on a hospital bed. It didn't matter if they could hear. What mattered was speaking to them. This was a language I could understand. "Alodia. It's been wonderful to meet you and spend time with you. I know you don't have much say in it, but I'm glad to have been welcomed into this house. And to share dinner with you and your husband. He's a great cook, by the way."

Elodie reached over and took one of my hands. She squeezed it reassuringly.

"I hope, in time," I said to Alodia, "you can come to trust me. I love your daughter. I really do. And that means I look at you like you're my family."

Elodie squeezed my hand again. I met her gaze. Saw radiant gratitude reflected there.

We read more poems to her. I looked up an Edgar Allan Poe poem, *Ulalume*, which had long been my favorite.

And I said: "She is warmer than Dian;
She rolls through an ether of sighs—

She revels in a region of sighs:
She has seen that the tears are not dry on
These cheeks, where the worm never dies,
And has come past the stars of the Lion
To point us the path to the skies—
To the Lethean peace of the skies—
Come up, in despite of the Lion,
To shine on us with her bright eyes—
Come up through the lair of the Lion,
With love in her luminous eyes."

But even as I grew more relaxed—helped by Elodie's actively comforting presence beside me—Alodia did not appear calmer. I noticed no slackening in her stiff posture, no relaxing of her shifting eyes. And when we bid her goodnight, she hoisted herself closer to the glass until her palms were white and her nose was pressed almost flat.

Elodie fell asleep spooned against me, cradling my arm against her chest the way a child might cuddle a stuffed toy bear. She twitched softly in her sleep, and I wondered what she dreamed. I wondered if they were good dreams, and hoped so.

At some point she readjusted herself and released my arm. I'd been lying awake for an hour, unable to move my mind away from tonight's dinner, or from Alodia's shifting eyes.

And, just as the idea had come unexpectedly earlier that I should join Elodie with reading to her mother, another idea sprung into my head as I lay in the dark.

Unlike the last idea, this one did seem immediately like a

bad idea—probably a terrible one. But I wasted no time letting it marinate in my head. I rose, dressed as if going out for a walk, left the room, and crept downstairs, headed for Alodia's side of the house.

20

Disbelief

It's odd—actually it's quite fucking annoying—the way people linger in our minds long after they're gone from our lives and are now, in reality, entirely different people.

I had once known Kendra so well. Considered her my best friend, my confidant, all that bullshit from my heart I never should've entrusted to her because she certainly didn't entrust hers back. Not all the way, not even at the peak of our relationship, when we'd been in love. Kendra never knew herself well enough to be able to give herself entirely to another person, not even to me. I should've known that, but I'm a fool without regret who gives people I love the benefit of the doubt—and when I say I give my heart, I mean it.

And I had learned the hard way: not everyone means it when they say things like that. Things like *I love you* or *I can't imagine my life without you.*

And I was beginning to learn the hard way—because there is only the hard way in these matters—that some people *do* mean it when they say those things.

But the important thing here is that I rarely thought about Kendra anymore. She didn't pop in my mind the way she used to—in fact, sometimes I didn't think about her for an entire day. And when I did, any semblance of the old pain was gone. I had someone in my life now who loved me in all the ways I hadn't known Kendra never did. Elodie opened parts of me I hadn't even known were closed—places Kendra had been too self-involved to ever care about searching for.

When I stepped out into the gardens behind Hugo Villeneuve's massive house, I stepped as if on thin ice. The silence of the night deafened me, encasing the wild beating of my heart.

And when I first caught sight of Alodia in the darkness, among the flowers, my mind did something unexpected.

I thought of Kendra. For the first time in several days, despite not having thought about her, despite no longer even caring much for her anymore, it occurred to me: What if Kendra could see me now? What would she think? What would she say?

None of these were serious thoughts. I spent no time mulling it over, or actually considering the answers. I didn't give a shit what Kendra would've thought, or what she would've said.

It's just that people linger inside of us, and no matter how certain we are that we've flushed them out of our system, they return sometimes. Some dormant aspect of them arises in our minds.

In this case, it came simply as that: What would Kendra think if she could see me now? Once, years ago, she would've cared. Would've been deeply concerned to know I'd one day be in this unimaginable position.

But *that* Kendra, the one that would've cared, didn't exist anymore.

And here I was standing on a cobbled walkway in the backyard of my girlfriend's father's mansion, facing my girlfriend's reptile mother—and there wasn't anything between us to keep her from me.

Her room had been empty. A lamp had been left on beside her bed of tangled sheets, allowing me to enter with confidence, past the barrier of glass. So I had come out here, to the gardens. And I knew I had to be out of my mind to be doing this alone, without Elodie, without Hugo, without some sort of weapon, without a barrier to protect me.

But the resolve burned like a furnace in my chest.

I had seen the way Alodia looked at her husband. In fact, I'd seen the way she fucked her husband—I can't call it *making love*. More important, I had seen the way Alodia looked at her daughter.

There was love in her luminous eyes when she looked upon them. Somewhere behind the manic blankness that was her bestial expression, Alodia was capable of love. Of trust.

And I couldn't get it out of my mind: I wanted that from

her. I *needed* it. If I was going to be this in love with Elodie, if I was going to give myself entirely—to *go all in*—I needed to know that her mother trusted me.

No matter what that meant.

Which is why this seemed like a good idea. A terrible idea, but a good one. At least... worth the cost. I hoped.

I caught sight of her as I was moving along the pathway. I was almost to the gardens, among the flowers, when I saw movement ahead. And I realized that if I had looked hard enough, I would've seen her from the moment I stepped outside. She'd been standing there all along, on the walkway ahead of me—standing perfectly still, blending into the night.

She still wore the tight black outfit. Almost a bodysuit. And her hair was like a wildfire encircling her head, shooting up and dancing in all directions.

The sight of her standing there, staring at me, was enough to kick my heart into panic and to make my whole body stiffen. And then I gasped—involuntarily, a lungful of a gasp—when Alodia's posture changed.

She'd been standing upright, sort of like a normal person and yet somehow not at all. Like an imitation of a person's casual stance. But when she realized that I had noticed her, she lowered herself. She bent her legs, splayed her arms slightly outward, hands wide open like extended claws.

She may have even bared her teeth. In truth, I didn't notice. Because the next second—a mere breath—she was coming at me. *Sprinting* at me with the limber speed and hungry focus of a tiger.

A brief thought passed through my mind as I willed myself into motion:

How the hell could a human move so fast? It didn't seem possible.

And then I realized that I may as well have been trying to move underwater. Like in a dream, when you try to run, it's like you're trying to run in low gravity, feet barely touching the ground, each step a glacial process. I didn't have the reflexes of a predator, nor of capable prey.

And by the time I understood that running was pointless, it was too late.

Alodia threw her entire body at me—lifted herself completely off the ground in a full-send lunge.

The force of her body's impact with mine made me huff as the breath was shoved from my lungs. I shot through the air. My head slapped against grass and dirt. If she had tackled me straight back onto the cobbled walkway, I would've lost consciousness, would've likely been bleeding from my ears. Instead, I felt the violent jolt through my body, felt a fuzziness—an aching in my head worse than any I'd ever felt—and when the purple blotches in my vision dissipated, I was staring into the animal eyes of Alodia.

I had never seen her so closely.

Those eyes were undeniably human, but the pupils were too wide to be normal—as if her irises had turned black, encircled by thin gold rings like the eyes of a reptile. And when she blinked—which wasn't often—I noticed, for the first time, a second fleshy film beneath her eyelids.

I may have moaned. May have cried out with disgust and with fear. But I could do nothing else. Couldn't move. Couldn't hope to resist. She pinned me to the ground and I could tell, without needing to try, that I couldn't move. She was unthinkably stronger than I.

Alodia's lips peeled back and she bared her teeth at me. And hissed.

I was hyperventilating; my breaths were shallow and it felt as though I were suffocating on air. The force of Alodia's tackle had knocked the wind out of me and I couldn't take a deep breath.

Gasping, surely with the appearance of a fish out of water, my vision blotted again, inked by approaching darkness, and my head pounded in unison with my wildly racing heart.

I thought, this is it. Whatever stupid fucking plan I'd formed—based on some misguided, optimistic whim—didn't matter. Nobody would know. Elodie would find my remains out here in the gardens. Maybe there'd be something left of my face for her to hold and cry over.

And I wondered—what would happen then? After I was found? Surely, throughout the night, Alodia would feast on me the way she had feasted ravenously on the raw, bloody meat at the dinner table. But what would happen to Elodie? Would she be able to forgive her mother? Would she be able to understand, maybe, why I had come down here?

And then another thought, this one more horrible even than the thought of my corpse being consumed by this feral woman...

Would Elodie ever find someone again? Someone who cared about her the way I did?

Would she ever trust someone again, the way she trusted me?

Would she be alone—alone like she'd always been—for the rest of her life?

My panic seemed to flatten, replaced by something that felt like the scorching fire of purpose. The fire that ignites inside a person who needs to do the impossible because there simply isn't any other choice, whether it's lifting a car to save a loved one, whether it's conquering an unconquerable mountain because of a drive that is never silent, whether it's burning the world down around you because it's the only way you will ever be heard by a system that silences and oppresses. That is the only way I know how to describe it. More than mere adrenaline, more than inspiration or powerful motivation, it woke me up.

And suddenly I gasped a full breath of air. My vision swam back into clarity.

"Alodia," I said, trying to lift myself up.

Alodia's face contorted into a wrinkled-nose snarl. She seized the collar of my shirt and pulled, lifting me up from the grass with a single arm.

For the span of a breath I hung, suspended by my shirt—

And then she flung me.

I landed on grass and rolled three times from the force of her throw. But the determination to take control of this situation hadn't yet died away. Using the momentum of my rolling body, I managed to get my feet beneath me. Almost stumbled back onto my ass, but didn't fall. Despite my vision clearing, my head still spun and swayed on the inside.

I faced Alodia.

She approached me slowly now, hunched like a bear on its hind legs, eyes gleaming in the dark.

"Alodia," I said, keeping my arms forward, palms open defensively. She needed to see in my body language that I meant what I was about to say. "Alodia, listen to me, please. I'm not gonna hurt you. I'm not here to hurt you."

A guttural sound emanated from her throat. A growl, I assumed. It was like the deep rumble of an idling engine.

If she screeched, as she had once—though behind the glass—it would probably break my eardrums.

"I promise you, Alodia. I won't hurt you. I won't even fight back. I promise. If I hurt you, it would hurt Elodie. And I would never, ever do anything to hurt Elodie. Never in my whole life. I promise."

That guttural growl again. It sent cold chills down my whole body. My outstretched hands trembled uncontrollably, and my voice was growing weaker, more desperate with each step Alodia took.

But I refused to back away. There was no running away from her. And no fighting back.

If Alodia had been a normal mother, a functioning person without the Bailey Family Condition, the equivalent of this encounter probably would've been a tense conversation in the kitchen. She would've been a critical, passive-aggressive mother who disapproved of me and gave me questionable looks. I would've found time alone with her and confronted her about her attitude, told her how much I loved Elodie, told her how important it was to me that she—Elodie's mother—and I get along, for Elodie's sake. I would've done my best to set boundaries, to act with respect for myself and for her.

But even as this had occurred to me, it was irrelevant, just as wishing always is.

Just as it would've been pitifully irrelevant to simply wish that Alodia—the real Alodia—didn't want to kill me. Wishing would never make it so.

Alodia stepped within a body's length of me. She lowered herself as if ready to pounce again. But instead she began to circle me, baring her teeth, growling louder and more ferociously. Drops of spit twinkled down her chin.

"I know you can understand me. I see the way you look at your husband, and at your daughter. And I'm sorry I didn't understand it before, but I do now. Okay? I want to be able to talk with you, Alodia. I want you to understand that I mean it when I say... when I say I love Elodie. I love her more than I've loved anyone or anything in my whole life."

She hissed. The sleeves of her bodysuit ended halfway up her arms, exposing enough wrist that I could see the snaking veins bulging. Her hands were rigid claws, palms open. Her dark curls slashed across her face but she made no move to swipe them away.

"You can understand what I mean, can't you?" I said. "When I tell you how much I love your daughter. You know what that feels like. You just want to protect her. She means the world to you. That's... that's what this is all about, isn't it?" I couldn't tell if my words were getting through to her, couldn't tell if she even cared what I said. But I kept speaking. And realizations came to me as I spoke, so I spoke them aloud.

"Alodia. That's what this is about, isn't it? Your family. *This* family, I mean. Your husband and your daughter—Hugo and Elodie. They're the only people in the world who've ever loved you the same way you love them. That's the truth, isn't it?"

I thought of the Bailey farm, where Alodia had grown up. I thought of this poor woman's twisted brother, Howard Bailey.

"They're all you have in this world, your family. Hugo and Elodie, I mean," I said, as she continued to form a perimeter around me. "They're all you ever wanted. And I know what you must feel. I mean... maybe I don't really know, but I can try to understand—you'd do anything to protect them. You'd kill for them. You'd die for them. I may not know what it's like to be a parent, but I can promise you, Alodia, that I love Elodie with all my heart. And I would do anything for her, too."

Alodia snarled again—it was almost a roar, arising in her chest and slicing out from her throat. She stomped a foot forward, causing me to jolt, but I stood my ground. Even with the aches in my body from how she'd tackled me and then tossed me, I stood my ground.

"I want you to know, also," I said, "that I learned more about you. More about your story, I mean—about who you were, what kind of person you used to be, and... and about what happened to you.

"Part of that was seeing the Bailey farm. Elodie and I went there. And it was the most horrific thing I've ever seen.

"And another part of that was reading some of your husband's journal. Elodie and I read some of it together—

especially the things he wrote about you, from back when you were starting to get worse. And after Elodie was born."

I saw something in Alodia's eyes, then. A flash of emotion so sudden, so unexpected, and so viciously primal, it hurt me just to see. The singleminded predator-stare softened as she physically grimaced, and then her expression widened into desperation.

It hurt her to be reminded of those times. It made her sad. Struck her somewhere deeply—more deeply than I could fathom.

"I read about how hard you tried to hold on—to your mind, your life, your husband who loved you and still loves you... and to your daughter. And I could picture it so vividly: you holding her and holding the image of her in your arms. It was all you ever wanted in this life. To have a life with your daughter. To be free from your horrible family, and to be able to live a life with this new family, the one you made.

"And I have to tell you something, Alodia. It feels so small with words, but I have to say it, just because... because of what it means to me.

"I'm sorry. I'm so sorry. I didn't know you before your condition... I didn't know any of this before a few days ago. But that kind of pain is something I can't even begin to imagine. To have fled from the horrors of your earlier life... and then to meet a man like Hugo. Someone you could make a new life with. Someone who cared about you that deeply, that meaningfully, that *thoroughly*, all the way down to your soul. Not everyone is ever so lucky, to find that kind of love. I know that now. In my own way, I know that. I can see it—in his eyes. In the way he talks about you. And... and I can feel it, when I look at Elodie, when I hold her and don't want anything else from this life.

"And then I think of you, sitting in bed, holding that little baby, your daughter, knowing you only have so long before you vanish into your condition. I think of you, finally having the life you wanted, finally knowing a love so full and so deep that it's all you could ever want—and more than you felt you ever deserved—but knowing you will have to leave it. Knowing you won't be able to live that life... not the way you would've wanted."

I lifted a hand to my cheek, felt tears there. Wiped them away.

"Alodia, I'm so sorry. I wanted to tell you that."

Alodia replied with a scream.

She slashed at me, and even with my arms up in defense I was propelled to the ground, my whole body rattled, wrists aching where she'd struck.

"Alodia," I said from the dirt, uncertain if she would strike me down once more if I tried to rise.

Alodia screamed again—a brief, wild shriek—and I say *screamed* because it wasn't a *screech*. There was something human in the sound—the lilt of raw emotion. And then I saw tears fall from her eyes. They welled up and then dripped down her face.

She dropped onto her knees then, hands digging into the ground, and her whole body shuddered. Strange sounds escaped from her throat. I could see that all of this effort had taken a great deal of energy out of her, but it was more than that.

She was crying. Or something like crying—her version of it.

Her eyes were wide open as the tears fell, her mouth gaped slightly ajar, and it appeared she was in pain, fighting back against something inside. And she was crying.

I thought about reaching out to her the way I would've to a friend, maybe to place a hand on her shoulder—to let her know I was here. But thought better of it and simply stayed there on the grass with her, unmoving, watching her cry. I said a few more things in whispers, kept apologizing to her and telling her it's okay, it's okay.

I don't know if she heard me. If she understood.

But this was the most human I had ever seen her. And even in the wideness of her eyes, I saw emotion there. Saw the desperation, saw the fight against the tears—and something else. Something that broke my heart:

Disbelief. As if she couldn't believe what was happening. As if Alodia—the human Alodia—was rising closer to the surface than she had in decades, and, looking out through those reptilian eyes, was in disbelief. In awe of what she was, what her life was—in awe and disbelief that any of this had happened and this was her life.

I felt a great weight in my chest, a weight like a block of ice crushing my sternum in, and I cried with Alodia until it felt as though there were no tears left.

21

A Good Plan

Elodie and I were downtown when the men came for us.

It was her hometown. I often forgot that. Whenever we were near Hugo's estate, the awareness of it drew all my attention. Nothing else seemed to exist around it, as if a house—and its legacy, its meanings—could exist in a vacuum, totally alone and without the context of its surroundings.

So when Elodie suggested we spend some of the day in the town of Hilltop, I looked at her with genuine surprise. "There's a town?"

She wrinkled her brow at me, unable to contain a laugh. "Babe…"

And, realizing how tunnel-vision I could be, I begged her to forget I said anything, and she teased me all the way out the door.

The town had been invisible to me before, but now it took on life and vibrant color. Knowing this was Elodie's hometown made it into something special, something sacred. The formative section of her life belonging entirely to her—sights she had seen, memories she'd lived.

The weathered stainless steel water fountains outside a visitor's center made me wonder if Elodie, as a child, had tiptoed to reach the faucet.

An ancient-looking used bookstore brought back memories of my own childhood, my own haunts, and made me wonder if young Elodie—before she ran away as a teenager—had ever lost hours along those dusty shelves the same way I'd lost so much time in libraries and bookstores.

Some places were boarded up, some looked abandoned.

Elodie brought me to a gazebo and we sat in its shade. The gazebo overlooked the downtown plaza, which was the most charming part of downtown so far, with its cobbled sidewalk, rippling water fountain, and a teeter-totter for passing children. There were no children, and the only passerby were solitary and on their way to places without a mind for much else around them. People pacing in the ruts of their lives, back and forth, losing sight of any other way of living or of looking at things.

This place was small, out of the way, easy to forget—which was exactly why Hugo lived here in his fortress, with his wife. It was exactly the place he needed, and surely all he wanted.

"Were you out here a lot when you were little?" I asked.

Elodie was leaning back against the gazebo's railing. All throughout our walk her eyes were somewhere else, as though she were seeing ghosts on the sidewalks with us.

"Not really," she said. "But the few times I was, I remember clearly. Somehow everything's the same... but so different at the same time."

"Did your dad bring you?"

She shook her head. "He attracts a lot of attention when he comes here. Too much attention, he thinks, even though sometimes he can't help himself. So he tries to stay away. No. Every time I hung out downtown, I had to sneak out."

"Not surprising."

"Not surprising that I did, or not surprising that I had to?"

"Both."

"And no, by the way, it wasn't to meet any boys."

"I wasn't gonna ask."

"I did have a friend though, once. David. He was an outsider like me. Come to think of it, he's the sort of kid who could've grown up to be a serial killer."

If I'd been drinking something, I probably would've spat it out. "That's... well, actually, that's not too surprising either."

She raised her eyebrows.

"Why would I be surprised that one of your childhood friends was a potential serial killer?"

Snickering, she leaned over and bumped into me. I put an arm around her shoulder and kissed her forehead.

She'd been asleep last night, when I returned to bed. Had stirred a little when I put my arms around her, just enough to find my hand with hers and bring it close to her face so she could kiss my knuckles with a faint moan. She hadn't asked about last night and I, not knowing how to bring it up, hadn't said anything yet.

Holding her in the gazebo, surrounded by a nostalgic world I could only see through her eyes since it was not my world, I wondered if I even needed to tell her about what had happened.

Maybe this was something to keep between Alodia and me. Maybe things would be different and that was all that mattered.

There are times when silence on a matter becomes as bad as lying. Just as there are times—these times rarer, I believe—when silence is a kindness.

Maybe, later today, once we returned to the house, instead of telling Elodie what had happened between her mother and me, I could show her. I could show her by suggesting we go spend time with her mother, and her mother would look at me differently. I felt certain of this.

Maybe Alodia would look at me with trust now. Maybe she understood, truly, what I had said.

And I wanted Elodie to see this. She deserved to see that it was possible for me to blend with her world. To be accepted by her parents, especially by her mother.

If I hadn't been caught up in these small plans in my head, if my attention hadn't been on the sensation of Elodie on my arm and against me, I might have noticed earlier the three men approaching the gazebo. One came from the direction of the street, one from the other side of the plaza, the other from the parking lot behind us. They had created a perimeter and approached us slowly, with their shoulders hunched, arms tensely at their sides. I noticed them when it was too late for Elodie and me to have a chance at running.

My heart kicked into gear. "The fuck."

We both stood from the bench and moved to the center of the gazebo. I tried to hold on to Elodie as if to shield her, but she slipped from my arms and instead put her back against mine. Like soldiers surrounded by enemies, we stood back-to-back, our hands clasped.

"Bennet," she said—and although she still called me by my name sometimes, it sounded strange in my ears because of the fear in her voice. "Look. It's the security guard. The security guard from the farm."

I recognized him, too. He wore an open button-up shirt, jeans with holes in the knees, and a tan sunhat with a half-mangled brim. The sunburn on his face—making the edge of his nose a shiny red knob—appeared to be a permanent feature, like the pale blue of his eyes. He'd been the one who greeted us at the gate of the Bailey farm. The asshole. The one who drove us there and back.

I scanned our surroundings. The town was nearly empty. "See any more of them?"

Elodie, clenching my hands, made a sound through gritted teeth. Maybe it wasn't fear I'd heard in her voice. She sounded angry, not afraid. "Just three so far."

"We have to get out of here."

"For their sake," said Elodie, raising her voice to make sure she was heard. "So that I don't claw this guy's fucking eyes out."

I couldn't help it—I laughed. But I had the tendency to laugh in some nerve-wracking situations.

My car was parked across the street, half a block down. If we'd been back in Wester, I'd have locked the doors, but this place was so small, so empty, I'd left it unlocked. The keys were in my right pocket, jammed in with my phone. No need to unlock the car doors before jumping in. Good.

But we couldn't just turn and run. There were three of them, and they'd be on us before we were even off the cobbled plaza. Right now, I realized we had a small advantage. We were on higher ground, and the gazebo had railings. That meant two of the men would have to cross the railing to get to us—there was only one small entrance, and three steps up into the gazebo.

Conceivably, we'd have a chance if one of the men came at us first. Or they'd crowd each other, giving us a second's headstart.

I said to Elodie, "If you're secretly a black-belt master or some shit and just haven't told me, now's the time to tell me."

"Same for you, babe."

"What about your mace?"

"In my purse." Which was in her car.

"I have a pen," I said. "That's it."

"I have these." She pulled small brass knuckles from her back pocket. They were thin, nothing special, but they gleamed as she slid her fingers through the loops. I'd never seen them before.

"Holy shit. You've always had those?"

"My dad taught me a few things." She raised her fists like a boxer.

I grinned at her over my shoulder, thinking of all the times when I'd tried to get on top of her in bed and she resisted me, managed to restrain me and keep me beneath her. I said, "Well... that explains a lot."

She nudged me with her elbow, and I could tell she at least smirked.

The men were closer now, having given up any semblance of discretion.

The security guard in the sunhat was nearest to the gazebo's entrance. He stopped walking a few steps from the stairs, raised a hand up to signal the other men to stop as well. He stood with his hands on his hips.

"Didn't count on meeting you two again so soon," he said. "But your Uncle Howie misses you. Says you got some unfinished business back on the farm."

"How kind of him to check in," answered Elodie, turning to face him. "You can tell him to fuck off. I'm doing fine."

"Well now, that just ain't how it works, missy."

"Works just fine for me, asshole."

The guard scowled. "You don't talk to me that way, missy. I'm a bonafide Bailey, I am. Head of security, a trusted member of the community. You're just one of them time bombs, you are. A ticking-clock wench." He chuckled, and it was a stupid sound, the sound of a halfwit gasping for air. "Can't wait to see how you look when it starts to happen to you, the way it happens to all of you. All blank in the face, staring off, not a care if you got a scrap of clothing on or if you just pissed yourself."

Elodie made another growling sound between clenched teeth. Her fingers whitened through the loops of her brass knuckles. "Can't wait to see what you look like with your teeth smashed down your fucking throat."

"You don't *talk* to me like that, girl. Howard said you needed reminding of your place."

"Please," I interjected. "Shut the fuck up, holy shit."

"Hey, Tony," said one of the men, speaking to the guard. So his name was Tony. "Howard said just the girl."

"That's right," said Tony as he adjusted the sunhat with one hand. "The name's Bennet, ain't it?"

"Don't speak to me."

"Oh we don't gotta speak—I'm just gonna say it. No one has to get hurt today. Hell, I'm sure it'd be fine if you wanted to come with her, you know. Emotional support while she goes through them tests and all."

Elodie and I exchanged a brief glance, and both of our facial expressions said the same thing: *Are you fucking kidding me?*

The man named Tony continued to speak, imploring us to come willingly so things didn't have to get messy. His words, not mine.

I said to Elodie in a low voice, "I have an idea."

"Tell me."

"Punch him in the face."

"Brilliant. Wish I'd thought of that, Bennet."

"I'm serious. If I run forward right now and punch him in the face, at least one of the other guys will try and help. And then you can run for the car."

She shot a glare at me. "I'm not gonna run. What makes you think—"

"There's a crowbar in the trunk."

"Ohh, gotcha."

"Good." While handing Elodie the keys to my car, I turned my attention back on Tony, who was still spouting something about how this is the way things are, and about how we only have two choices, which really comes down to the two choices we have in life: resist what's coming, or accept what's happening. And he seemed quite proud of this speech. I wondered if he'd rehearsed it.

Without waiting for a pause in his musing, I walked forward as if it were the most natural thing. When I reached the steps... that's when I charged.

The last fight I'd been in was early high school. Over a girl, of course, but in my defense I wasn't the one who started it. I've been in a few fights, all of them in school—the first being third grade—and in this way I learned that I didn't care much for fighting.

Which isn't to say I wasn't good at it.

Sophomore year, an upperclassman approached me during lunch, accusing me of convincing his girlfriend to leave him. I remember the way his whole face popped with red, eyes wide and stupid as he jammed a finger at my center, already raising his other hand into a fist.

I remember I heard my father's voice.

And although my father and I never understood each other and never got along, not since my earlier youth, there are some things I will always remember about him, and in that moment his voice came to me saying these words: *If you have to hit them, hit first and hit hard.*

Simple and to the point. Maybe that's why I remembered it. You can be the one that ends the fight.

Which is what happened with the upperclassman. As soon as he was in reach, I swung for his face as hard as I could, connected with his cheekbone, and he dropped.

Tony stood with his sunburnt face beneath the mangled rim of the straw sunhat, raising his eyebrows at me with bewilderment at my audacity as I came upon him.

There are plenty of people I've wanted to punch in the face throughout my life. But, not being a violent person, the idea of swinging a fist with the intent to hurt someone is strange to me. But this didn't hold me back.

I put my whole body into it, the momentum of my legs and then the thrust of my arm.

Tony realized what was about to happen at the last second, and threw his arms up to try and shield his face, turning his body at the same time—but he was too late. My fist connected and he went stumbling back, a slew of curses emerging from his mouth.

I turned in time to meet one of the other men. He ducked, collided with my torso, and my back hit the cobbled plaza ground.

The second time I'd been tackled in the past two days. A new record, as far as I could tell.

The man began swinging at me, striking my feeble defense of

raised wrists. Scrambling, I reached up, grabbed his face, and *shoved*. I was on my feet in moments, moving away from the two of them, my stance wide and fists raised.

Tony had let his sunhat drop to the ground. I noticed something in his hand that hadn't been there before, and, realizing what it was, my original plan dissolved. Maybe I could've held off the two of them—maybe long enough for Elodie to come back with the crowbar. But Tony had a taser in his hand, and that changed everything.

Elodie, I saw, had made it across the street and into my car, but the third man had followed close behind. They were struggling in the front seat, him clawing at her, her trying to maneuver away and kick at him. From across the street, I could see them flailing in the car's front seat, but couldn't make out if Elodie was winning. Couldn't tell if she stood a chance.

Tony pressed a button on the taser and it buzzed and snapped like something wild and hungry. A purple spark flashed between the taser's teeth.

"Could've made this a hell of a lot easier," he said, spittle flying from his lips. He had that stupid look on his face, eyes glassy and yellow against the sunburn-red of his face.

"Lucky for you we didn't grab the cattle prods," said the other man.

Across the street, Elodie had just landed a full-booted kick to her attacker's face. The man fell through the car's open door and toppled onto the asphalt, clutching his smashed tomato of a nose.

Any second now, Elodie would find the crowbar.

Tony moved toward me, brandishing the taser, swiping it in my direction. I stepped back, stepped back, trying not to imagine how that snapping electricity would feel against my skin.

"Tell you something," said Tony, beaming. A few more feet back and I'd be up against a railing. On the other side of the railing was a ten-foot drop to a parking lot. "I'm glad you decided to fight. Howard said he hoped to see you again. Said there was some things he wanted to tell you."

He lunged at me, clicking the taser into life. And rather than jump backward again, I slipped to the side, turning my shoulders so that Tony's arm went past me by inches. Then I had my hand on his wrist, gripping as tightly as I could. He swung at me with his other hand, and I lifted mine to absorb the impact with the side of my elbow.

And then he jerked his head forward into my nose. I recoiled, throwing my head back, nearly falling over my own heels.

Hot and unbearably sharp pain exploded in my side, causing the entire left side of my body to stiffen and shoot down with sudden numbness. I toppled onto the ground, trying to hold my side with my other arm.

When I looked ahead, however, I saw my car jumping the curb into the plaza.

Elodie hadn't taken the crowbar. She took the whole car.

The man with Tony was first in line. He managed to turn halfway around before his legs met the grey hood of the car and he went spinning to the side like a straw scarecrow taken in a gust of wind.

The car sped toward us—toward Tony and me.

The tires squealed across the cobbled plaza, and the car came to a rocking stop only two or three feet from me—enough to have sent Tony backward. He stumbled, then tripped over me, and rolled somewhere off behind me.

I heard Elodie call "Get in!"

Despite the numbness in my left side—and the sharp echo of the pain—I pulled myself up, flung the car door open and climbed in, and in the next instant we were speeding away.

"What the fuck." I looked over my shoulder once we were out of downtown, on the road back to the house. No one was following us, but not that it mattered: they knew where Hugo lived. "I can't believe—"

"You okay?" asked Elodie.

"I'm fine. That thing fucking hurt."

"I'm sorry. It was a good plan, though."

"Yours was better."

She looked over at me and smiled briefly. "Thought it might save a little time to just hit them with your car instead."

"It worked." I tried to stop rubbing the spot where I'd been hit with the taser. "Elodie, we need to leave town."

"No."

"What?"

"If we leave," she said, "they'll just follow us."

"I didn't say we should go home. We just have to get out of here and go... *somewhere*. Anywhere, honestly."

Elodie let the silence sit, her focus on the road ahead. Without her saying anything, I was beginning to think I was wrong. Where would we go? What would it accomplish right now to run and hide?

But what else could we do?

I thought of Hugo, waiting for us. Hugo in his massive home, on those beautiful, colorful grounds. Hugo and his beloved wife, the half-monster half-woman, Alodia.

And suddenly I didn't feel as afraid of being followed. Hugo's home didn't just *look* like a fortress, it *felt* like one. And a lot of that had to do with Hugo himself—the imposing air of him, the sensation of standing in the presence of a threat cloaked in a friendly smile and articulate phrases.

"Elodie, we're leading them straight to your dad's house."

"They already know where he lives."

"Still. What'll he think?"

She didn't look my way, kept her eyes on the road. Her next words sent chills down my body.

"He'd want us to come back," she said, her voice dropping in volume. A shadow fell across her eyes. "And he would hope they follow us. He's wanted to see Howard Bailey again for a long time."

22

Alone in the Dark

It was my second dinner with the Villeneuve family, and as Elodie and I sat at the table waiting for Hugo to bring in Alodia, I couldn't sit still. For awhile I tried sitting on my perspiring hands as if to stifle the energy coursing across my skin, but this only made me feel awkward. I put a hand on Elodie's leg and smiled at her, searching for reassurance in her eyes. She gave it, but it changed nothing about how I felt.

I hadn't seen Alodia since last night. I had no idea how she would react to me now.

Hugo had put together homemade gumbo with an array of appetizers and sides at the table's center, spread across the velvety crimson cover. Tall candles set in curling silver candelabras lined the table, and the effect was that the entire room gently flickered.

I regarded Alodia's side of the table. She would sit across

from us again, and hopefully wouldn't spend most of the evening staring at me with a murderous gleam in her eyes. Her cutting-board plate sat ready for the placement of raw, bloody meat—a stark contrast to our elegant white bowls and plates.

"You know... I didn't thank you for saving me," I said without looking over at Elodie. "The bastard had me on the ground, and half my body was numb. I don't think there's anything I could've done to get away." I slid my hand from her thigh to her knee. "You saved me."

When I looked over at her, I knew immediately that something was wrong. A cold feeling cemented inside me, starting in my chest but spreading its debilitating grip to my limbs. It was a lonely feeling, like standing alone in a room gone suddenly dark as you wonder—where did everyone go? Why would they leave me here?

Wasn't I worth bringing out of the dark?

I'd felt this three times in my life.

The first was in the moments after I realized my mother had died. When I had come into the room and started talking to her like I always did, ready to make mostly one-sided conversation to compensate for how weak she'd become, ready to sit and read to her, only to realize that her eyes weren't following me across the room and that she was too still.

The second time I felt it was at Night Owl, when I'd seen Kendra dancing with that other guy. The feeling followed me for days, amplified, of course, when I saw him in her bed.

The third time was on the night that Elodie and I returned home from the Bailey farm. The night when I'd turned to her, our faces close together on the pillow, and she was staring blankly, no expression on her face, no comprehension in her ashen eyes which were like pebbles in the dark. I'd been overcome with such a rushing feeling, a feeling that filled me coldly all the way to the surface, blotting out all other thought and all other awareness of place or time.

The feeling of standing in the dark, knowing you're alone, knowing you've been left there.

Beside me at the table, Elodie's head was turned in my direction and her eyes were trained on me. It wasn't a blank stare, necessarily—not in the same way as before. Rather, there was emotion on her face but it was subdued, as if she were observing her own emotions and trying to make up her mind about whether to feel them.

Her lips parted, mouth slightly agape, like she was about to say something but couldn't find the words.

And her eyes...

It was as though she didn't recognize me. As though she'd just now turned in my direction to say something, but found that a stranger sat beside her.

I saw all of this in the way she looked at me. I pulled my hand away. Stared back, waiting for the punchline—waiting for whatever had come over her to pass so she would recognize me again and this terrible moment would give way to a flood of relief.

My voice came out small and choked. "Babe." I reached out to her, put my hand on her arm, then her shoulder. "*Elodie.*"

Her lips trembled, dropping open to form a gaping *o*. And her eyes, stricken wide, were fixated on me.

I realized something about the way she was looking at me. And this realization filled me with freezing cold—all through my body—followed by desperate panic.

I held her by both shoulders now, pulled myself close.

"*Elodie. Wake up.*"

I could see her underneath the haunted mask of her face. She had fallen under a lake of ice, and I could see her down there, could hear the muffled sounds of her fists pounding against the underside of the ice... and there was nothing I could do to help her. But I could *see* her—she was trying to break through.

Tears formed in my eyes, dripped down my cheeks. I shook her once. Twice. Lightly, and then harder than I wanted to.

"Elodie. You're okay. Take a deep breath. Please. Just breathe and it'll pass. Come back. Come on. Come back to me. Come back to me."

She broke through.

It could've been half an hour, it could've been no longer than two or three minutes.

The light in her eyes swam back to life, and she gasped with all of her breath—as if she really had been underwater and was now breaking the surface. One of her hands flew to her chest, the other gripped my shoulder so tightly it hurt.

"Bennet," she said, the color returning to her cheeks. Quicker than I would've thought possible, she was sobbing and clutching at me, holding me tightly and burrowing her face into my shoulder. "Bennet," she managed to say. The desperation in her voice chilled me. It wasn't the Elodie who'd been with me in the gazebo today—the strong, guarded young woman who had taunted our attackers as she slipped brass knuckles over her fingers. This was the frightened girl that Elodie had locked underneath the surface for most of her life. This was someone thrown into a cage too small for them and with the key in sight but far beyond reach.

With her whole body pressed against me and arms wrapped around, I could feel, through her chest, the manic pounding of her heart. I held her as she sobbed, and I tucked my face into the folds of her hair and closed my eyes.

I'm not sure I've ever felt more scared in all my life.

You will lose her one day, Bennet. That's what Hugo had said to me.

And I still didn't want to believe he'd been telling the truth.

The doors leading to the living room slammed open, swinging until they struck the walls and rattled on their silver hinges. And then came a guttural sound, a throaty, inhuman growl and the sound of swift footfalls.

"Alodia!" Hugo called, and there was more fear in his voice than I'd ever heard. "Alodia, no!"

I knew I should've separated from Elodie and ran. I knew it would've been the smart thing to do anything at all. Instead I merely held Elodie tighter and kept my eyes closed, waiting for Alodia's hands to tear me away from her sobbing daughter. And I knew how strong she was, knew resistance would be impossible. The way she had lifted me with one arm and tossed me across the grass. The way she'd pinned me down, leaving me immobile and at her mercy.

How would this look to her? How would it coax her instincts? Her daughter, terrified and hysterical; and the young man whom Alodia didn't trust, holding Elodie close. Would she think I was killing Elodie? Attacking her? Upsetting her? Would she be able to tell the difference between a threatening hold and a comforting embrace?

I held onto Elodie, clamped my eyes shut, and waited.

The clawing hands, the violent attack and separation from Elodie—it never came. When I opened my eyes and looked, Alodia was crouched on the dining table, leaning so she was within arm's reach of us. Her ashen eyes were curious and sorrowful, completely ignoring me as she was fixated on her crying daughter. With each sob and sniffle from Elodie, Alodia flinched as if someone had flicked cold water at her. Her eyes—with their outer and inner filmy lids—blinked with each flinch, and I noticed how she instinctively bared her teeth for the briefest of seconds.

Maybe, I thought—realizing it for the first time—her emotions were so volatile and difficult to read because they were primarily instinct. Maybe her emotions were visceral for her in this way, and, judging by her reaction, it brought her genuine pain to see Elodie in pain.

Maybe that was how she felt emotion. It explained so much.

At one point, as she calmed down, Elodie let go of me so she could stand up and embrace her mother. Alodia at first didn't react, simply accepted Elodie's embrace, but after a few moments she wrapped her arms around her daughter. She did it more as a mimicry of Elodie's gesture, while her eyes stared blankly ahead over Elodie's shoulder.

Only once, as we settled down to our seats, did Alodia's eyes fall on me. And I didn't see that murderous gleam, nor did I feel any sense of animosity. She simply looked at me across the table before turning her attention to her food—a slab of raw, bloody meat—and ravenously tearing into it.

Elodie explained to her father what had happened. He listened silently, a shadow on his face, as Elodie told us how it had felt. As if she'd been looking at herself from the outside, like in a strange and hazy dream. Like she was sinking into some mental darkness, screaming on the inside. By the time we all finished dinner—Elodie barely touched hers, but did her best—Hugo had barely said a word. And his silence was somehow so much louder than anything he could've said.

23

Artificial Moonlight

I stayed with Elodie as she fell asleep. Stared at her and she stared back, sorrow and pain clear in the shimmering of her eyes—the weight of knowing—and I couldn't think of anything to say. So I ran my fingers through her hair gently, keeping the rhythm of the ocean tide in my mind, until Elodie's eyes finally closed and her breathing became tranquil and deep.

I went downstairs, wanting to have some alone time with Alodia.

But I found Hugo down there, too.

He sat on a bench overlooking the gardens, and he wore a deep magenta robe under which I assumed he wore nothing else. The garden was lit up tonight by the soft lamps that lined the walking paths, illuminating the grounds in moonlight-white.

Hugo sat contently, hands folded in his lap, head tilted slightly as though he were possessed by a pleasant memory that took him away from here.

Or maybe the memory in his head—assuming that's what he was doing: remembering—maybe it didn't take him away to some other place. Maybe he was remembering this very spot years ago, when he was young and had first met Alodia as she danced nude in the moonlight. Surely this memory returned to him often, like a recurring dream.

And as I watched him—as he sat unaware of me—I realized I had my own version of this dream, but for me, of course, Elodie was at the center.

Elodie's dark form moving through flashing beams of lights and shadow-pools of dancing bodies.

Elodie moving toward me, phantomwise, gently smirking, eyes gleaming as if reflecting the light of a distant fire

Elodie beckoning me toward the edge of a cliff, toward the leap into dark water.

This memory seemed a blend of many memories, but still it jumped out from my mind with bright clarity.

Elodie. That fire inside her. That challenge—equally an invitation, or a dare—in her eyes.

These very things were fading from her. This fact had crossed from suspicion to undeniable reality. Last night being one of the final steps into knowing, into understanding.

When Hugo noticed me, he asked me over. I sat beside him on the stone bench and for awhile we looked out at the colorful grounds. The garden. The walkways. The lamps that cast dim white light, as if they were miniature moons floating above the beds of lavender broadleaf lupines, white avalanche lilies, and pink fairy slippers.

I almost leapt from the bench when Alodia emerged from behind one of the flowerbeds. She wore a flowing white shawl that was transparent, revealing through its folds that she wore nothing else underneath. But this didn't matter to me, didn't even strike me as unusual. She was dancing. And as soon as my panic abated, I was entranced.

The way she floated on her toes, twirling here and there, skipping sometimes, swaying her hips and extending her arms. The way her dark hair bounced and fell all around her shoulders and her face with each turn and spin.

The absurdity of it struck me—a nearly naked woman, conscious only in the unknowable animalistic sense, dancing in a garden late at night without music. I felt the urge to laugh, but when I looked over at Hugo and saw the pure awe and adoration in his eyes, the urge departed. I thought of how I would feel if it were Elodie out there, dancing.

But the thought filled my stomach with a queasy feeling, a weight not previously there, and made it harder to breathe.

Mid spin, Alodia's leg gave out beneath her and she tumbled onto the ground, catching herself with her hands but landing hard on her side.

Hugo reacted physically by jolting, almost shooting up onto his feet. But this must've happened before, because the look on his face went from surprise to understanding and then to sorrow.

Alodia, in the garden, picked herself back up and stood for a long time, staring vaguely upward, not moving at all. I held my breath in suspense, felt as though time stood still. And then she resumed her dancing as if she hadn't just fallen and stood in one place for several quiet minutes.

"It's getting worse week by week," said Hugo, his voice heavy. "Worse than it's ever been."

I felt sorry for him, much more deeply than I would've thought. Beneath his enigmatic veneer, I saw, in that moment, despair.

"I need to ask you something," I said, and caught even myself off guard. The question I needed to ask him had been sitting in my head long enough that it had rooted itself and crept up toward my skin, aching to be spoken.

And there was just something about Hugo. For all the ways he made me uneasy, he was easy to talk to.

Without taking his eyes from his dancing wife, Hugo said, "Ask."

"What was it like to lose her?"

Hugo sighed, his shoulders dropped. He kept his head up and his eyes on his wife.

I said, "I read some things from your journal. I'm sorry I took it. I don't know if I ever said that—"

"You did not." He crossed his arms. "Is this something you do often? Take things without asking?"

I felt heat in my face. "No. No I... I don't know what I was thinking."

"You were curious."

"Yes... I guess I was. And I was terrified."

The edge of his mouth threatened to twitch upward, but his face otherwise remained the same; his eyes followed Alodia's dance. "I do not blame you for your curiosity. I receive the impression, time and again, that you cannot help yourself. In order to dispel of your fears, you plunge into those fears, using your curiosity as a driving force. I simply wish you had asked first."

"I'm sorry."

"You apologized already." He surprised me, then, by reaching over and patting my shoulder. It was an awkward gesture—perhaps the only awkward thing I'd ever seen him do—which only made it that much more disarming, and that much more touching. "And I accept your apology. There are no locked doors in this house. And if you had asked, I assure you: I would've let you take it."

I resisted saying sorry again, recognizing this as Hugo's way of putting an end to the discussion.

He waved his hand. "You were saying, about what you read in my journal..."

"Right. Um... I read what you wrote about the time Alodia tried to kill Elodie. When Elodie was a baby. And the things you wrote about that time, in general."

"I take your meaning." He gave me a brief look for reassurance. "You know what I wrote in the journal, and you're aware of the events of that time—some of them, at least. But what you want to know is, what was it like. How did it feel to watch her slipping away."

"I don't mean to... to make you talk about difficult memories—"

"But you do, Bennet, and this is fine. You want to know if you can learn something, or if, perhaps, I can warn you about what's coming."

My throat felt dry and I'd lost all awareness of the rest of my body. All my attention was aimed at Hugo, while my thoughts spun incessantly around Elodie. Elodie and the way she'd looked at me tonight, barely any emotion on her face except for the bewilderment of not recognizing me.

"I guess that's what I'm asking," I said. "You loved her. You still love her. And... and even though I struggle to understand, I'm trying to."

"To understand why I love her?"

"No. To understand how it is that you seem... that you seem okay. Almost like you and her have a, um... a normal relationship, emotionally... or something resembling normal, maybe..." I took a breath, felt the tingle of sudden panic in my chest. I'd probably just insulted him. A *normal* emotional relationship? Would he think I was judging him? *Was* I judging him? "I'm sorry," I stuttered. "That's not what I mean."

"I do take your meaning." He looked off toward the garden again. Alodia was out of sight, probably on the other side of a row of bushes, still dancing. "Surely this very thing has been a subject of much uncertainty in your relationship with my daughter. This gap of understanding between your world and hers."

"I wouldn't have put it so eloquently, but yeah. We've had obstacles."

He laughed. "A polite way of phrasing it. This being my life, Bennet, I cannot see it from an outsider's point of view. I cannot imagine what, in your life, has informed the way you look at the world, and therefore cannot imagine what you must think of my life."

"I'm trying to understand," I said, certain to hold eye-contact. "And it's important to me to understand, because I love Elodie. And because I just... I have to know."

Hugo surprised me by grinning. "There. Your curiosity. That is a depth of honesty I appreciate. So let me tell you what it was like, Bennet."

And Hugo told me what he knew of heartbreak. Which is to say, far more than I had ever known.

One thing that is true of love, of any love—but especially the deep romantic love, deep enough that it transcends any conventional ideas of *romantic*—is that it creates a shared private space between two people. It is the space of connection, of friendship, mutual to those who share such love but exclusive to all else. Others may look and may be happy for you, for they understand what it's like to share a space like that with somebody, even if theirs is starkly different from yours. Others may even judge, for they don't understand—aren't capable, perhaps, of loving somebody else that much, with such honesty and privacy.

It is this shared private space that comes to mind when I

remember Hugo and Alodia. No one understood them. *I* didn't understand them. But the love Hugo felt for her was palpable, it filled up his life, and he did everything he could to make it fill hers. Even as I tried to understand, there were aspects of it I couldn't, or didn't necessarily want to.

But the closest I came to understanding fully was when Hugo told me what it was like for him to watch Alodia, his beloved, descend into her condition, knowing full well she might never re-emerge.

"She wasn't like the rest of her family," he said, folding one leg over the other and entwining his hands atop it. His eyes were aimed at the garden but not really looking at it. "And I mean that not merely in the sense of her soul. Most of the Bailey family comprises pedophiles and misogynists and psychopaths—for my money, the lot of the Bailey men are sick degenerates who belong in cages. The way they treat the women is unconscionable. You saw this for yourself, I know. But even some of the healthy women are complicit in this family's actions. It is the reality they are born into, and they believe the world is this way. It is one of the great tragedies of this family, and of so many others. The highly contagious nature of their particular inherited madness. That is a matter for another time, I suppose.

"What I mean to say is, Alodia is unlike her family both because she is kind and because of how her condition manifested. For most, the process begins gradually, coming in small waves upon the onset of the first symptoms, and then it worsens exponentially. The regressive waves become longer and longer until one day they do not awaken from the dream that this condition puts them under. If you take my meaning.

"For Alodia, it began in childhood far, far earlier than it begins in most others. But it occurred only at night. During the daytime she was a perfectly healthy young girl. But something would change at night, you see. Not so much that she regressed behind her mind, as is the best way I know how to describe the Bailey Condition, rather she would descend into a dreamlike state. This meant a great deal of sleepwalking, waking up in strange places with only faint memories of the interactions she had in the night.

"This is how I met her. She was in such a state when I found her dancing in the gardens one night, when we were young. I perceived nothing wrong with her, and did not find it strange that, in the morning, she only faintly remembered what had happened. Which is, I suppose, strange in its own right." Hugo laughed. "Especially when you consider how passionately we made love that night. But, though her memories were faint, she did remember me, and we spent the rest of that next day getting to know each other more intimately. As though a primal part of her had been drawn here, to this place, and to me, and the rest of her simply needed to catch up.

"And when I think about it, about what she was like at night —back when her condition manifested solely in this way—I realize an important thing. Whatever the dreamlike state meant, it seemed to remove her fears, it seemed to be an emergence of the desires she normally chose to conceal or hide beneath the surface. As if her inhibitions and ideas of herself melted away with the setting of the sun, and all pretense faded under the stars. You understand, Bennet, for we've discussed this very thing. We all know this feeling. We have all experienced what it feels like when the walls of our identity—our sense of control, our fears, our masks—crumble away in the face of something deeper, more meaningful, more *immediate*."

I stared at him, bewildered. "I'm not entirely sure if—"

"Nonsense, Bennet. I speak of what lies primally within us. When passion or desire take control, and you are moved by something deep within you rather than moved by conscious choice. Perhaps while in the throes of true lovemaking, you understand."

And I did. Of course I knew what that felt like. So yes, I understood. And I told him so.

"That is what happened to Alodia at night," he said. "That is how she became. For the first couple years of our being together, it only happened on some nights. On these nights we sometimes slept very little." He grinned. "Or we danced in the gardens. Or went driving through the forest roads, sticking our faces out the window, headlights off."

I knew that feeling, too. And I thought of that cliff edge again, out at Farewell Lake where Elodie had said to meet. Our second date.

"And, if I'm being honest, there were a few years when we tried not to talk about the possibility of her condition. It was, as you can imagine, a profoundly sensitive subject for her, and I respected this. Only when we'd been together for three years did she open up to me about her family. There were things I'd gathered, clues she'd given me in conversation, but not until then did she tell me everything. It took a matter of days for her to tell me everything, and let me tell you, they were an emotional few days."

"Did she take so long because she was afraid?"

"Afraid, yes. But not of her family, not like you think. I believe she was afraid I would not accept her anymore. Afraid that, if I learned where she came from, and her family history, I might look at her differently. Even now, I wish I'd found a way to let her know, earlier on, that this was a ridiculous fear. As if anything could have made me look at her differently. As if my love were conditional upon some conceived notion of a... status quo.

"What do you know of my life, Bennet?"

His question caught me unprepared. I simply looked at him, not knowing what to say.

"I speak of my life before Alodia," he said. "What do you know about me as a man? My history? Where I come from?"

"Almost nothing. Elodie's referenced some things... like some of your family being from South Africa, some from France, and she said something about the family business, but I never pried."

Hugo nodded somberly. "I was born in this country, brought by my mother—the only member of my family in the country. She died when I was very young. So I was alone, and learned to make a life on my own. And life has never been especially difficult for me—do not get me wrong, Bennet. My inheritance is inexhaustible and always has been. Despite this, I spent a decade on the road, moving from place to place, searching for something in the world when I should've been looking inward."

It occurred to me, watching him speak, that I'd never really heard Hugo talk about himself.

"There are many stories I could tell you from this time, as you can surely imagine, but what I mean to say is I have been alone in this world for almost as long as I can remember. Never did I feel seen, or understood, or as if I'd met anyone the equal of me—someone capable of meeting me as I am, on my level, as some would say.

"That is until I met Alodia. Someone whose fire cast such heat as to frighten me. Someone who awakened something in me no one ever had. Someone who did not pull her hand away when the flame got too hot—and would hold my eyes all the while, daring me to pull *my* hand away first. You take my meaning?"

I was trembling—though I couldn't explain why. "Yes," I said, thinking of Elodie, of the first night we'd met. "I think I do."

"I felt as if I'd been moving through my life half-asleep, numb to what others cared so passionately about. Friends of mine gave their whole lives to matters I truly couldn't care for. But I awoke when I saw Alodia dancing in my garden. And it was not a brief thing, this newfound sense of being acutely alive and awake. It carried on through every conversation, and with every time I met her eyes or made her smile.

"She is everything to me, Bennet. She brings to my life all that is important to me about this life. She has given me so much simply by opening my eyes to what I might even, ever, want.

"So when her condition reared its ugly head into our life, there was never a question for me about what to do. And never did it occur to me to walk away from her. My love for her was challenged, was transformed to its shaken foundations, but all it did was grow stronger. And all of this..." He lifted his hands, palms up and fingers splayed outward, gesturing to all of his estate at once—the house, the gardens, the grounds. "All of this, and the life I have crafted for her, is my love for her. It is not without its rewards, for she is not truly gone. She is merely... she is merely here in a different way." Something like a smile crossed his lips and tilted the edges of his glistening eyes.

"So," he said. "As she worsened and her regressive episodes lasted longer and longer, becoming more and more frequent, my heart broke anew each morning. I tried to be an influence of strength and equanimity for her, but all I could offer was my vulnerability. She grew frail and weak for a time—sitting in bed, staring off into nothing, for hours. Eventually, it became *days* at a time. I fed her. Bathed her. Helped her move so she could spend time outside on nice days. Got a wheelchair for her. All of these things. But it broke my heart, over and over again. To see her that way. To watch her diminishing, and to see the light in her eyes fading.

"You see, Bennet, we had planned a life together. The home we wanted and hoped to expand. The places we wanted to visit one day. The children we wanted to have. For a few years we were able to live that life. To begin it, I mean. But then the episodes began, and I don't mean the strange, dreamlike nights. I mean clear signs of the condition..." He sighed. "Not unlike what happened to Elodie at dinner.

"On one of Alodia's clearer nights, we were sitting out here, and there was no moon. She pointed the constellations out to me, as she often did. I know them just as well as she, but only because of how often she'd tell me about them when we were under the night sky. I can recall it so clearly... the way she clung to my arm, rested her cheek against my shoulder, and released a deep sigh. And she said to me, *This is where I want to stay. Right here. In this moment, forever.* And sometimes I like to imagine that's where she is, somewhere in her mind. In that moment exactly."

And Hugo told me about Elodie.

He told me that he and Alodia had always wanted children, had even discussed the risk of having one. But Alodia insisted, with all of her heart, that she wanted at least one child. At least one, who might remember her, who might get to experience the world and get to live in it and discover how deeply beautiful it could be.

"Even if that meant risking having a daughter?" I asked—rather, I demanded. "How could she want that? A daughter who might one day develop the same condition?"

"Because the world desires to be witnessed, Bennet. What are we here for if not to give ourselves to it entirely, with part of the function of existing being the desire within us to push life forward? To give ourselves to each other, and create more life of ourselves? Our children are our legacy, they're the new world that is to come, because the world, like us, grows old. Desires to be reborn, if you will, through the eyes of youth. Do you want children, Bennet?"

I blinked at him as if stunned by this question. The audacity of it, as much as the reality of what it made me realize. Answering was easy.

"Yes," I said, and realized I meant it. Yes. But now there was so much more to that question. And to my answer.

"Yes," I said again. "I want children."

"Then you must understand," said Hugo, "that Alodia and I wanted a child in spite of *any* risk. Because, when Alodia spoke of the beauty of the world, she meant the *real* world. She'd been raised into a completely different one—the horrible world of the Bailey Family—but she'd escaped from it. And she knew what the world could be, and told me, once, how she wanted her child to have a chance to live in this real world.

"Needless to say, she hoped with all her heart that she would have only boys. That way, the curse of the Bailey blood would lessen with the next generation. If she had sons, they wouldn't need to fear that they would one day regress to a primal, animal nature. If she had daughters, there was still the hope—though a slim hope—that they wouldn't develop the condition.

"When it became clear that Alodia would not have much longer," said Hugo, "and we would not have the life we'd planned, we decided to try. Just for one child, if we might be so lucky. Maybe this was foolish, I know. Selfish beyond imagining, perhaps. Maybe it is not something even I can rationalize now."

I tried to remember what Elodie had once told me.
Do not judge my family.
I tried as hard as I could.

"But you must understand, Bennet, that if I could do it over again, I would change not a single thing. At the time, all I could think was that I needed to have a baby with Alodia. I needed her to have my child. My love for her was equally this craving. This is deeply selfish, I know, from the foundation of my being.

"But Elodie is my heart, you see. I knew this from the moment I held her in my arms for the first time. And even if there is nothing that can be done..." Hugo dropped his eyes down for the first time in the conversation. He'd been watching for Alodia, who still danced in and out of view every few minutes. "Even if Elodie, too, slips away... and I fear that is what's happening to her... Even if she slips away—then to have tasted of life at all, to have held the candle in the darkness for awhile... isn't that worth it, no matter how swift or brief it is? She is my heart. I cannot imagine this world without her."

"Neither can I," I said, thinking of a gray world.

"Then you must understand, Bennet—given the chance, I would not do a single thing differently."

With stricken eyes I watched him, my heart feeling so large and so vulnerable in my chest. Hugo looked at me. His eyes glistened in the garden's soft lamplight. "And that she has tasted deeply of the love you have for her," he said, "that she can hold your love like light in a chest, and that she can carry it with her into the darkness, when she goes... knowing this brings me peace amidst the impossible grief."

I couldn't seem to find my voice, nor any words to say.

"You say you are trying to understand me and my love for Alodia. It is—and will be—easier for you to understand than you think, Bennet. Believe me."

As I formulated a response in my head, wondering if there were more questions I wanted to ask—wondering if there was anything else I'd come out here seeking from him—something happened.

Alodia came twirling out from around a hedge, her transparent white shawl wrapping and then flowing all around her hips and down her thighs—like a dress of silky artificial moonlight—and then, halfway through her spin, she froze. Her head snapped in one direction—toward the white arch of the garden's gate, which led to the house's front driveway—and even from this distance I noticed the change in her facial expression as it tightened from plain-eyed serenity to ferocious glare. Her lips peeled back, revealing teeth in a bestial sneer, and her arms dropped, hands curling into claws. Her posture became hunched, her legs widened into a firm stance.

The silence between Hugo and me deepened, became urgent as we watched. We both turned toward the garden gate where Alodia's attention was fixated. My assumption was that Hugo had to have been as baffled as I. Looking off across the darkness of the yard, at the black garden gate beneath the elegantly curving arch, my whole body stiffened and it became difficult to move air through my lungs.

What—who—could be there that would give Alodia pause? Make her readjust herself to a stance suggesting she felt threatened?

When I looked to my right, seeking answers from Hugo, I saw he shared none of my fear.

Hugo stood from the bench. He had shed his robe but wasn't nude beneath, as I'd suspected: he wore a loose shirt and a vest that gleamed emerald. With his walking-stick held in both hands, he looked ready to fight.

24

The Attack

"Close your eyes," said Hugo, and then he clicked a small button on the top of his walking stick. The house—looming in the dark to our left—erupted in light.

The lamps in the garden burned brightly, too, filling the gardens and the grounds, scattering them with long shadows from the hedges and bushes and fountains and statues.

I hadn't quite closed my eyes in time, so the explosion of sudden light into my corneas made my head flash with pain. I stumbled back as if I'd been struck, waiting for my pupils to adjust.

My vision was just decipherable enough that I noticed movement ahead. By the sound of many rapid footsteps, I realized: we were being attacked.

Seconds later, still squinting in the light, I saw a group of them. Seven, maybe eight shadows racing toward us—and they were coming fast.

Most of them veered off toward the gardens. Toward Alodia, who remained where she was with a wide stance, ready to pounce forward or to scramble away. I watched just long enough to see her lower herself and then charge forward at her attackers. She moved with frightening grace, a banshee's shriek belting from her lungs.

And then the other men—four of them—came within tackling distance of Hugo and me.

One of the charging men actually ducked down as he got near, spreading his arms out to the side, ready to smash into me and drive me to the ground. I was still useless, my eyes throbbing, vision full of obscuring blots, and—momentarily lacking balance—my tottering made me an easy target.

Hugo stepped directly in front of me. He spun and ducked, making his back into a launching pad—managing to tuck himself beneath the charging man's body to collide with his waist—and with a sudden thrust upward, he tripped the man and sent him flipping forward and slamming into the grass.

The other two men hadn't charged forward with the same blind enthusiasm, rather they slowed down and raised their cattle prods.

Hugo ignored them. He looked down at the man on the ground; the man was holding his tailbone, which he'd landed on, while at the same time trying to rise to his feet. Hugo didn't even hesitate—he slammed his foot down onto the man's throat. With a meaty slap—almost a snapping *crack*—and the sound of dry, breathless choking, the man died. Just like that. A flip onto the grass, a stomp on the neck. A wild thrashing, bulging eyes, hands clawing at a collapsed throat.

Something like a gasp of air through a narrow pipe. Silence. Dead.

Just like that.

I paid no more attention to the pain behind my eyes, or to the imprint of the flash of light when I blinked.

I stared at the dead man on the ground. Stared at Hugo, who gave the man only a passing expression of hatred and then disgust before turning to face the other two attackers.

It had meant nothing to him. No hesitation. No hint of regret in his eyes. He simply turned to the others, walking stick held out now like a fencing sword. And I had no doubt he would kill these other two, if he managed to hold them off.

From the direction of the garden, a man screamed.

Well, he screamed for two, maybe three seconds. The scream was muffled by a hand over his face, and then cut off completely after the sound of a muffled snap.

Alodia had broken a man's neck. All of us—me, Hugo, the two men with cattle prods—turned our heads in that direction.

There were four men over there trying to restrain a wild woman who was more animal than woman. There'd been five men, but the fifth lay on the ground, half-splayed across the cobblestones of a garden pathway, his neck bent at an unusual angle halfway up to his head.

Alodia had been holding onto this man, had gotten her hands around his head and been able to twist. But the four others were grabbing at her, taking hold of her arms, reaching for her legs. With every swipe of an arm or kick of a leg, the group of men were pulled along, tripping over each other, falling over her.

She was stronger than all of them, and dangerous enough—I had no doubt—to take all of them on. Or maybe it's better to say, there was a time when she would've been strong enough. She was weaker now. There'd been the way she fell earlier, while dancing through the garden. The paleness of her skin which had become more noticeable since the first time I'd met her.

She was deteriorating, and when I looked over and saw her struggling with her attackers, I knew she wouldn't be able to resist them for long. But what could I do?

The two men with cattle prods were still watching this unfold, as was Hugo. I saw my opportunity—a brief window— and jumped for it. I charged past Hugo and threw myself at the man on the right. My hand gripped the neck of the cattle prod and I slammed myself into the man. But at the same time, I felt a familiar stab of hot pain against my body. The electric bite of the other man's cattle prod against my back, shooting pain up through me in paralyzing jolts. I tried to lift an arm so I could punch the man beneath me in the face, which would hopefully stun him long enough for me to wrestle the cattle prod from his grip. But the stab from the other cattle prod shot through my body again and I spasmed off my prey and onto the ground, my body instinctively trying to leap away from the pain.

The pain stopped when Hugo stepped in.

Hugo bashed the end of his walking stick into the side of the man's head. The sound was a hollow *clap*. The man stumbled, free hand flying up to his head as he cried out.

I turned to this scene for only a moment, since I knew I needed to get back to my feet. But I saw Hugo lay into the man with a sense of eloquence I would've thought impossible in a fight. Wielding the walking stick like a sword, he swiped, stabbed, slashed at the man, twirling the walking stick, pulling it back, arcing it forward again. It struck the man in the face, then the ribs, then across the face again, then in the stomach, the shoulder, the back of the head. All with such expert, flowing swiftness. I'd never seen anything like it.

But I remembered what Elodie had said earlier, when she and I were driving back from town.

I had asked her what Hugo would think, that we might be leading members of the Bailey Family back to his home.

He'd want us to come back, she had said, and now I knew what she meant. I knew why she went to him, felt safe here with him.

Hugo was dangerous. I'd known this from the very beginning and yet continually forgot it, such was Hugo's charisma. But here was a man capable of killing. A man capable of unspeakable acts of violence when his hand was forced.

The man beside me was reaching for his cattle prod, which lay a few feet away in the grass. The force of my body's impact with his—and the sudden drop to the ground—had knocked the wind out of him, apparent by how he clutched at his chest with one hand while reaching for the cattle prod with the other. I reached it before he did, and didn't hesitate driving it into his side and powering it on.

The whole rod buzzed, electricity snapped at the end, and the man spasmed and writhed, trying to scream between clenched teeth. I released the button for a moment, pressed it again—jabbed it, jabbed it, my own face becoming a rigid contortion of rage.

Fuck the Bailey Family. Fuck these sick bastards.

In seconds the man's eyes fluttered closed and I released the button, pulled the cattle prod away.

I looked in time to see Hugo finish off his attacker.

He had disarmed the man of his cattle prod with a mere spin of his walking stick—a flourish I'd seen in movies but never in real life. The man put his hands up, started to say something like "You got me," and then Hugo swiped his walking stick into the man's knee. The man collapsed. And then Hugo swung the walking stick into the side of the man's head, sending him all the way to the grass where he moved no more.

Hugo and I locked gazes for only an instant before turning our attention, at the same time, to Alodia.

She had tossed one of the four attackers several meters away with a mere swing of her arm. The other three were on top of her and were succeeding at restraining her. With every nearly fatal bite at their necks, or claw at their faces, or kick at their bodies, she was growing weaker, and they were able to hold her down for longer.

Hugo and I were only halfway across the yard to her when—
BANG!
We froze.

"Well," said Howard Bailey, stepping out into the yard, a shining revolver in his grip. The lights from the house cast strange shadows across his bulbous face. "Can't say this is exactly how I pictured our reunion, Hugo, but I'll admit it's how I hoped it'd be." Four men trailed Howard, each with unusual rifles in their grips, rifles with small bodies and long barrels. I could tell they were tranquilizer guns. But for us? For Alodia?

Hugo, in response, returned his walking-stick to the ground, gripped only in one hand. He stood up straight, examining Howard Bailey as he would an animal of some kind—an animal he pitied, I should add.

To our right, the men were pinning Alodia to the grass. She snarled and wailed, snapping at them like a threatened reptile biting at prey. From her throat emitted that deep vibrating growl.

Hugo took a few steps forward, seemingly unfazed by Howard's revolver or the men with tranquilizer guns. "Howard, I must admit I'm surprised you and your men haven't burst into flames on my property. Such cowardice these grounds have never seen before."

"Cowardice?" said Howard in that stilted, high voice of his. "You're the one who keeps my sister prisoner here, Hugo. Acting out your sick delusions with her. Using her all these years."

"I won't dignify *your* sick delusions with a response, Howard. What are you doing here?"

Howard tilted an eyebrow as if to ridicule. "Why don't you ask this young man?" He gestured to me, grinning idiotically. "Call it an overdue appointment."

"Elodie is quite beyond your reach," said Hugo before I could say anything. "In case your men at the front doors haven't yet noticed, the lights are not a mere parlor trick. Every door in the house is locked from the inside."

Howard's grin became a frustrated sneer. He had shed all of the awkwardness I'd seen in him on the farm. This was him in his element. This was the real Howard Bailey. "You're a sneaky man, Hugo Villeneuve, that's what you are. A disgusting, slippery man. Well, never mind, then. We'll just... we'll... we'll see about that, then, now won't we?" He gestured to the men behind him, then to us. The men approached us. "Don't get any funny ideas now. This don't gotta be a messy affair." Howard aimed the revolver at me. "And you... Bennet, ain't it? That's your name, right? See, I ain't some monster. I've got manners. A sense of right and wrong, unlike Hugo. You go on ahead and drop the stick, yeah?"

I hesitated only a moment. There was no way out of this one. I let the cattle prod drop to the grass. And although my mind raced through the hopes of a plan, I had nothing, knew I would do nothing even though a primal part of me wanted to charge—against all logic—and smash Howard Bailey's massive face into the cobblestones of the garden walkway until nothing remained of his features but a bloody pulp.

I'm not sure I've hated anyone the way I hated him.

The two men approached Hugo and I, handcuffs ready in their hands, tranquilizer rifles slung over their shoulders.

I didn't resist, knowing what would happen if I did. My hands were cuffed behind my back.

But the man who approached Hugo asked for the walking stick.

"You wouldn't rob an old man," said Hugo, his voice strong with defiance. It was difficult to imagine him ever having been someone who easily followed orders.

"It's not a question, you fucking zoophile scum," said the man, seizing the walking stick. Hugo didn't let go, merely held on, refusing it.

Howard Bailey didn't seem to notice. He was preoccupied with watching his men struggle to restrain Alodia. He wore that terrible self-satisfied grin. "Oh how I've missed my dear sister. *Oh* how I've missed her. Can't wait to get some alone time with your daughter, too, Hugo. Never seen a specimen quite like her—"

And that was all it took to set Hugo off.

Hugo let go of the walking stick—rather, he let go of its sleek shaft and gripped the rounded top. When he pulled his hand away, releasing it to his assailant, a thin blade slid from the rest of the walking stick.

A sword.

In one quick motion he slid the blade through the man's throat as though to sheathe it there. He did this without a moment's hesitation, without seeming to even notice that he was taking another man's life: no sense of conflict, nor of struggle. The man reached for his throat as blood spattered out over his clothes, and he choked on his gasp for air.

Hugo's next movements were quick. He did two things at the same time:

First, he swiped the thin sword out of the man's throat—the swift motion elicited another gurgling choke from the man—

and, at the same time, Hugo grabbed his walking stick from the hand of his victim.

Second, he spun and threw the walking stick like a spear toward Howard Bailey.

The walking stick flew through ten feet of air and struck Howard Bailey in the face, making a *thwap!* sound on his skull. He stumbled back, raising the revolver haphazardly in our direction.

BANG!

I acted instinctively by throwing myself, shoulder-first, at the man who'd handcuffed me. I hit him in the back and knocked him onto the grass, and I fell beside him, flailing my legs to try and regain my balance and stand without use of my hands.

Another cannon blast from the revolver: *BANG!*

Hugo was charging at Howard Bailey, a concentrated glare of untamable determination on his face. He intended to drive the sword into Howard's chest, to pierce the blade through his heart and watch the light drain from his eyes like the sunlight from the evening sky. It didn't matter that, even as he drew within a few quick strides, Howard was aiming the revolver toward him, was steadying himself from the prior blow to his head.

I had risen from the ground and was now on my knees, but I stopped. I saw what was about to happen and I screamed Hugo's name.

BANG!

The flash of brief fire from Howard Bailey's hand.

At the same time, someone's boot struck the side of my head. Everything went black.

25

Monsters

I awoke with my face pressed up against cold concrete, a ringing ache in my head and throbbing in my temple where I'd been kicked. I could feel a fresh pain in my cheek, too—they had probably thrown me, unconscious, into this cell.

There were voices of men, and after a few moments, I caught a few words:

"...plenty of stock for your wildest dreams, you fucking zoophile."

Followed by the slamming of a metal door.

When I lifted myself to sit, rubbing my head all the while, I saw I wasn't alone in the cell. A man was seated against the wall. *Sprawled* is a better word than *seated*. It appeared to take a great amount of effort for the man to remain upright, as both his hands were pressed up against a bloody wound in his stomach—a wound that stained his shirt in a wide red rose.

It was Hugo. His eyes were closed, but I could tell he was awake—he breathed carefully in through his nose, out through his mouth. Every few seconds he grimaced slightly. Beads of sweat wrung from his forehead. And even with the darkness of the cell and Hugo's dark complexion, I could see a pallor in his sweat-beaded skin.

I crawled over to him.

"It was a foolish thing I did," he said, opening his eyes. "But it does not matter now."

"Let me help." I moved his hands and applied pressure to his wound. "Maybe we can make something to wrap you up—"

"I already have. But it does not seem to be helping much."

"It's gonna be okay, Hugo."

He grinned—not for effect, but genuinely—and released a laugh that sounded like a dead leaf being ground into pieces. "I would not expect bullshit from you, Bennet. Come now."

"I'm trying to help. Maybe I'm saying that for myself, you know. Reassurance."

He laughed again. "Then you are kinder to yourself than I have ever been to *my*self. But to a fault."

I glanced around. This really was a cell, not merely a room turned into a place for holding. Three concrete walls, a small barred window that showed it was still dark outside, a cage wall, and the door beyond.

"We on the Bailey Farm?" I asked.

Hugo nodded. "They brought Alodia to the corral. To a private cage for tests. When Howard arrives, who knows the things he will do to her."

"Howard isn't here?"

"No. At least, I do not think so. He stayed with a few of his men with the hopes of breaking into my home and reaching Elodie."

"You think they've gotten to her by now?"

Hugo gave me a look, one eyebrow tilted up, something like a smirk in his eyes. "The house is designed for such things. The safety protocol I initiated ensures every door is shut and locked in the house. If Howard found a way inside and through the many doors that await him, Elodie would either be gone by then, or prepared enough to put up a fight."

"Jesus, Hugo. You think she'd try to fight them?"

"She is my daughter, Bennet. You know her well enough. You know what she is capable of."

"No, I really don't. I have no idea what she's capable of."

Hugo's expression suggested doubt until, after a few seconds, he realized I wasn't joking.

I understood. Elodie had told me more than once about how she ran away from her life. How she pretended, sometimes, to be a different person with no family, no fucked up past, none of these unthinkable realities in her rearview mirror. If Hugo had taught her how to defend herself—considering the way he'd fought, the way he'd killed those men in the garden—then she wouldn't have been forthcoming about it.

But there'd been that moment in the town, when the Bailey men had come for us. Her lack of fear, her fighting stance. *My dad taught me a few things*, she'd said. But how much had he taught her?

"Why do you think they're keeping us here?" I asked. I had

no way of telling the time. It didn't even feel like it was the same night as when we'd been attacked in the garden.

Hugo's gunshot wound bled slowly no matter how he bandaged it or how consistently we kept pressure on it. Every few minutes we succeeded in stopping the flow altogether, only for it to start again—thankfully much slower than it had been—a few minutes later.

And I could tell he didn't have much strength left.

"Perhaps, at this point, they use us as bait," he said. "If Howard and his inbred goons have failed in capturing Elodie, they know she will come for us."

"Right. And what's with their obsession with Elodie?"

Hugo chuckled through his nose, more of a pity-laugh. "Put your mind to it and I'm certain you can figure this out, Bennet. Think of the kind of man Howard Bailey is. Think of what this entire operation—the farm, the cages—think of what it symbolizes to a man like Howard Bailey."

"Howard Bailey and his fucked up family." I shook my head. I sat with my back to the bars, arms draping off my raised knees. "Seems like some kind of sick fantasy they're all playing, only it's reality. Like... domination."

The corner of Hugo's lips wrinkled upward. "Very good. Control, I would have said, but domination is a perfect word. Whatever unthinkable delusions drive the Bailey patriarchs to perpetuate their family culture, it is almost sexual in its single-mindedness, wouldn't you say?"

I felt my stomach churn and the blood drain from my cheeks. "If you wanna put it that way, sure."

"How else would you put it?"

I shrugged. "I guess that *is* how I'd put it. It sure... s-sure *seems* sexual when Howard talks about Alodia. Which is fucked up, since that's his fucking sister."

Hugo nodded. None of this was new to him. "From the moment Alodia and I first heard our child was a baby girl, I knew Howard Bailey would one day come for her. Since she is of Bailey blood, the desire to subjugate her, to control her, to *dominate* her, is, shall I say, indomitable in Howard Bailey. He is sick, you see."

I met his eyes and laughed. "Gee, Hugo, if you hadn't said anything I'd've had no idea."

Hugo chuckled. It hurt him to laugh.

"So what we need to do," I said, "is burn this place to the fucking ground. And castrate old Howard Bailey before we kill him."

Hugo laughed so hard he sputtered, and a drop of blood slipped down from his bottom lip. He wiped it away without saying anything.

He really isn't okay, I realized—though I already knew it—and the thought reverberated through my mind as though it'd been shouted into a room of tin walls. I tried not to wonder how much longer he had. Tried not to envision telling Elodie that her father was dead.

And I thought about Howard Bailey. I thought about the way he spoke of Alodia—the lilt of bursting passion in his voice, the tenderness that took hold of his mostly unreadable stare.

Did he think of Elodie like that? Had he looked at her like that, when we'd come here?

What would he do to her if he caught her?

Heat poured through my body at the thought.

Later, the metal door of the building opened. Of all the people I'd expected to come through to join us, Alodia Villeneuve wasn't one of them.

I don't know how long it had been when we heard the lock coming undone on the door. Both Hugo and I turned to watch. Four guards came in, ushering Alodia who was in cuffs and chains.

Hugo gasped. I felt my whole body tense up, and then I felt the primal boiling rage deep in my stomach.

Alodia wore only a tattered gown—rags, more like—and there were fresh purple bruises on her arms, her legs, her face. She was pale, shuffling along at the prodding of her captors with simpleminded obedience. A horrid contrast to how, hours ago, she'd been dancing in Hugo's gardens, in a flowing nightgown.

"You..." Hugo tried to stand, but the effort made him wince and groan with pain. But, with his hand over his gunshot wound, he managed to rise to his feet. "You monsters." He accused the men. "You vile animals!"

"Nah," said one of the men. And I recognized his voice. It was the man named Tony, who'd attacked Elodie and me in the gazebo. A rifle was slung over his shoulder—a real rifle, not a tranquilizer. "We're the ones who deal with them vile animals. Like your wife here."

The men unlocked the door of our cell.

"Howie went and called us a few minutes ago," said Tony. The men undid the cuffs and chains around Alodia and shoved her into the cell. She collapsed onto the cold ground. Hugo went to her. Tony scoffed. "Howie said your daughter—Eleanor?—he said she went and got away. Stole one of our vans and is probably on her way here. Don't know what the fuck she plans on doing, but she'll have a hell of a time getting through us." Tony drew his baton and clapped it against the cell's iron bars. "You two have a good time keeping her from eating you alive, now."

And the men were gone.

"Oh, my dear," said Hugo, adjusting so he could both sit and hold his darling Alodia. "Oh, my dear… I'm so sorry. I'm so sorry this is happening."

His arms were wrapped around her, holding her close. She didn't seem to mind, in fact when she blinked she kept her eyes shut for a few seconds as she let herself be held. This was, I supposed, her way of leaning into his love. She did what she could. Felt it how she could. Acknowledged the warmth of him, even if affection wasn't exactly in her repertoire of emotions.

But as I watched the two of them, Alodia made a strange sound. Like a whimper. A crackly, childish moan. She seemed so weak. So frail. So beaten. And though I have never considered myself capable of breaking easily, part of me broke when I heard those sad, morose sounds coming from Alodia as she trembled with pain and weakness.

I understood, as I watched the two of them, that Hugo

would do anything to protect her, all the way to his dying breath. Just as I would do anything to protect Elodie, if it came to that.

"Hugo," I said, breaking the stony silence. "Can I ask you something?"

"Of course, Bennet."

"Did you ever feel like something was lacking? From your life, I mean?"

He appeared to consider this. Alodia was either asleep or simply resting in his arms with her eyes closed, and Hugo fought to hold onto consciousness.

"No," he finally said. "Never."

And all the answers I'd needed about him, about Alodia, about their marriage and their inexplicable love for each other, was answered with those words.

While my stomach grumbled, while I struggled to find things to say to keep Hugo from falling asleep, a strange sound exploded from somewhere on the farm, reaching our cell from the barred window.

The sound of a car—probably one of the trucks on the property—speeding suddenly up, engine revving, tires clawing through dirt.

And then a metallic screeching crash—

—followed by something like a chorus of siren's cries rising in volume, becoming a thunderous roar.

26

The Open Cage

This is what happened to Elodie.

When the lights came on in the house, and every door slammed shut and locked itself, Elodie shot up in bed with a gasp.

This hadn't happened in so many years, she'd forgotten her father's house had an emergency system in place. There'd been a time, in the dark dream of her childhood, when Hugo had feared attacks from the Bailey family. Every few months, men would try to sneak onto the property to kidnap Alodia, to bring her back to the Bailey farm. Elodie had been seven years old when it first happened.

Three men had snuck onto the property, coming through the woods and across the grounds. They broke in—this was before any advanced security measures had been implemented in the house—and found what was, at the time, Alodia's space. At this point in time, Hugo hadn't finished construction on his more elaborate space for Alodia: there was no giant plexiglass wall, but instead a series of connected rooms dedicated to her. The Bailey men crept into her space and assaulted her.

Hugo did not divulge the intricacies of this event in his journal, and I can understand why. It would've hurt too much to write of such things. To lay such honesty upon the page for reflection when it would be so much easier to hide those things away inside the mind, and try never to look at them.

When Hugo, a few rooms away, heard the commotion, he flew from his bed, through the hallway, to Alodia's section of the house.

Two men were pinning her to the floor while the third was attempting to mount her, fondling her naked body all the while. She had been sleeping, so her strength had not yet returned to her. But the urgency of the situation was apparent nonetheless as she writhed and tried to kick and claw at the attackers. In minutes she would be strong enough to take them, but because of her condition, awakening from restful sleep was a slow process, so for now all she could do was squirm her body and screech.

Hugo hadn't drawn the sword from his walking stick by the time he burst into the room, but when he saw what the men were doing, when he realized what they intended to do to Alodia—despite that they were related to her by blood—Hugo drew the sword.

The first one he killed by stabbing the blade through the man's throat from behind. This was the man who was climbing atop Alodia; this was the man whose idea it had been to "have some fun with her" before bringing her back to the farm.

The two others tried to attack Hugo. He badly injured one of them, while the other was getting the upper hand before Alodia seized him by the shirt and tossed him across the room as though he weighed less than a pillow. This man—the third one—ran for his life and escaped.

But the other... Hugo didn't kill the other. Not for weeks after.

Instead of killing him, Hugo dragged him out to a hidden door in the forest. This door led into a cellar, where Hugo stored food for Alodia, as well as emergency supplies like canned food, gas masks, and a collection of weapons, mostly guns and knives.

This was where Hugo kept the man, torturing him slowly, for weeks, learning what he could from him. But he didn't do it for information on the Bailey family, not really. He did it to punish the man for what they'd done to Alodia.

These were the span of weeks, Elodie told me, that her father lost his mind.

Only after this event did he design the security system for the house. The locking doors, the lights burning on. Later he installed fencing around the property, some of it electric. And in the months to come, more Bailey men came to the Villeneuve estate.

Elodie's memories from those years were interspersed with being awakened in the middle of the night—so often—by all the doors in the house slamming shut, and every light buzzing brightly on.

Even on nights when it didn't happen, when the night was calm, she would wake up with her heart pounding, a gasp in her throat, muscles taut with fear and anticipation.

So this was the first time in years that it happened to her, that she was torn from the gentle rest of sleep by the bright lights and the sounds of doors slamming shut. And her body reacted before her mind even processed what was happening.

Elodie bolted upright, gasping, eyes wide and alert. And she knew within seconds—

The Baileys were here. They had come, after all. And if her father had engaged the house's security system, it must be bad.

She dressed in a hurry, jeans and a simple black shirt and sweatshirt, and checked the windows. From her room there was no view of the gardens.

Her father had told her, many times, not to try and explore the house when the security systems engaged. The safest thing was to stay where she was: every door locked from the inside. She was safe in this room.

But I wasn't there in the room with her, meaning I was in

trouble, too. And Elodie wasn't about to sit around and wait for someone to come knocking at her door.

While she was checking the house to make sure no one else was inside, she heard the gunshot. Elodie darted across the house to Alodia's side. She propped the double-doors so they wouldn't lock behind her—in case she needed to make a quick exit—and stood before the plexiglass. Then she entered through the plexiglass door—which she also propped open—and went to the windows in time to see me and her father being dragged across the lawn.

Her mother struggled against a group of men who were dragging her as well. And she was clearly too weak to put up much of a fight.

Elodie's first impulse was to grab a weapon—a fireplace poker, a knife, anything—and rush outside. But there were too many men out there, and at least one of them had a gun.

So she did the only thing she could do: nothing. She watched as we were dragged off the grounds.

By the time some of the men tried breaking into the house, Elodie had devised a plan.

While Howard Bailey and his goons were smashing windows downstairs, Elodie was back in her bedroom. She broke one of the windows of the room and slipped onto the roof in the dark. And, like she had so many times as a young teenager, she shimmied down one of the drainpipes and dropped into the house's front yard, beside the porch.

She sprinted down the driveway through the dark.

The Bailey men had parked their vehicles on the road, before Hugo's front gate. The gate was locked, so the men had found their way onto the property by walking the fence line until they found a spot where they set up two ladders. Elodie made use of these, and—for the hell of it—knocked both ladders down on her way over the fence.

There had probably been three or four vans on the road before, but the others had already driven away with Hugo, Alodia, and me trapped within. Only one van remained, idling at the edge of the driveway's pavement. A man leaned against the driver's side, arms crossed, head reclined against the side of the car's roof, eyes aimed skyward. Which was to Elodie's advantage.

She came around the other side of the vehicle, rushing but not sprinting, and threw herself at the man before he even realized what was happening.

Speeding through the woods, adrenaline pumping in her blood, Elodie rolled the windows down and let the road soothe her. It would be a few hours before she was close to the Bailey farm, and she intended to drive through the night.

In the passenger seat were two items: an identification card, and a .38 revolver with a nickel finish that gleamed under passing streetlights.

These, she decided, were all she'd need.

And, of course, the man tied up with rope in the back seat, duct tape over his lips.

She pretended like she had done this before. Not to pretend would've been to admit, especially to herself, that she had no idea what she was doing, which would be to risk being overcome by fear.

But after a time, she didn't need to pretend. Something like courage settled into her blood and gleamed in her eyes. And she felt no fear, only the relentless need to push forward.

So, not long before dawn, once she pulled the van up to the gated entrance of the Bailey farm, Elodie grabbed the revolver from the passenger seat and climbed into the back. She aimed the gun's short barrel at the head of the bound man and warned him that she wouldn't hesitate killing him if he screamed when she pulled the duct tape off. He didn't scream. He simply stared at her with wide, frightened eyes, beads of sweat popping from his hairline. His odor filled this part of the van: body odor and dirt and... shit?

"What's your name?" she asked.

The man stuttered. "Tim."

"You'll be driving, Tim. And you're not gonna say a goddamn thing."

"Y-yes, ma'am. Not a damn thing."

"You're gonna pull up to the intercom, type in the code or show them your ID card or whatever you have to do, and then pull up past the gate once it opens."

"Yes, ma'am."

"I'm gonna be right behind you, pointing this into the back of your seat." She leaned in closer, despite the smell. Glared into his eyes. He must've seen something there, in her glare, because he trembled and looked away. "Look me in the eyes." He did.

With a strain of effort. "Do you doubt for a second that I don't give a fuck about your life?"

He tried not to start crying. Shook his head.

"You get me past the gate, you can live. Get it?"

"Y-yes, ma'am. I got a wife, see, at home, and she—she—"

"And she won't have to worry about you if you get me past the gate."

He started to cry this time, to really cry. She waited until he was done, and tried not to feel disgusted by him. This man had a wife. Did *she* know what went on here, on this farm? How could he look at her and treat her well—assuming he did—and then come here, to this farm, and treat all of those Bailey women like animals?

"And here's just one piece of advice," she said, purposely stalling on untying him to keep him in suspense, to ensure he would do everything she told. "Your family's had this coming for a long fucking time. I don't care if you agree with me, I don't care what you believe, or what bullshit you've been brainwashed into believing so you can justify what you're doing here. I don't care what you tell yourself so you can sleep at night. It isn't worth it. And I swear to god, if I ever, and I mean *ever*, see you again, if one day you end up in my life again with any more of my fucked up family coming after me or my mother, I've got two fucking bullets with your goddamn name on each. And, Tim, they're going straight into your kneecaps. And then I've got plenty of other ideas for what to do with the rest of you."

"Oh my god, s-s-sure, of course... I... I swear, ma'am, I swear—"

She untied him and backed away, keeping the gun trained on

him all the while. He complied, submissive and trembling, by climbing into the driver's seat and buckling his seatbelt, though he fumbled with it for several seconds.

Elodie noticed a red gas can among the miscellaneous supplies, here in the back of the van.

"Well," said the voice over the intercom at the gate. "Howard sounded pretty sure that you were dead, Tim. Said we should expect that girl... Hugo's daughter, whatever her name is... Howie said we should be expecting her to show up. You say you ain't even seen her?"

"That's right," said Tim, his voice shaky. "All's good. Just panicked back there, but Howie's basically right behind me. Guess I better start getting r-ready to apologize to him, huh?"

After several seconds—maybe a whole minute—the intercom buzzed and the gate opened.

She told him to stop after he'd driven a few feet past the gate, down the winding path through the trees. He put the van in park. Perspiration shined slick on his skin.

"Get out," she said. "And go home. And don't come back to this farm, if you've got any sense of fucking humanity left in you."

He flinched at her every word, and was out of the van in a moment. As she sat in the driver's seat and buckled the seatbelt, she cast him another glare. He met her gaze only for an instant before turning away and closing his eyes.

It didn't matter now, she thought, if he went back and used

the intercom to alert the others. It was too late to worry about that.

She held onto the revolver even as she gripped the steering wheel with both hands. Turned her eyes forward, along the winding path which would open up onto the Bailey farm, and she pulled the van out of park. Pressed her foot on the gas pedal, and kept pressing down.

The first gate stood open, allowing Elodie to fly by it without any problems. From all sides she heard Bailey men yelling—some of them calling for her to stop, others simply sounding the alarm that something wasn't right—and Elodie turned toward the corral. The van trailed billowing dust. Her headlights illuminated the fence, casting shadows across the corral.

When she blasted through the high fence with a rattling crash, the speedometer had climbed to sixty. She struck where the fence was a gate, and it folded and snapped off from its hinges, leaving a wide, broken space.

In a rolling cloud of dust the van dragged to a stop within the corral.

And just as Elodie wondered what to do next, whether the van would be riddled with bullets or whether she should jump out and make a run for it, she heard the sound—

—of dozens of rising shrieks coming from the feral women around her as they realized, for the first time in years, that their cage was open.

27

Listen Closely

"It's Elodie," said Hugo in a voice that was too soft, too withered. It appeared to hurt him when he breathed, and his eyelids seemed weighted down as he attempted to stay awake. But he held on tightly to Alodia. Tears slipped down his cheeks, but he didn't remove his arms from his beloved, not even to wipe the tears away.

I thought of what he'd said earlier, when I asked him if he'd ever felt there was something lacking from his life.

And he hadn't even hesitated in answering. Here was a man with no regrets for what he'd given his life to—for *whom* he'd given his life to. And he was looking out, now, from his own fading twilight.

Maybe they both were. Maybe this was how their story ended.

When I had first come to Hugo's estate, pulling up the long driveway into view of the house and grounds, I'd been deeply nervous, almost terrified, of a man capable of loving a woman of Alodia's condition. A man capable of loving a woman whom some would call a monster.

But as I looked at the two of them now—Hugo with his arms around her even as he slowly, in pain, faded away, and she with her bruises, her soft whimpers—my heart swelled and broke for them. And I thought: *they're beautiful*.

And I wondered if we were going to die here. How could Elodie save us? What chance did she stand against the entire farm of Bailey men?

Even as I thought this, the sounds I heard through the cell window told a story of violence and hope. Screams both of an inhuman sort and a perfectly human sort. A battle was taking place out there as the Bailey women, it sounded like, escaped from the corral. Maybe that was the crash we'd heard—Elodie driving a vehicle straight into the corral, leaving an opening in the fence. But how many Bailey women were there? How many men to try and hold them back?

How much longer before the next sound from outside was the sound of gunfire?

"We need to get you out of here," I said to Hugo. "Both of you. And get you to a hospital or... or something." I went to the bars of the cell. This wasn't some advanced prison, therefore it actually had the iron bars. Very old-fashioned, very fitting of the Baileys. "I just don't know how Elodie will find us..." I leaned against the bars, shut my eyes, tried to think of something, anything. "I don't even know if... if she—"

"Bennet." Hugo spoke through a cough, more of a sputter. When I looked, I saw blood dribbling from his bottom lip. His eyes were bloodshot.

God. Maybe this was it. My breath began to leave me.

"Bennet," he said again.

I came closer. "Hugo... I need you to hold on. For her."

He managed a feeble smile. And still held onto Alodia, who appeared to be asleep.

"I am under no illusions, Bennet. Though I thank you."

I didn't know what to say. Words felt unbearably insufficient under the certainty in Hugo's stare.

"You need to get Elodie," he said. "And you need to get out of this place."

"If I can get out of here, I'm not leaving you."

He coughed again, and more blood dripped down his chin. "You are many things, Bennet, but naive is not one of those."

I reached out and placed a trembling hand on Hugo's shoulder. He nodded. A single tear slipped down his left cheek.

"You know what to tell my daughter for me."

I nodded back. Words continued to fail me.

"Do not turn back for me. You understand?"

"Hugo..."

"And do not ever come back to this place. Whatever becomes of it is not in your hands, nor should it be. Your responsibility is to my daughter."

"Yes. Yes, always."

"There is more gratitude in my heart for you, and more love in my heart for her, than I can say. So understand what I mean when I say, Bennet, do not regret. Do not think back, not even to this very moment, with wishes of what you should have done, or should have said—anything of that sort. Do not be so foolish. You... you are part of my family, you understand? And there are no locked doors in this house."

"Hugo... there's so much I want to say to you."

"I know, Bennet. Now... stand away."

I gave him a questioning look, my eyes full of tears, but I did as he said.

Hugo straightened up and pulled Alodia even closer to his chest. He held her, then ran his hand through her hair. The patience of this motion, the familiar way he knew how to plunge his fingers through, moving the strands from her face and above her head and over her ears—he had done this hundreds or maybe thousands of times. She stirred. Her eyes fluttered beneath their lids and then opened, staring blankly ahead.

"Alodia," said Hugo in a tense whisper. "Alodia." His breath tickled her ear.

I saw the way her eyes widened at the touch of his breath and the sound of his voice. Wrinkles of tension appeared in her forehead, and her body twitched as if she were trying, and failing, to sit straight up. How hurt was she? Knowing how sick she was, how weak... how much longer did she have, too?

From outside on the farm, the sounds of screams. And a few pops of gunshots, and what I assumed to be the snapping electricity of cattle prods. From in here it was impossible to tell what was happening, whether Elodie and the Bailey women were overrunning the farm or were, themselves, being overrun.

When I looked to the small window, I saw an orange glow. Fire.

"Alodia, my love." Hugo plunged his hand through her hair again. "My sweet, sweet love. Listen closely to me.

"You have been the love of my life, as I have told you again and again, night after night. Dancing with you under the moon and the stars, in our garden... that is what I will take with me into the darkness. And I will be holding you, always. Here." He placed his hand to her chest, over her heart. "This is where I will hold you, forever. Just as the trees hold the sky. And the land holds the sea. And the moon holds the ocean. You see?"

I couldn't believe what I was seeing.

Tears were dripping from Alodia's eyes. Those eyes remained blank, staring forward, but there were tears. Like on the night I had confronted her in the garden. As if Alodia were there, somewhere beneath the surface, beneath the veil, still with enough agency for tears to fall.

"You have all of my heart, my love. But I cannot hold you any longer. We both knew this day was coming... for both of us. So what if it is sooner than either of us thought." He released a heavy breath that gurgled with blood, followed by an involuntary moan—not just of pain, but of agony. "I would have grown old with you, my dear. I would have danced with you until our legs could no longer keep us going. I would have sat by your bedside and taken care of you long into your illness. I would have sung to you as you slipped away.

"But this is the way things are. No matter how much time we

had, my love, my dear Alodia, it never would have been enough."

Alodia found her strength, then. Just enough.
She pulled away from Hugo, only to turn on her hands and knees so she was facing him, her face only inches from his. And she was crying. No sound escaped her. Silent tears streamed down her cheeks.

Hugo lifted a hand to the side of her face and smiled at her. "Elodie is in trouble, sweetheart. And I would go to her, if I could... and protect her from these monsters. As I have always tried to do. I would've done anything to protect her... and to protect you. But I can't anymore. I can't." Their foreheads touched. "Alodia, dear... I don't have much time. But neither does Elodie. Whatever strength you have left, my love... find it. If you can. Bennet will help you. He will do whatever he can to save her. Hear me, my love. Elodie is in trouble. She needs us. She's in danger. *Elodie needs you*, my love."

For a moment, I thought maybe Alodia had snapped out of her condition entirely.
Moving away from her dying husband, she stood straight up. It was as though the illness hadn't weakened her, as if the beatings she'd taken over the last couple hours hadn't occurred. She stood straight up, her entire body flexing rigidly as though she were not a body of muscles but rather a single muscle, sheer force and will. Her arms hung at her sides, hands splayed and curled into claws.

The frail, beaten animal was gone. A beast stood in her place.

When she turned to me, I literally jumped back and fell, gasping.

Her eyes were on fire with a glare so blunt, so simmering, it seemed uncontainable. Her teeth were gritted and bared like those of a jungle cat defending its young.

Which is exactly what I was witnessing. A mother realizing her child was threatened. A vengeful predator called to the hunt.

I didn't believe what I was seeing—not entirely—when Alodia went to the cell door and took hold of the bars. I didn't believe it could possibly be happening, not even when, as she tensed her whole body and began to pull—muscles pulsing from her skin as if trying to burst outward, a guttural sound bursting from her lungs—when the bars made a high-pitched squealing sound.

But I believed it when the metallic clanging exploded suddenly in my ears, followed by a violent metal snapping, and the cell door came furiously loose and clattered onto the concrete floor.

I gaped at Alodia, hyperventilating, heart pounding.

It didn't seem possible, but it had happened in front of my eyes.

She looked back, but not at me. She looked back at Hugo, who lay crumpled against the wall, hand to his stomach, skin ned of its ripeness, eyes shut. He still breathed, but his breath was shallow and quick. Alodia looked at him and, after several seconds, released an anguished cry. An animalistic, sorrowful cry. And then she charged at the door that led outside, and with a single throw of her body she blasted through it, and went sprinting out into the predawn chaos to find her daughter.

Only seconds behind, still dazed from what I'd just witnessed, I followed.

28

Chaos

The pale light of dawn was spilling into the darkness on the edge of the sky.

The corral was entirely empty except for the gray van and the folded piece of fence.

Chaos was everywhere.

The largest building on the farm—the building where Elodie and I had been taken, where Howard Bailey resided and ran most of the operations—was a pyre of angry flames. Most of the Bailey men were running frantically away from the fire, but some were running toward it with fire extinguishers or buckets of water while, in chaotic motion all around, the feral Bailey women were hunting.

A pale woman down near the corral leapt ten or maybe

fifteen feet and collided with a man who waved a cattle prod at her. But the woman drove him to the ground with the impact of her body, then grabbed his face with one hand and smashed his head against the ground. And then again—and again—and again—and again. Blood spilled in a crown on the dirt around his head, matting his hair, and his muffled screams became elongated grunts—and then he was silent. The woman released a victorious cry—a screech—then dismounted him and tossed him inside the corral as though he weighed no more than a raincoat.

Outside the open door of a nearby building—which, it appeared, was the mess hall—two Bailey women had ganged up on one especially large man. He was stabbing his cattle prod at them, snapping the electricity, screaming in an effort to intimidate but unable to hide the terror from his voice. The two women were closing in, pinning him against the side of the building. Every time the man stabbed at one, the other would move in closer.

The man, realizing this, swept the cattle prod in a wide arc, attempting to push both the women back, but one of the women met the swing with her wrist. And the second woman jumped forward and sunk her teeth into the bulbous flesh of the man's neck, driving him to the ground in a spurt of blood that spattered in a line across the building wall behind him as he dropped to the dirt.

There were bodies strewn across the farm, most of them men. Security guards and staff in uniform. But there were plenty of corpses of Bailey women, as well. I stepped over two, each with bullet holes in their heads. And then the horribly mangled body of a security guard. One of his legs had been torn into at the thigh, and I saw the white of bone beneath puddling blood.

And the main building wasn't the only one on fire. Another had been set ablaze on the other side of the corral. This, I assumed, was one of the sleeping quarters for the guards. And the flames *roared*. I had never realized how loud fire could be.

The building looming to my left had the appearance of a home, or perhaps a hotel. It was untouched by violence or flames except the front door stood ajar. I ignored this and continued pursuing Alodia.

Some of the Bailey women, I saw, were fleeing from the fire. But not merely from the fire, they were headed for the farm's perimeter. They were headed for the woods—they were headed for freedom from this terrible place.

Outside the main burning building—a collection of silhouettes against the fire's glow—three men with cattle prods were surrounding a single Bailey woman. She was still on her feet, swiping and growling at her attackers, but they kept stabbing her with electricity, kept closing in, prepared to jump on her and restrain her.

And there was Alodia Villeneuve, sprinting at the group to help her struggling sister. I pursued, knowing that Alodia was weak despite her sudden burst of adrenaline, knowing she had only so long before she would become nearly immobile again.

But she threw herself at one of the attackers, essentially body-slamming him to the side. He flew maybe six feet and then hit the ground rolling and flailing in clouds of dust, the cattle prod flying from his grasp.

One of the other men swung their cattle prod at Alodia, but with his attention turned, the other Bailey woman lunged and dug her fingers into his throat.

I came to a skidding halt, mouth agape, eyes wide with shock. The woman had literally driven her fingers into the man's neck. He was clawing at her arms and at his own neck as blood spilled down onto his clothes. From his throat came burbles and the sound of wet choking. Within seconds his movements became dying spasms.

The third man turned and bolted away, headed for nowhere. Alodia pursued, gaining on him from the start.

The thunder of gunfire cracked through the dark morning air.

A man with a rifle stood by the corral, aiming up the incline toward a group of three Bailey women by the burning building. He wore a familiar sunhat and a security guard's uniform.

Tony. I'd recognize that lanky form, and that sunhat, anywhere.

He took aim toward the Bailey women again and fired off a shot. The crack echoed off the sides of nearby buildings.

One of the Bailey women let out a shocked cry and dropped into the dirt, convulsing.

I looked back and forth between Tony with the rifle and

Alodia, who had caught up to her target and was tearing into him, clawing and biting and slashing.

Another shot from the rifle cracked through the air. Alodia lifted her eyes toward it, growled, and charged. She had maybe fifty feet to cover, and would reach him in seconds—she was unnaturally fast. And Tony... one turn of his attention and of the rifle—one thunder-crack from the muzzle and she'd be dead. But she was closing in...

And so was somebody else. A woman was coming up behind Tony, and she wore dark clothes instead of rags.

Elodie?

Before I could think of what to do, Tony turned in my direction and waved a hand.

"Howie!" he called, waving a hand. "Right there! Right over there!"

I would've bolted away to try and take cover, or else dropped onto the ground in the hopes of making him miss a shot if he tried, but that wave of the hand, and his yelling that name, gave me pause.

And then it was too late.

Something flew over my head and fell around me. I realized it was a rope, or some kind of wire, as it fell over my shoulders, around my chest, and then it constricted and I was tugged onto my back.

"Hey!" I called, trying to shift around enough to get at least one of my arms out, to try and pull the wire free. And then I heard the weighted, booted footsteps near my head, and I looked up.

Howard Bailey's massive form hulked above me. His eyes

gleamed, along with half of his gigantic face, in the dancing orange glow from the fire. Like Tony, he wore a sunhat, though the straw had come undone in crosshatches across the brim. There was a fresh wound—a gaping red gash—down his face. It was still bleeding. It must've been Hugo's sword. He'd gotten at least one slash in before being shot.

A pleased grin had spread across Howard's lips. In his hands was a long metal pole, at the end of which was the wire restraining me. As though I were an animal he'd come to catch.

How many of the Bailey women had been subjected to this treatment? To this very tool?

Two more gunshots rang out in quick succession. My heart swelled with fear for Alodia and for Elodie. Either one of them —or both—could be dead, and I couldn't see.

Without a word, Howard grabbed me by the collar of my shirt and pulled me to my feet. And, using the pole, dragged me into the two-story building behind us, the one that resembled a hotel—which was, I found out, all too accurate an impression.

29

Open Your Eyes, Boy

Ever since Elodie came up to me at Night Owl and told me to *shoo*, I had witnessed some unbelievable things. My life was beyond any notion, any idea, that I could've ever imagined. And some of those things were seared into my brain, would likely linger with me for years to come. Some of those things had shaken me. But some I had begun to process, for Elodie's sake. Some of them I had come to see in a new light. Especially Hugo and Alodia. Their marriage. Their love—which tempted to warp any preconceptions I'd ever had about what love could be, or necessarily *should* be.

What I saw in the rooms and hallways of the building that Howard dragged me into… those images shook me as deeply, maybe even more, than anything I'd witnessed the past few months.

It was called The Hotel. When healthy female members of the Bailey family were brought onto the farm for testing, they were often kept on the property for weeks at a time. Months, for some. And The Hotel was where they stayed when they weren't being tested on.

Howard dragged me through a lobby, then down a hallway of many rooms. The rooms were close together, the simplest of hotel-style rooms each—no luxury, no aesthetic, no comfort. And as I was shoved along at the end of Howard's cattle prod, I peered into the passing rooms, all with doors ajar, some of them with broken locks. Someone had kicked most of the doors down from the outside.

From the hallway, as I was prodded forward, I glimpsed women's bodies. Some lay in the entranceways, blood leaking from gunshot wounds in their faces. Blood stained the thin carpets around their heads. A woman's blonde hair splayed out, soaked by a pool of blood.

Other bodies I caught only parts of—legs draping over the edge of a bed, an arm tossed out from a bathroom—but the scene was clear in each one. And none of the women wore any clothes.

"Howard you... you sick *fuck*. You killed these women?" I tried to look at him over my shoulder but he jabbed the prod into my back and shoved. The pain was blunt—he was kind enough not to electrocute me, rather he just pushed me along— and I stumbled forward and tried to avert my eyes from the open doorways we passed. Each one contained the scene of someone's violent ending. Dead women. On the right, it was a woman in her seventies, hair curly and gray. She didn't have any clothes either, meaning this was how the women were kept here. Like inhuman specimen. A room past this, a woman who probably wasn't older than twenty-one.

"You did this?" I said. Tears were sliding down my cheeks. My arms trembled and, with the next prodding from Howard, my knees nearly gave out from under me. "You did this, you twisted—"

"Don't judge what you don't understand, boy," he said. We came to a set of stairs and he urged me up. I climbed them clumsily, tripping over every other step. I couldn't feel my legs. Couldn't feel much of anything except for the blunt points of pain in my back.

"You sick, sick fuck."

"Your girlfriend's the one who's the cause of all this," he said. And I could tell he believed it. "You think I wanted to do any of this?"

"Yes. I think you did."

"Well then, I don't know what to say. You got me pegged wrong."

We reached the next floor. Into another hallway of rooms with open doors.

I was wrong about not being able to feel anything. I could feel my stomach twisting itself into a knot. And my breath felt like fire in my body.

There had to be more than a dozen rooms with open doors—a dozen rooms each containing the naked body of a murdered woman.

Howard directed me into a larger room, probably where

staff convened for breaks and meetings and maybe sleep, for some. It was part office, part bedroom, part kitchen.

Howard sat me on a wooden chair in the middle of the room and zip-tied my hands behind me. Plopped himself in his own chair a few feet from me. He looked around the room and sighed heavily as if settling down after a long day of work. The gash in his face bled at the edges. He wiped it away—along with sweat from his forehead—with trembling hands.

When he looked at me, he looked at me with something like pity. Sympathy, maybe? It wasn't anger I saw there, or necessarily contempt. It was almost as if he felt bad for me.

"I hope you die from that," I said, meaning the slash from Hugo's sword.

"Listen closely. I know what you're getting at... and I know how this must look."

"Like you're a fucking psychopath," I said. "And a monster."

"You saw what's going on out there, Bennet." He gestured vaguely to the window. "Right? You saw that? You of all people gotta have an understanding, at least, of what our women are capable of. I mean..." He gestured again to the window, implying the scene outside. With dawn spilling into the sky, the glow of the burning building was no longer the prominent source of light. "I mean, imagine if they were allowed to run free out there in the world. Imagine if they were allowed to procreate. Even the healthy ones can pass on the gene, you know. And if this got out... it could spread exponentially. There'd be monsters out there, spreading like a disease. You ever think about that?"

I fought against my restraints, glaring. "They're only monsters if you *treat* them like monsters, you fucking psychopath. You were right when you said that I, of all people, know what they're capable of. I've seen how Alodia's capable of love, and compassion, and... and forgiveness. I've seen what she'll do to protect *her* family from real monsters like *you* and *your* fucked up family, Howard. That's what I've seen."

Howard wiped beads of sweat again from his face, then blood from his wound, and shook his head. "So old Hugo Villeneuve got into your head, did he?"

"Hugo loved Alodia."

"Hell, *I* love Alodia. I'm her brother."

"You don't love her. You have no fucking clue what—"

"You don't got a clue what you're talking about, boy. I'm the one that protected her all them years from our parents, made sure she was treated right while she was here—back when she was healthy. Me. Good old Howie. I'm the one that watched out for her all those years until Hugo brainwashed her. And he kept her like a damn sex slave, he did."

"Hugo *loved* her. He loved her selflessly."

"Hugo's a sick man."

My whole body quaked from the trauma of what I'd seen on the way up here, and from the hatred boiling in my blood for Howard Bailey. If the ties around my wrists hadn't been restraining me, I wouldn't have been able to help throwing my hands around the man's massive neck. My vision pulsed with my pounding heart, burning toward red. I kept thinking of Hugo in the cell...

Hugo holding onto his wife, holding her close with his fading strength.

Hugo whispering into her ear, telling her how she was the

love of his life, telling her he would've stayed with her, taken care of her, until it all went dark.

Hugo telling me he never felt he lacked anything in his life, even after everything that had happened, even after all he'd lost, even after all he'd done and given for Alodia.

I kept seeing him urging Alodia to go, as he slowly collapsed.

Howard leaned toward me, his stare regretful. "You love her, don't you? Elodie, I mean."

I forced myself to breathe slowly between my gritted teeth. Her name didn't belong in his mouth. He didn't deserve to say it. I said nothing.

"You wouldn't be here if you didn't love her. So I gotta ask you, Bennet... is she worth it?"

"Don't fucking talk about her. Don't say her name."

"Now don't be petty, Bennet. I'm asking you a simple question, that's all. Chances are, she won't make it another few years before the condition sets in. It's always been strong on Alodia's side of the family. And besides... last you two was here, I could see it in her eyes. Sometimes they've got a look about them, when they've got it. And oh, boy, she's got it."

There was something strange about the softness of his voice as he spoke about Elodie. It made me feel even sicker. My head spun, but the adrenaline in my blood—fueled by the angry volcano in my chest—kept me steady.

"Tell me something, Bennet. She act different at night? You ever wake up and find her sitting straight up in bed, staring off into nothing? Or how about feasting on some roadkill, or a critter she killed in the dark? Any of that start happening yet?"

"Shut the fuck up."

"No? Maybe? Sounds like a maybe to me. How you gonna handle that, huh? You think you've got what it takes? You think you're anything like Hugo Villeneuve?"

"Shut the *fuck up*, you son of a bitch."

"I'm trying to open your eyes, boy. That's all. You might've thought what you saw was love—I can tell, since you're all worked up about it—but think about it, man. Think about what it takes to love something like that."

"Some*thing*? She's a *human being*."

"I'm just saying, Bennet. Think about what it takes. You think you can sacrifice your whole life to a blank slate? An animal that won't respond to you, won't ever care for you back, won't ever *give* back? Except, of course, when it comes to the wedding bed, but we don't gotta speak about what that'll be like. I'm sure you've imagined it plenty of times."

I was hyperventilating now, despite my best efforts.

"And I get it," he said. "You're hopeful. You think there's maybe some kind of nobility, a deep sense of romance and love, in the idea of it. That's Hugo, getting inside your head. You saw how sick he was and mistook it for... well, I don't know what you mistook it for. Clarity? Reality? Love? I hate to be the one to break it to you, Bennet, but you've gotta have something off about you in the head to be anything like that man. You think Alodia loved him? You think it wasn't just hopeful projection? You think you'll be happy like that, one day, when Elodie's no better off? When she feasts on raw meat and critters she finds out in the yard? When you visit her from across cage bars, or plexiglass, or anything like that? You think you won't regret what could've been a normal life when one night you're holding her and wish she'd hold you back? When you go out in the world and see all those happy, normal couples, and understand you'll never be able to walk down the street, hand-in-hand, with her?

"I know what that's like, that feeling. Believe me, I do. I've suffered it over and over, for that dear sister of mine. I get it. You love Elodie. But listen, Bennet. You're a young guy. You've got a whole life ahead of you. I can promise that you can walk away from it safely, without anymore trouble from me. And if you do walk away—which, I don't lie, is the smart thing—you'll be heartbroken, sure. Maybe it'll take a long time for you to stop dreaming about her. But you *will* get over it. I can promise you that. You'll meet somebody who'll make you see this in a new light. You'll find someone who fills your heart as much as you fill theirs, you see, and then it'll be okay. Then the pain will have had meaning, and you'll wonder how you ever considered the things you're considering now. You understand what I'm saying? You considered these things?"

He had come even closer to me, scooting the chair so he wasn't even a foot away, staring into me.

Tears still stained my cheeks and I was shaking out of control. With my arms wrapped around the backrest and zip-tied, I didn't have much movement.

Yes. I had thought about those things. Yes, they kept me up at night, sometimes. And I dreamed, every now and then, about waking up in the middle of the night to find Elodie staring directly at me but not really seeing me.

"Yeah," I said to Howard, shaking as if freezing cold. "I've considered all of that. And you're right... maybe you're right about all of it."

"What I'm offering you, Bennet, is a way out. You're the outsider here. You can just walk away."

"Yeah?"

"Scout's honor, boy. It's not like I've really got anything against—"

I whipped forward and head-butted Howard in the face. His nose crunched and splatted against my forehead, and then he jolted back with enough force to tip the chair over and spill himself onto the carpet, one hand over his nose, the other flailing off to the side as if to catch his own titanic weight.

I had no way of escaping, no hope of putting up any fight. So, watching him roll around and lumber back to his feet, I started to laugh. And once the laughter had me in its grip, it had all of me.

I lost my mind for the first time in my life, and couldn't stop laughing. It escaped my throat without any filter, without any shame. Forced itself up through my lungs, came hoarsely out of my throat. More tears fell in streams, and I kept laughing.

And laughing. And laughing.

Howard Bailey, swearing, moved to kick me, but I leaned to the side with such abandon—hardly able to breathe—that my chair tipped over, too, and I dropped onto the carpet. My coarse, hysterical laughter—rising in pitch and volume—filled the room. It seemed that I was laughing inside my own head, too. There was no escape from it.

"Should've known you were fucking crazy," said Howard, towering above me, holding his nose. Blood trickled around his mouth, down his neck and to the collar of his shirt.

Howard lifted one of his massive feet, placed his booted foot against the side of my face.

The certainty struck me that I was about to die. And all I could do was laugh.

From the hallway there came the sound of shuffling—two, maybe three people running. And then—

CRACK! CRACK!

Two thunderous shots in quick succession. Like thunder detonating, even from out in the hallway.

The rifle had been in Tony's hands, and that sounded like the same rifle. But who was he firing at? Elodie? Was she—

The door slammed open and slapped against the wall.

Both Howard and I turned abruptly toward it.

"Well," said Elodie, covered in blood and hoisting Tony's rifle up to her shoulder so she could aim down the sights. "If it isn't Howard fucking Bailey, just the monster I was looking for."

I recognized the fiery look in her ashen eyes, how the irises appeared preternaturally to glow. It was the look that sometimes came over her at night. Like the fire burning inside of her grew beyond control and took the driver's seat in her mind. I could even hear it in her voice.

Like the Bailey women. She was hunting.

Howard bared his teeth as if to growl. He didn't raise his hands. "What now, Elodie? Gonna slaughter your own kin?"

"Already did plenty of that," she said. "Tony screamed when Mom ripped his throat out." And, without another second's hesitation, she pulled the trigger.

The sound was deafening in the room—more like an explosion, it seemed, than a gunshot.

The bullet struck Howard directly in the considerable swell of his stomach. Blood spatted out from the wound and he stumbled back, hand over the place where the bullet had entered, his eyes bulging, mouth agape.

"But you aren't mine to slaughter," said Elodie, stepping aside from the doorway. "Mom? It's your brother Howard."

I never would've thought I could feel such relief at the sight of Alodia Villeneuve, but I felt just that—a bursting of relief. Relief that she'd survived, at least for now. Relief that the shots I'd heard as I'd been dragged into this building hadn't indicated her death.

She was even paler than before, and I noticed how the muscles in her legs were shaking under her own weight, but she stayed on her feet. And her face—as well as the entire front of her gown—was soaked in blood, and I guessed it wasn't her blood.

Alodia was hunched—clearly still on the hunt—and her reptilian eyes settled on Howard, her long-estranged brother. Her lips peeled back and she growled—that low, vibrating, guttural sound. Her fingers splayed outward and curled into claws. Maybe I was projecting, but I'd swear she recognized him. I'd swear she knew exactly who he was.

Howard Bailey lifted a hand as if to dissuade her, or to shield himself from her. He had started to keel over, and his voice had to gurgle through blood in his mouth.

"Alodia, my sweet. It's... it's me. It's Howie, your brother. You remember Howie, don't you?"

She stepped toward him, half-circling, preparing to attack. It was so clear in her eyes, I thought, that she recognized him. It was similar to how she'd looked at me from across the dinner table, when I thought she wanted to lunge at me. Except, for me it had been a fireplace burning. For Howard, it was a forest fire.

"It's me. Alodia, it's me. You remember me, don't you? We used to sneak out at night to pick berries from the river. Before... before you started getting weird at night, I mean. I... I stood up to Dad for you when he said you should be sleeping here, in The Hotel, instead of at home. I've always been on your side, Alodia. Sis. All this time I've just been trying to get you back. Everything I did—"

Howard never got to finish his sentence.

Alodia leapt at him, covering several feet of ground in that single leap, and sunk her claws and her teeth into him. He screamed, but her screech drowned him out.

I watched for a moment and then closed my eyes against the image of blood, having seen enough traumatizing horror to last a lifetime.

Elodie cut me free of my restraints. And then she held me. Before I even realized it, my hysterical laughter turned to sobs. I put my arms around her and cried against her, and I think she may have sobbed with me.

We stayed that way for a long time, in each other's arms.

Outside, the farm was burning. Before we went on our way, we made sure the rest of it would burn, too.

30

Silences

The Bailey women were gone. Whether they'd gone off together into the woods, or simply went one-by-one away from this place of horror where they'd been kept most of their lives, I hoped they'd be okay. I hoped they found each other out there and got to live.

We took one of the farm's pickup trucks—for all we knew, it may have belonged to Howard Bailey. With the truck's bed covered, we were able to keep Alodia in the back. She had plenty of room. And she laid down beside the body of her husband.

I had hoped that Hugo might've held on long enough to say goodbye to his daughter one last time, but no. When we returned to the cell, he was on the floor against the wall where

Alodia and I had left him. His eyes were shut, blood marked his chin, and he was entirely still, as if under the spell of perfect sleep. None of the tension of his pain showed anymore on his face; he appeared at peace, in fact it almost appeared as though he'd been overcome with a sensation of relief in his final moments. A sensation, perhaps, of letting go.

I hoped that's what he felt, at the end. He had known more pain, more loss, more heartbreak, than anyone I'd ever met. And he'd borne it with an eccentric grace uniquely his own.

Looking down at him in the cell, neither Elodie nor I said anything. Elodie bent down and put her hand on his hand, maybe to test for warmth, maybe just to touch him. I heard her say, in a choked whisper, "Dad..." but that was all.

Later, after burying him in the ground, in the gardens of his home—marked by an elegant black stone and chiseled letters lined with sparkling gold—I struggled with what to say about him. He was, in everything but name, my father-in-law. And if Elodie and I ever had children, maybe one day I'd tell them stories about their grandfather.

Or would I? What stories could I tell them that they would ever understand?

For the entire drive back to Hugo's estate, Alodia kept her arm over her husband's body. I thought of what Howard had said to me.

You might've thought what you saw was love... but think about it... Think about what it takes to love something like that.

And when he'd referred to some*thing*, he'd meant Alodia. He'd meant Elodie.

I glanced back at Alodia, holding onto her husband's corpse as if it was all she had left.

I looked at Elodie in the passenger seat, and felt Howard's words gnawing at me from the inside.

Could I love her?

Was I stepping out over open air, into darkness, by loving her?

We buried Hugo in the garden, as had been his wish. Beside him, an empty plot—clearly designated—awaited the coming day when Alodia would join him in the ground.

There was no funeral for Hugo. No drawn-out process of preparation. Not except for the legal matter of his will.

He gave everything to Elodie, of course. And his only words for her were words of love, and wishes that she do with the home as she saw fit.

Silences, sometimes, are easier to remember than the words we fill them with.

Elodie and I stood in front of Hugo's grave for a long time. I remember how the silence stretched on. A gentle breeze wafted through the yard. We'd shared a glass of champagne after we were finished digging, and were dressed up now—me in a suit, she in a long black dress. We would've had Alodia with us, but at that point she could hardly walk, so we let her stay in bed.

And, after a long time of standing there in the soft breeze, in the gold-tinted light of evening, I spoke first. I don't remember what I said, but I remember it made Elodie cry. She'd been holding the tears back all day, but she cried when I spoke.

And she cried harder when, after I'd finished, she said what she wanted to say. Then it became a conversation. I told her what my first impressions of him were like. And it was easy to be honest with her about it, now that there was distance between us and that first day when I'd been introduced to her family.

Elodie laughed and cried all at once.

And then came the hard part. She started to tell me about why she went four years without speaking to her father, and then dropped down onto her knees in front of the grave, barely able to get the words out. She spoke no longer to me, but directly to the memory of her father.

"Dad. I never got the chance to apologize to you." She covered her face. "I know you didn't care about me apologizing... you would've told me not to be sorry. You would've hugged me and said you loved me, and would've just waved off my apology. But I wish I could've said it to you anyway. I needed you to know..."

Her whole body shook. I crouched and put my arms around her, and held her the way Hugo had held Alodia in the cell, in their final moments together.

"You wouldn't have wanted it," she said to her father's grave, between stifled sobs. "But still... Dad, I won't ever get to tell you I'm sorry."

I thought for a long time—probably too long—about what

to say as I held her. In truth, Howard's words kept reverberating through my mind, bouncing off my thoughts and clinging to them.

"He knew," I finally said to her, and meant it. "Elodie, you should've heard the way he talked about you. Even at the end. He would've forgiven you like it was nothing."

She nodded, knowing this was true, completely out of words.

And we stayed that way until the golden evening light burned red, then grew pale, then sank into the horizon as if retreating from the encroaching dark.

31

More Time

My sister, Nat, was rarely shy about sharing her opinions with me, especially if she disagreed with my logic or thought I was being stupid, but after I finished telling her my plan, she stayed silent for a long time.

We were at her house, sitting on her back porch. Nat was two months pregnant—having undergone insemination. Her wife was somewhere in the house.

And Nat, over the steam that curled up from her mug of coffee, was staring at me with a stunned expression. She said nothing.

But what she was stunned about, I couldn't be sure. It either had to be the story about Elodie's worsening condition, or it had to be the last part: that I had a ring and planned on proposing to Elodie during our upcoming trip to the coast.

I suppose she could've been stunned at either of those things. Or both.

Last time I'd come over, I had told her about the Bailey farm. I told her everything, because Nat was one of the only people in the world I told everything to. She'd nearly gotten sick, then, but she hadn't judged me. Hadn't condemned any word of what happened.

She'd seen the old photos of the farm, after all. She was the first person I'd shown those to.

And she surprised me with all the questions about the women. Where had they gone? Had Elodie and I tried to help them?

And I told her what I knew, which was very little. News stories began to circulate of human-like beasts living in the forests for miles around the town of Olympus—and those stories were spreading. Some said it had to be a cult of wild women. Some said it must be a primitive tribe. Others—veering closer to the truth—described a frightening illness, or condition, taking over and spreading across the population.

These stories—and telling them to Nat—made me feel glad. Whether anything would be done about it wasn't yet known. All I knew was that the women were free, they were thriving in the wild, and the Bailey men no longer threatened them.

"Ben..." said Nat in response to the news I shared with her. Her eyes slowly dropped to her coffee. "You're sure? I mean... I don't want you to think... to think that I'm..."

"Of course not," I said. Knowing Nat, she wouldn't want to

offend me. She knew how sensitive this was. How important. I'd been waiting a few weeks to share it with her.

"But... you've thought about this. You've run this through your head."

"I have. Over and over. It's even kept me up at night, lately."

"I'm not surprised. Maybe it's the kind of thing that *should* keep you up at night."

I nodded. "I'll give you that."

"But I need to know. You've really thought this through."

I released a heavy breath and raised my head, looked her in the eye.

Just the night before was when I made the decision. It had been spinning through my head for weeks.

Alodia had died in the spring. It was a slow fading away for almost two months after Hugo's death. She might have lived longer—a year, maybe more—but she was so weak after all that had happened. And it seemed for the best, which Elodie agreed with. The two months of watching her mother fade away had weighed on her at every waking moment, depriving her of sleep, ruining her appetite, making it hard for her to breathe. She drifted through the estate as if sleepwalking—and, sometimes, she did sleepwalk. Elodie's condition worsened during the two months of her mother's decline, brought upon by her weakened emotional state. Her constant state of fear and uncertainty and depression like concrete in her limbs.

We held another two-person funeral for her mother. Digging the grave, then the burial and then sharing a glass of champagne

—our own reception. And the words and the tears shed over the two graves: the final resting place of Elodie's parents.

"When strangers asked about my parents," she told me, later that night, "I used to say I was an orphan. I never told anyone about them. But now, I just wish I had more time with them."

Over the grave, she spoke of her mother's deep love for her, which could be felt even through the irreversible wall that was her condition. She spoke of how she wished she could've known her mother as a person, before she'd disappeared into the fog.

"I think I would've loved who you were, Mom. And I think you would've been proud of me."

And when I looked at Elodie, at the way she carried herself through her grief, at the way she moved with grace through her own gradually emerging condition, I knew Alodia—the person, Alodia—would've been proud of Elodie. Would've, like me, been in awe of her.

And Elodie would've deserved that. She deserved love that didn't come with conditions.

This was what I realized the night before meeting with Nat.

There'd been a few nights when I awoke to discover Elodie sitting up in bed, staring into the dark.

There'd been nights when she opened her eyes on the pillow and stared at me but didn't seem to see me.

There'd been nights when she made love so wildly, with such mounting abandon, that I felt something animalistic in her movements and saw something primal and thoughtless in the gleam of her eyes.

This night, she rested without problem, without interruption. I found myself awake and looking at her, just looking at her. Hugo had told me that it wouldn't be so hard to understand how he could love Alodia the way he had. He told me it would be easier than I thought. I chanced brushing my hand softly through Elodie's hair, and she stirred faintly without waking.

I looked at her and realized I couldn't live without her. Nothing could've made me leave her—not the fear of what was coming, not the memories of what we'd been through. Not even the ghosts of Howard Bailey's words haunting my dreams. No. The memory of Hugo's words spoke louder—

"...and that she has tasted deeply of the love you have for her, that she can hold your love like light in a chest, and that she can carry it with her into the darkness, when she goes... knowing this brings me peace amidst the impossible grief."

I loved her. I wanted to love her for the rest of my life. My life being *our* life.

"I've thought it through," I said to Nat, my sister. "I promise."

After awhile she set her mug of coffee aside, her face showing mostly fear, then reached a hand out for mine and simply said, "Okay."

32

Dancing in the Garden

Hugo's estate became our home. We'd had our wedding in the garden, accompanied solely by my sister and her family—and my father, who I'd invited into my life, who embraced Elodie already as a daughter-in-law even though he rarely remembered her name. Seeing him was easy—easier than it had ever been. I found none of the bitterness inside me which I'd once held onto with such firmness, nor any of the impatience with his fading memory. And, to my surprise, he was filled with joy to be around me again.

"It's a brave thing you're doing," he said to me, when we had a moment alone in the garden. Elodie was off with my sister; the two had become fast friends. And my father cheered me with his glass of wine, clinking it to mine, and stood somewhat awkwardly beside me.

"Getting married?" I said.

"That too. But I mean... standing by this girl. After she's lost everything. Her parents, one after the other like that."

"I don't know about brave." Between sips of wine my thoughts flashed back to the Bailey farm. In my memories it was always at night, aglow with spreading walls of fire.

"You're a braver man than I am, son. I... um... there's..."

"Dad..."

"There's a lot of regrets I have, you know, about how I was when your mother—"

I turned my whole body toward him and looked at him with a directness I once would've been incapable of.

"You're here now, Dad. That's all that matters."

Through teary eyes he managed to smile. Lifted a hand up and put it on my shoulder.

Neither of us said anything more. We didn't have to.

It was a few weeks later—a few weeks since I'd stopped thinking of this as Hugo's estate and started thinking of it as our home, hers and mine—when Elodie told me. We were sharing a bottle of wine out in the garden, seated at a metal table for two. Or, rather, I was having wine; she hadn't touched hers. Night had fallen and the full moon shone silver, a bright eye, casting dim shadows of us on the grass.

"It's not as scary as it used to be," she said, meaning her episodes. They still occurred with varying frequency, at least a couple times a week, but some of the urgency had faded. This was a conscious effort on her part. "It seems like it gets worse when I panic about it. Like... when I become aware of what's happening, as long as I can remember that it's happened before and that there's nothing I can do about it, then I don't panic. And I don't feel as afraid. And it doesn't last as long."

"I noticed that. And maybe I'm just being hopeful, but it seems like it's not exactly getting worse, right? Am I imagining that?"

She smiled and shook her head. "I don't think you're imagining it."

Neither of us had any delusions that she wouldn't eventually grow worse, or that she wouldn't one day—even if it was years from now—descend completely, the way her mother had. But things had been evening out. Things were, for now, okay.

"You know... every time we come out here, and I mean every time," I said, "I think of your parents."

Elodie nodded softly. "Me too. I think of them dancing. They used to do that all the time when I was little. When I couldn't sleep, I used to look out the window and watch them. Sometimes they danced for hours."

"I can picture it," I said.

And I realized something that had never occurred to me before, about Elodie's childhood.

Even though the years of her youth were full of darkness, full of loneliness, she'd had parents who loved each other, in their ways. Parents who went out to dance in the garden at night.

Elodie and I had only danced back here once, on our wedding. She had been crying through most of the dance. Crying through the biggest of smiles.

In a burst of inspiration, I took a larger-than-usual swig from my wine, stood, and held my hand out to Elodie.

She raised an eyebrow. "Well this is... cheesy."

"You have to risk being cheesy if you're gonna be romantic."

"Bennet, we don't have any music."

"Neither did your parents."

"Yeah, well... my parents were weird."

I tilted my eyebrow back at her. "Okay, yeah, your father was uncommonly theatrical. But come on. It's practically a tradition."

"That is *definitely* not a tradition."

"We're in charge of what's tradition and what isn't. Now come on and at least stand with me."

Elodie titled her head at me, appearing as though she were ready to deny me, but she set down her still-full glass of wine on the table. "There's something I have to tell you."

"You can tell me on your feet."

She rolled her eyes but failed at restraining a grin as she took my hand and let me pull her to her feet. We swayed softly, close together.

"You know," she said, "we didn't even dance on the night we met. And it was in a dance club."

"What we did was better than dancing," I said. "In a manner of speaking."

"True." She rested her head in the crook of my neck; her breath softly tickled the skin beneath my ear. "It feels like nothing's changed."

"What?"

"Since we got married. It's like... like we're the same as before."

"In a good way or a bad way?"

"It's just how I like us. This is where I'd want to stay, if I could. Right here, forever."

I smiled. Ran my hand through her hair. Sometimes, when we held each other, I was struck by the reality of my life. That I had the love of this strange and incredible woman. That we would love each other for the rest of our lives. That we both had a chance for a life about which we might be able to say, one day, we had no regrets.

Maybe one day I would have to follow her into the dark. And I knew I would. And I wouldn't look back.

"What did you have to tell me?" I asked.

She pulled her face away from my neck so she could look into my eyes. And, just like that, she told me.

We hadn't talked much about it yet, only because it hadn't seemed like the right time. But the conversation was always going to come up. I simply didn't expect it to come up the way it did—before we'd had a chance to make a decision with any certainty.

"Elodie," I gasped. "Oh my god."

"I know. I only just found out, just this morning. And I didn't know what to think, or..."

"I thought we were gonna talk about this—"

"I know, Bennet. I know. It's not like—"

"No, no... that's not what I mean. Elodie. I mean... you're sure?"

She nodded.

I kissed her. She looked at me, surprised, and then kissed me back. And we kept kissing until we started to laugh, and pulled apart to look at each other.

Dozens of thoughts spun through my head. It came to my mind to ask the pressing question—

What if it was a girl? What if we had a daughter? A little girl with Bailey blood in her veins.

And I could see that fear glinting in Elodie's ashen eyes. She knew I was thinking it; surely it was what she'd been thinking about all day.

So I chose not to say it. Not now. The time would come for that conversation, but for now the fear of the possibility was shrinking beneath what I felt. And I could only say—

"We'll be a family, Elodie. We'll be a family."

She leapt up, wrapping her legs and arms around me, and she kissed me. Deeply.

Hugo's words about Elodie, about whether he regretted having a child, returned to me.

...to have tasted of life at all, to have held the candle in the darkness for awhile... isn't that worth it, no matter how swift or brief it is? She is my heart. I cannot imagine this world without her.

You must understand, Bennet—given the chance, I would not do a single thing differently.

If we had a daughter, I thought, I knew what I would do. I

would love her. With all my heart I would love her. And do anything to protect her.

I looked into Elodie's eyes. She looked into mine.

Under the moonlight, just the two of us in the silver darkness, we twirled amongst the sleeping flowers and the shapes of our own shadows on the grass.

THE END

Acknowledgments

Although writing is solitary work, no writer reaches any measure of contentment or success alone, no author stands up except on the shoulders of those that came before, and no novel reaches completion without the support of many individuals.

To my parents. Kevin, my dad, has been my first reader since I first started writing books at the age of ten. Eileen, my mom, may not personally enjoy the genres I write in, but her love and support has sustained and defined me for longer than I can remember.

To Anjali, my partner, whose relentless encouragement and patience, even when I disappear obsessively into my work at certain stages, is unconditional and for whom my gratitude is fathomless.

To my coworkers turned friends of the former Quarantined Writers group: Cain Wright, Shannon Hawkins, and Maribell Borjon. And, Cain, I'm sorry (only somewhat) about the nightmares.

To the earliest readers of this book, friends and family members, who were willing to subject themselves to the strangeness, the depravity, and the darkness.

To my dear friend Espen Aukan, screenwriter, wordsmith, film buff, and overall amazing person; a kindred spirit in many ways, and unconditionally supportive, sometimes without even realizing it.

To my friend, the author Mike Salt, whose prolific nature and excited approach to writing has long been inspiring.

To the filmmakers and authors I've never met, but whom I've come to know through their work—work that has influenced me, inspired me, and amazed me from a young age.

And to you, the reader. There will be more to come, and I hope you're there for it. But for your time and attention now, with this strange, dark book, my gratitude is inexpressible.

Photo by Kevin Lakin @kjlakinmedia

Cody Lakin is a writer and bookseller living in Southern Oregon.

codylakin.com

CPSIA information can be obtained
at www.ICGtesting.com
Printed in the USA
BVHW040759180423
662560BV00008B/217